BLISTERING FURY

Hot rage mastered Billy English and made him shake. That was his greatest enemy, that blind rage which leaped on him and blurred his eyes with red. He shook the passion off instantly, and, cold and ready for action, gripping his smashed and bleeding left hand, in spite of the pain, around the handrail, he slipped up. He changed his footing, and then dived over the top of the steps and at the knees of the guard, shooting himself in with the full strength of his arms and with a lucky sway of the train to drive him in all the faster.

Other *Leisure* Westerns by Max Brand:
RED DEVIL OF THE RANGE
PRIDE OF TYSON
THE OUTLAW TAMER
BULL HUNTER'S ROMANCE
BULL HUNTER
TIGER MAN
GUN GENTLEMEN
THE MUSTANG HERDER
WESTERN TOMMY
SPEEDY
THE WHITE WOLF
TROUBLE IN TIMBERLINE
TIMBAL GULCH TRAIL
THE BELLS OF SAN FILIPO
MARBLEFACE
THE RETURN OF THE RANCHER
RONICKY DOONE'S REWARD
RONICKY DOONE'S TREASURE
RONICKY DOONE
THE WHISPERING OUTLAW
THE SHADOW OF SILVER TIP
THE TRAP AT COMANCHE BEND
THE MOUNTAIN FUGITIVE

MAX BRAND

KING CHARLIE

LEISURE BOOKS **NEW YORK CITY**

A LEISURE BOOK®

February 1997

Published by special arrangement with Golden West
Literary Agency.

Dorchester Publishing Co., Inc.
276 Fifth Avenue
New York, NY 10001

KING CHARLIE

PART I

Chapter One

Behold him on the top of the hill!

His head is high, his eye is bright, his posture is that of a King looking down upon his own country. He is four-and-fifty years of age, and his birthday fell last Sunday, though he himself does not know it, for a dozen years ago he purposely lost track of time. He is four-and-fifty years of age, but he seems at least ten or fifteen years younger, for his step is long and elastic, his gesture quick and nervous, his voice vibrant; there is not a deep line in his brown, brown face, or a single grey hair on his head.

Who is this who has come through the desert and out of it without a pack on his back or a canteen at his side? Behind him lies that desert, a riot of colour—a freak of a desert it is, having cast those grey garments in which the mountain desert usually appears; for the sands are orange, and the rocks are black, the sky is its own heavenly blue with dazzling white clouds blowing gaily across it, and far away a

9

ghost of smoke-trees fill a depression in the hills and flow out, winding slowly, across the sands, until they seem to be a ghost river.

It is a land of allurement, that desert. There are some who hold that those who catch the germs of the fever of love for it can never be happy in other places, not even in other deserts. They must come back here to where the sage climbs the northern mountains or the cactus grows on the southern hills. But whatever lure may be in the mountain desert, this tall fellow does not feel it. He has turned his back on it. He is not even staring down at the little town at his feet, but far away he sees a sign of his kingdom, and his lips part in a slow smile, as though he were drinking a draught of pure joy. That sign of his empire is the swiftly drifting smoke of a railroad train driving towards the horizon, and the empire of the man on the hill is the empire of the steel tracks.

Yes, he is a tramp. It is the absence of all care that has permitted his unweighted shoulders to remain so straight; and it is the absence of remorse that keeps his hair so luxuriantly thick and dark and leaves his face unseamed. Peering at him more closely, one may see that the skin is a little thick and rumples over the knuckles of his hands, and that the skin of his face seems tough and dense, with a rough texture, while the high colour seems stained permanently into the cheeks and cannot fade, no matter what grief or terror he may feel. Life in the open has kept him young, and when he was perforce constrained by the heavy hand of the law to live and sleep in one place for years together, his thoughts were still roving under the stars and in the wind.

He is a tramp, but never dream that this is any cold handout hobo, for he is a hot diet man. Mistake him not, at the same time, for a gay-cat, one of those wretches who work from time to time when their courage as beggars fails them. Neither is he sponger upon his own kind, the lowest of the low. No, for this is the highest order. He is no bindle stiff. He scorns to carry his blankets as he roves, but trusting to divine chance with a courage worthy of a greater cause, he throws himself ahead on the long road and never loses heart whatever its windings. When he begs, it is from house to house. And he does not take the first thing offered him in the matter of food. No, no, far, far from that. He is a fellow of preferences which will not down. He has been known to beg at twenty houses because on that particular morning he felt like sausage for breakfast and would not be content with less.

How could twenty doors be opened to him? No, rather ask how could they remain closed when he presented himself. For see how neatly he is dressed and with what pains he now produces an old rag and wipes the desert dust from his shoes, and then finds a small pocket whisk-broom and gives similar attention to his hat. Hat and shoes, those prime objects of a tramp's attention, satisfactorily attended to, he continues his work with the brush until coat, vest, trousers, have been thoroughly searched and every atom of the dust is driven off into the wind. Then he removes from around his neck the handkerchief which was tied there to prevent the sweat from soaking the dust into the collar of his coat. Last, he brings out a little round mirror, and in this views his face attentively from many angles, at first shaking his head dolorously, but presently plucking up more cheer and going briskly about giving his features a rubbing which will almost answer the purpose of soap and water and towel.

With all done, he looks down again on the little town, a small cattle town, where the only two roofs of any importance are the red roof of the school and the blue roof of the hotel-merchandise store. His destination is the railroad yonder, which will end the curse of this long walk across country. But his next station on the journey is to be the little town immediately below him. He cocks out his elbows, inhales a deep breath, and swings off jauntily down the hill.

Such is King Charlie!

No, the picture is not yet complete. For part way down the slope he pauses to light a cigarette. From an inside coat pocket he produces a leather *case,* and from the case he selects a "tailor-made" smoke. He places the cigarette between his lips and the case is restored to his pocket. He draws out now a matchbox preserved from crushing—oh luxury!—by an iron frame. He opens the box, he selects a match and lights it, but when the flaming little stick is almost at the end of the cigarette a sudden tremor seizes him. There is only that one word for it. He is *seized* as though a hand had taken him by the shoulder and was violently shaking him. From head to foot he quivers. The bright colour in his cheek pales, though it does not quite go out. He makes a desperate effort, his nostrils dilating as though a great terror had fallen upon him. But still he cannot put that flame to the tobacco, and presently the match is shaken from his finger-tips. He removes the cigarette next, but it, also, falls through his fingers to the ground.

It is the prison tremor which some men get after two or three years in the penitentiary, and which it requires fourteen or fifteen years, split up into many terms, to give to a more hardened character. It is the shaking which comes from the haunting dread that, in another moment, the hand of the "cop" will be clapped upon his shoulder. It is the dread of society; it is the horror of the law that is the invisible hand shaking King Charlie even here in the wilderness. Other men get it in other places. It stops the sneak thief, perhaps, with his finger-tips working at the watch. It wakens the murderer with a leap in his sleep, the sweat streaming down his forehead. It has interfered in the midst of the commission of the greatest crimes and made the master criminal helpless. That, of course, is a rarity, and rare indeed was it to see a man with such nerves as those of the "King" broken and made to shudder by a thing which did not appear as even a wraith.

He mastered the shaking, however, after a moment of fierce effort. Perhaps it was the excitement of seeing the railroad in the distance and the prospect, just before him, of the termination of his long tramp, which made him lose his nerve. And he wondered, grimly, if the tremor would ever come to him when he was riding the rods. If so, it would be the end of King Charlie. Yet he considered that prospect without again turning pale. Real cowardice did not exist in the body of King Charlie. Out came cigarette-case and matches once more, and he lighted his smoke, inhaled a deep breath of it, and snapped the smoking match into empty air with a challenge to the world to beat him yet.

Then he went on, jaunty as ever.

Chapter Two

He slackened his gait as he entered the town, and his face assumed a more thoughtful expression. Not that he had the slightest doubt as to his ability to secure food for the evening meal, it being now hardly more than mid-afternoon. But he had to readjust himself a little whenever he entered one of these small Western towns. There was always food in plenty to be had in one of them. But there was also an immense amount of trouble lurking for him just around the corner unless he proceeded with the most extreme care.

These Westerners, when they once started to ask questions, could be most embarrassing. Also, they had a way of enforcing answers, even at the end of a revolver, if need were. Such a need should not be in his case, he resolved. He would talk fluently, no matter how untruthfully. But as a rule it was easy. They were so used to being hospitable to whoever came along, these men of the desert, that he had

King Charlie

hardly to ask at all. He simply presented himself, and was asked to step in and sit down.

Even as he walked along the street now, who could tell when a man might accost him and they should fall into conversation which might lead to a handout of a sit-down meal and a bunk thereafter, to say nothing of tobacco *ad nauseam*, if he wished it. It made the wary old tramp shake his head in wonder at the simplicity of human beings: If he himself were a man of property, for instance, his dealings would be far other than this. He would make his residence respected—dreaded—if he had to hire a day watchman as well as a night watchman. He would kick every loafer down the steps who dared present himself at the door—he would have steep steps constructed for that special purpose. He had reached this point in his reflections, and had kicked a stone viciously from his path at the same instant, when a voice from the side accosted him.

"H'wayeye, stranger?"

"Hullo," said King Charlie, and looked up into the face of a dusty man, who was reining a dusty horse towards him. Perhaps this was the man who was to take him home to food and a place to rest. He eyed the other curiously.

"What you doing this far West?" asked the man on horseback.

King Charlie was startled. This was certainly not a hospitable manner of beginning a conversation.

"I dunno why I shouldn't be this far West," he declared.

"Well," said the other without heat, "I *do* know a pile of reasons."

"You do? Why?"

"That ain't the point. Them reasons suit me. Besides, I seen you knocking at doors in New Wilmington a month ago."

King Charlie continued to smile as calmly as ever. "You must have me mixed up with some other

15

gent," he said. "I dunno how—"

The other exploded with sudden wrath.

"You rat!" he said furiously. "I know you and I know your kind. You're the carriers of the germs that go around the country spilling wrong ideas into the brains of the youngsters. Damn the lot of you! If I had my way I'd hang you up and shoot you to make sure you died!"

"You're a kind-hearted sort," remarked Charlie, still smiling. "I'm certainly obliged for all this free information, but—"

"Mind how you talk!" A hand was snapped out, and a grim forefinger pointed like a gun at the head of the King. "Mind how you talk! I've got this to back me up!" He flicked open his coat, and the expert eye of Charlie caught a glimpse of a badge of some sort. "A hobo less would be a gift to the world," declared the venomous man on horseback. "Damned if I ain't tempted every time I look at one. But I'll tell you what—unless you want to land in the gaol, and trot out from the gaol to a woodpile for thirty days, you get out of town before night. I don't mind you so much during the day, but when I catch a bo at night I'm death on 'em!"

He waited for no answer, but twitched his horse to one side and loped down the street. A cupful of dust was scooped up by a hind hoof and flung into the air, where it dissolved into a cloud that blew straight into the face of King Charlie. He busied himself removing all traces of that dust before he permitted himself to think, far less speak.

Then he said to himself: "For that I'll get even with your town! You're a watchdog, are you? Bah! I'll steal half the town right under your nose!"

And the King snapped his fingers carelessly in the air.

After trying one or two doors, however, he became more concerned. The doors were locked, and there seemed hardly a soul in town. Of course, he could get into any of those houses that he wished to enter, but he had not the slightest desire to commit burglary by forcing a lock when he had no idea of what the lock might be guarding.

Then he learned the cause of the exodus. There was a bucking contest on the outskirts of the village; and, indeed, from the top of the hill he remembered now that he had noted a drift of men and horses out of the town.

"They're picking the best rider out of Carterville," said the old woman who was his informant. "And they're going to send him down to the State bucking contest with all expenses paid. It's about time that we folks waked up and done something like that. There's Saunderstown and Four Oaks on each side of us have won the prize two years running. And we got better men right here than ever was growed in Saunderstown and Four Oaks put together."

"You certainly have, ma'am," observed King Charlie. "Everybody inside of five hundred miles has heard some sort of mention of Carterville."

And with the smile which this brought to her lips left behind him, he turned his face towards the far end of the town with purpose indistinct in his own mind, but with a determined will to do the greatest possible mischief to Carterville with the least possible cost of time and effort on his part.

He found that the grounds for the bucking affair had been laid out in a small pasture on the verge of the village. Around the fence two or three hundred men, women, and children were gathered, and above their heads drifted a mist of fine dust, now and then reinforced with a great upburst, white as a cloud; and from time to time the hoofs of horses thudded in broken rhythm on the ground, and the snorting of horses was heard as they landed with all their force in crooked positions.

But these noises and the shouting of the spectators had ceased as the King came up with the onlookers and squeezed a way to the fence between an old man and a young woman. He saw that in one corner of the lot there were corralled a dozen ugly looking horses, wild as the wind, every one of them. They were sweating with fear, and some of them bore the marks of the saddles which had been cinched on them. But for that matter, the riders bore even more distinct marks. Here was one with a rag bound around a face as swollen as though he were afflicted with the mumps, and yonder was another who limped feebly, supporting himself with one hand resting on the fence.

"Them Dirks hosses are sure mankillers!" chuckled the old man at the King's right. "My, my, this reminds me of the days when—"

"But think of that little Billy English having got clean into the finals!" cried the girl, interrupting.

And the King made out that he had worked his way in between two members of a single family.

He eyed them nonchalantly. The old man's lower right vest pocket was bulging with a big watch, but the practised eye of the King estimated, from the rim which was visible, that it was plated gold only. At the breast of the girl's dress there was a diamond pin, but the jewel was not worth twenty dollars.

He would not risk such petty thefts in so small a crowd or so far from the railroad.

"He ain't so little," said the old man.

"Why, dad, he's only fourteen!"

"Well, when I was a boy fourteen was old enough to do a man's work. I recollect well milking fourteen cows night and morning, besides ploughing all day long—when I was under fourteen. Yessir! Little Billy English ain't so little after all. He's as tall as you be, Bess!"

"Nonsense, dad!"

"I say it *is* sense! It do beat all how you womenfolk can't let a boy grow up. You're as bad as your ma already, Bess."

18

King Charlie

"What's that?" cackled a shrill voice near by. "What's that you're saying, Lester?"

"Aw, nothing!" answered the old man, a good deal abashed. He continued to the girl in a lowered voice: "Yep, Billy English is plenty big enough to be riding a hoss. He kind of reminds me of the way I used to sit the saddle myself when I was a kid—sort of slanting to the right."

"H-m-m," murmured the girl. "Well, I sure hope that little Billy wins out!"

"You hope, do you?" scoffed the argumentative father. "Well, your hopes ain't going to win, Bess, and I'm here to tell you that!"

"Why not? Why ain't Billy going to win?"

"Why, Bess, ain't you got no eyes? I ain't denying but what he's done noble so far. He's done enough to make anybody proud of him, and in a couple of years he'll have 'em all hustling down to the State fair. But he ain't going to go there this year. No, sir. Don't you see who he's got to beat?"

"I see, Joe Fairview. Is Joe such an awful wonder, dad?"

"No wonder, no wonder," said the father hastily, by no means willing to deal out such unstinted praise to a member of a generation later than his own, "he ain't no such rider as Cracker McGee used to be, or Paul Chester, or a dozen more I could name, because he ain't got the style and the easy way in the saddle, and he don't work all the bucks out of a hoss the way they used to do. Still, Joe is a right pretty rider, and he sure is a pile better than a kid like Billy. Land sakes, Bess, d'you want us to send down a mere kid like Billy to represent us at the State fair?"

"You just said he was big enough to do a man's work."

"Don't you go taking my words out of the places where I put 'em. I said he was big enough to do tolerable well for chores. I didn't say that he was to go and stand up and call himself a man among men.

Why, we'd be a laughing-stock if we sent down a kid like little Billy."

The testy old gentleman shook his head and stamped. "Tush!" he said. "The ideas of you women—"

"Hush!"

"Well?"

"See them shake hands. They're going to ride it off. They're going to ride off the tie. See Billy and Joe Fairview shake hands over yonder. They're going to fight it out to a finish."

"No, no!" muttered the ancient, peering first through his glasses and then over them. "You ain't telling me that, are you?"

The King followed the direction of all the staring eyes around him and at once found the centre of interest.

A tall, hard-featured cowpuncher was in the act of shaking hands with a tow-headed youngster who swung his sombrero in his other hand, and whose whole manner was that of one embarking on a tremendous lark. His blue eyes shone, and their blueness could be distinguished even at that distance.

That, beyond a doubt, was little Billy English.

But as the old man had said, he was not so very small. He was already, in his fourteenth year, a matter of five or six inches over five feet. Moreover, it was not a purely gawky height. His shoulders were both wide and well rounded out. And every move of his body and gesture of his hand indicated lithe muscles at play in his young body.

Indeed, to the keen eye of the King, practised in estimating the abilities of pugilists, Billy English seemed rather a little man than a big boy.

Chapter Three

The King now observed that three men were furiously engaged in the labour of capturing a long-legged brown horse who battled with insensate fury, knocking the humans about as though they had been ten-pins; except that these ten-pins clung by means of ropes whose hold could not be slipped, and in the end the brown was down, blindfolded, and eventually saddled and brought out, dancing and fretting himself into a foam while the crowd of onlookers gasped.

A bulky man, robed in a light linen duster, now advanced towards the centre of the arena.

"Ladies and gents," he said, when his raised hand had brought silence to the circle around the fence, "you've all seen how Joe Fairview and Billy English have rode to a tie. Leastwise, that's the way that me and the other two judges make it out. We all voted for a tie, and now that tie has got to be rode off. We're picking a bad one to try out the two gents that are still competing for the honour of representing Carterville. Jim Dandy is the hoss they got to ride. And the first thing is to see if each of them can stay on Jim Dandy's back for one minute without no spurs locked nor leather pulling, but riding straight up and taking what's coming to 'em, according to the rules. The gent that does the first riding is apt to get the worst of Jim Dandy's work. So we're going to pick him by tossing a coin. All right, ladies and gents. You won't need to start hollering to make Jim Dandy buck. He'll do his best all by his own self! The gent ain't yet showed up that's been able to rake him fore and aft while riding, and they's been a hundred of the best that's tried to stick to Jim Dandy."

He waved in conclusion and went back to his post, where the brown was now saddled and prepared for his test. Next, little Billy English and tall Joe Fairview stepped forth to see the coin flipped up from the broad thumb-nail of the judge. A rush of whispers came from the onlookers.

"I can't help praying that Joe has to ride the hoss first," said Bess, at the King's elbow.

"Don't make no difference," declared her testy father. "He ain't got a chance. Yes, he might of stuck it out if they'd kept on using ordinary hosses the same's they've been trotting out up to this time. But he ain't got the legs or the experience to stay with Jim Dandy for ten seconds, let alone a full minute. But Joe, yonder, he's got the makings of a real hossman. I could show him a few little pointers about the way he catches back with his legs. But take him all in all, he does a pretty good job. He rides by balance, and that's the main thing. Most of the boys nowadays just try to squeeze a hoss in two for a few seconds that wears them all out and don't do nothing but get the hoss fighting mad and warm him up to his work. And the next couple of seconds—zip!—off they go like a water-melon seed that you snap out of your fingers."

"But don't you think that even little Billy rides the same way pretty much?"

"How else can he ride with them short kid legs of his?" asked the illogical old gentleman. "Now don't be asking questions but watch and see what happens. The boy has done noble, but this is the end of his rope."

There was in the King something which responded with a thrill at the thought of a lost cause and those who maintained it. And staring across the space of blazing sunlight at the tow-headed youngster, he felt that unfamiliar leap of his heart in sympathy. Not a dozen times before in the long course of his life had the King been so stirred to hope luck should fall to the share of anyone other than himself.

Who would have to ride the formidable horse first?

The judge delayed as long as possible the drawout, the suspense, before he snapped up the coin. The two contestants involuntarily leaned back to see the coin rise to the top of its arc and hang there for a glittering, winking instant before it fell in a streak of light to the dust. And then they leaned to examine it and read their destiny.

But it was covered a quarter of an inch deep in the dust. The judge got laboriously to his knees, blew the dust away in a great cloud, and then removed all doubt as to who was the winner by jumping up and clapping his hand on the shoulder of Joe Fairview.

The latter shrugged his lean shoulders as who should say: "It really makes little difference to me."

But little Billy English, on the other hand, waved his hand most gracefully to his competitor in sign that he accepted the judgment of chance without malice against the successful man. Then he clapped his loose brimmed sombrero on his head and hitched up his belt before and behind, leaning forward the while and staring at the brown horse in so aggressive an attitude that the King stepped a long stride forward and hung his arms over the top rail.

"There's a gamester!" he breathed in devout admiration. "Oh, he's a hundred and thirty pounds of iron and fire, that Billy boy!"

He turned abruptly to the ancient Lester.

"I got a ten-spot that says the kid is going to beat the lanky guy," he declared. "What d'you say, father?"

The old man blinked.

"I dunno that I know you," he murmured.

"Make it five," said the King. "I bet you five dollars that the little kid you think ain't big enough to ride like a man will stick in the saddle longer than Joe Fairview."

Old Lester peered wistfully across the arena until his eyes rested on the difference in bulk between the tall brown horse and the little blond-headed Billy English.

"Maybe them five dollars are trying to burn their way out of your pocket, son," he said. "I'll take you up."

He produced that sum in one-dollar bills, counted it with great care, and fluttered it before the face of the King.

"Put up or shut up," he said with boyish enthusiasm, and snapped the fingers of his left hand while he spoke. "Let your money talk."

King Charlie brought out his small roll, detached a five-spot as agreed, and turned with a smile to the girl. Perhaps that smile, at some date unascertained as yet, might be the means of bringing him one or two lucky meals. Besides, under no circumstances did the King overlook an opportunity to place a woman on his side. They never did much in a material way beyond giving food and old clothes; but for such a thing as testimony in court, one smile would buy more from the average woman than a thousand dollars would buy from the average man.

Bess took the stake and held it in both her hands, while she laughed up at the bettors.

King Charlie

"I can't help hoping that you lose, dad," she said.

"Stuff!" exploded her father. "You don't know nothing, girl!"

"Who is the boy?" asked the King of Bess.

"I don't know," she answered. "Well, I know as much as anyone knows. He just happened into town when he was about five years old and said that he'd walked in from the railroad. Of course, everyone tried to find out who his father was, but we couldn't learn. And after a time Mr. Shaw took him in."

"Well," said the King, "he done a good job in raising that kid. I suppose he's out here giving Billy a cheer? Where is the old boy?"

"He ain't here," said the girl, laughing without mirth. "And I guess he wouldn't give his own son, if he had one, a cheer. He ain't that kind. Yes, it may have looked good of him to take in Billy when Billy was five years old, but everyone says that Mr. Shaw was simply foresighted. In three years Billy was doing as many chores as a grown man could have done almost. Mr. Shaw has hardly given him a chance to go to school in the winters. And for the last three or four years, Billy has rode the range just like any grown man. Everyone says it's a shame."

"Then why doesn't somebody do something?"

"I dunno," said Bess, troubled at the thought. "I guess they don't want to get into trouble with Mr. Shaw. He's such a fierce man, you know."

"Huh!" grunted the King, "then why don't Billy run away?"

"Why—I guess he's never thought of doing that."

"Then—" But the King left this final thought unexpressed and turned rather abruptly to watch Billy English climb into the saddle.

In another instant the long-legged brown was off, unrestrained by a bit and bridle, leaning into his longest stride with his long, ugly neck thrust out, snake-like, and his ears flattened. Never in his life had King Charlie seen so ugly a head. Inside of half a dozen jumps, having gained enough impetus to suit himself, the outlaw flung himself high into the air and began such a set of antics that old Lester cried out: "Boys! boys! boys! Never in my days have I seen such educated pitching, eh, Bess!"

King Charlie had crossed and recrossed the great mountain desert, but his stays in that region of much work and little play had not been long. However, he had seen horses buck before, but even had he never laid eyes on one he would have been able to say that the brown was a master hand at his own work. He seemed intent on smashing his own legs like pipestems, so fiercely did he throw himself about, and yet—"Look! look!" cried Bess. "He's using the spurs!"

"By God!" shouted her ancient father, taking off his hat and forgetting all about his bet in the enthusiasm which sprang from watching such fine horsemanship. "By God, lass, you're right! He's raking him fore and aft, too!"

For the rules of good, honest bucking are that each rider shall not only endeavour to stick in the saddle, but he shall also do his utmost to induce the horse he sits upon to display its worst wares. To merely ride straight up is often a small thing, but a horse which will hardly buck at all under straight riding may hurl itself into a maelstrom of bucking at the first scratch of the spurs. And little Billy English was to the full urging Jim Dandy to his utmost.

Swinging his short legs, he swung his spurs the entire length of the body of the brown, rolling the rowel along the hide and driving Jim Dandy into a perfect frenzy. More than this, to pile Pelion on Ossa, he swung his ragged hat and with it slapped Jim Dandy alternately between the ears and on the flanks. And it seemed to the King, as the outlaw horse reached the height of his efforts, that the air was converted into a semi-solid—that it was at least like water, in which Jim Dandy turned and twisted and writhed like a fish, and ever and anon dropped down and struck the earth a tremendous blow that knocked the head of the rider forward or back or to the side. And every one of those terrific shocks must have been like the thud of a great fist against the brain of the boy.

"What's the time—what's the time on him?" cried the King, thrown into a wild excitement. "They ought to stop it. It's more than a minute. It's two minutes he's been riding."

"Thirty seconds," replied old Lester, glancing down at his watch. Indeed, every man around the fence was alternately yelling and then glancing at his watch. Beyond a doubt everyone wished to see the boy conquer.

"Look!" cried the King, all his poise gone in a flash. "Look at him bleeding! He's sick!"

For those merciless shocks had forced a thin trickle of blood from the nostrils of Billy English. Now his head rocked wildly. His face was convulsed with desperate effort, and yet not for an instant did he relax his beating of the hat and his raking with the spurs to keep Jim Dandy at the height of his work. Suddenly—it was a spin of the brown, a leap into the air, and a side spring that did it—the young horseman was hurled from the saddle. No easy, slipping fall. He darted as a stone from a sling, and, amid a yell of dismay, he turned over and over on the ground.

"He's killed!" cried King Charlie.

Now, up he leaped, shook back his hair, clapped on his head the sombrero upon which he had never relaxed his grip, and started racing towards the brown shrilling: "I'll get you this time, you long-legged sinner."

The burst of laughter from the audience—laughter which came from relief as well as amusement—stopped him and recalled him to the fact that he had fought his fight and finished his chance. Instantly he stopped, brushed the blood from his cheek with a careless flourish of his bandana, and cried to Joe Fairview: "Good luck, Joe!"

"Game—game to the last inch," muttered the King. "And made of indiarubber, too. You could drop that kid off a cliff and he'd land on his feet and laugh at you. He looks lucky."

Chapter Four

"What time?" breathed the King next, wiping the perspiration from his brow.

"Fifty," said old Lester. "He only lacked ten seconds. Only ten. I misdoubt that Joe can stick to Jim Dandy that long—unless the kid has taken some of the buck out of Jim."

That, however, was apparently what had happened. Joe Fairview rode well and honourably. He urged the brown horse with beating hat and raking spurs just as the boy had done, though with much less fury of gusto, but it seemed that Jim Dandy, and very rightly, considered that a day's work had been done. He only bucked twice as hard as an ordinary horse could buck, and the result was that the dauntless Joe lasted through the sixty seconds, and then slipped out of the saddle victorious.

"Give your pa the money," said the King to Bess, without turning his head to watch the transfer take place. "He's won it. He outguessed me. But I guess

I've seen five dollars' worth. Now what's the kid going to do? Now what's he going to do?"

He was not left long in doubt. Straight across the field walked tow-headed Billy English, thrust out his hand, and shook that of the victor with a broad grin. Then he sauntered towards the fence, swung himself over it with much agility, and still smiling and laughing at those who crowded around him offering condolences and praise, he declared that he must hurry home to finish some chores, and straightway disappeared down the street, while the others turned their attention to the man of the hour, Joe Fairview, who was now to carry their hopes and their ambitions down to the State fair.

That is, all turned towards him saving one man among the spectators, and that was the King. He detached himself from his place at the fence, glided through the crowd with the ease of an eel through muddy water, and started down the street in pursuit at his long, swinging stride which devoured distance with an amazing speed and lack of effort. For fast runners may be made; but fast walkers must be born and then made afterwards.

All the way he was saying over and over again to himself: "Clean as a pebble. All grit. No give up. That's a white kid as ever I seen! Clean white!"

He touched the shoulder of Billy English in a few moments, and the latter turned towards him a white, smiling face, with the expression just a little set.

"You're pretty sick, ain't you, son?" asked the King.

There was a sudden change in the expression of the boy. The smile vanished and left him wan and with his forehead covered with a sick sweat.

"I'm all right," he gasped.

"Come in here," insisted the King, and showed the way between two houses and behind a shed, leading Billy English with a grasp which the latter had no apparent strength to resist. "Now lie down," he or-

King Charlie

dered when they reached their destination—a small stretch of dead grasses.

Billy English slumped down and lay flat on his back, his eyes closed, his nostrils dilated, his lips parted and gasping for air. The tramp watched him with quiet concern. Then he opened the boy's shirt at the throat, pulled his shirt out, and fanned rapidly with his hat, so that a current of air passed over Billy's breast. After a moment he was able to gasp through set teeth:

"Thanks. I'm—all right now!"

"The hell you are!" said the King quietly. "You stay right where you are till I tell you to move."

It was ten minutes before Billy English sat up and flushed with shame as he looked at the tramp.

"I dunno how it was," he confessed. "I got sort of sick."

"At the stomach, eh?" asked King Charlie.

"That's it, Mr.—"

"Smith—Charles Smith."

"I guess it was the sun that got to working on me, Mr. Smith," said the boy.

The title affected Charlie oddly. It was long since he had been a Mister, far longer than he had been a "King."

"The sun, eh?" he murmured. "I don't suppose the bucking had anything to do with it?"

"Oh no. I just lost a stirrup, that's all."

"You'd like to try it over again, maybe, now that you are rested up, and Jim Dandy is rested up too."

The boy flushed and his eyes gleamed.

"Will they give me another whirl?" he breathed.

"You can't go to ride in the State fair, anyway."

"I know that. But me and Jim Dandy ain't had it out yet, you can bet on that."

King Charlie sighed and looked far off, over the distant hill-top and past the mist of the horizon, and into his own youth, when he, also, had not known the meaning of surrender, but every fall had simply been a signal for fiercer battle.

He answered curtly: "You've had your chance, and you weren't good enough to take it."

"I ain't whining," said Billy English, rising to his feet and shaking himself together. "Next time—well, so long."

"Wait a minute. Where you going?"

"Why d'you ask?"

"I got particular reasons for wanting to know."

"Why—I'm going home, that's all."

"And what you going to do when you get there?"

"What business is that of yours?"

"Look here, son, how much older am I than you?"

The boy flushed and cleared his throat. "Well," he said, recognizing that age gave the other the right to talk to him and ask as many questions as he chose, "when I get home I'll get to work. They's a string of cows to be milked before night, and every one of 'em is my work."

"D'you always work when you're at home?"

"Why, no. I live the same as everybody else. That's my home, you see. I sleep and eat there, and every-thing."

"You sleep and eat and work there seven days a week?"

"Why, not on Sundays—"

"You milk the string of cows on Sunday, don't you?"

"Ye-es."

He seemed vastly reluctant to admit that he had duties even on the day of rest.

"And besides, if they's anything turns up that has to be done on Sunday you're the one that does it, ain't you? Extra wood, or a fence to be mended, or anything the like of that?"

"Sure. That's only nacheral. Me being the youngest man around."

"So that on Sundays you're about as busy as any other day?"

King Charlie

"That can't be helped."

"Well, I suppose you get good pay working seven days a week that way."

"Pay? Why, nobody gets paid for working in their own home."

"Don't they? What makes a home a home?"

"Why, it's where your father and mother lives and—"

"*Your* father and mother?"

"Well, not exactly. Mr. Shaw took me in, though, which makes him have a pile more claim on me than most fathers have on their own sons."

"I guess Shaw has told you that pretty often."

The boy flushed.

"Well?" he asked, strictly on the defensive.

"To make it short, that ain't your home any more than it is mine. If Shaw wants to treat you like a son, why don't he adopt you and give you his own name, and make you heir to his land and house? Why don't he do that?"

The boy paused. He was unable to answer.

"He's a terrible religious man, Mr. Shaw is," he explained at length. "I guess I ain't quite good enough to suit him."

A tremendous oath exploded from the lips of the King.

"Now talk up," he said. "Are you happy?"

"Why—I never thought of—"

"Are you happy the way the other boys in town are?"

"Sure—I—"

"D'you have a chance to play games with 'em, and—? Billy, you don't. You ain't happy. You don't even know what happiness means!"

There was such a lump for Billy to swallow that he touched his throat, staring vaguely at the stranger.

"How come you're making all this talk?" he asked wistfully. "It ain't going to make me any happier."

"Why not? Why can't you leave old Shaw?"

"Leave him after him taking me in that way?"

"Taking you in! Why, boy, you're talking like a fool. The whole village is laughing at you for the way you lct old Shaw use you! He ought to of been paying you regular man's wages for years, the old skinflint. Everybody in town's laughing at you, Billy English."

Billy crimsoned. Ridicule is the thing which children dread most.

"If I ever hear any of 'em doing it," he threatened vaguely, "I'll sure as nation—"

"What?"

"Nothing," said Billy.

But he fell into a brown study, and the King gave him time to think, for that blackening forehead meant a storm ahead for Mr. Shaw.

At length there had passed a sufficient space of silence in the judgment of the King. He rose, walked to a pile of tin cans, selected one, and tossed it, without warning, high in the air and to a considerable distance.

"Hit that!" he cried while the can was at the height of its rise.

Automatically the boy obeyed. He was in an awkward position, with his arms folded and his hands as far as possible from the butt of his gun. But the weapon came out like a flash, and just before the tin can struck the ground the weapon exploded, and the can darted off in a long, straight, sparkling line under the ringing impact.

Billy put up the gun with an exclamation.

"That was a fool thing to do!" he said.

But the King walked over, picked up the can, and examined the hole, exactly in the centre.

"It was a damned hard thing to do," he said at last.

Chapter Five

As he turned towards the boy again, his mind was made up. Billy English must go with him. From the first moment when his eyes had fallen on the boy something had leaped up in him in recognition. It was not the mere exhibition of modesty and courage and skill combined which he had witnessed in the horse-riding, and again in this small but significant bit of gunplay that influenced him, he told himself. It was more, far more.

Every rascal likes to feel that there are mysterious impulses behind his rascality. Yet, having made up his mind, the tramp hesitated before he ventured on the one real hold—in appearance—which he might use to bring Billy along with him.

"I got to be going now," Billy was saying. "I sure can't stay any longer, Mr. Smith. Mr. Shaw'll be plumb mad if—"

"Well? Let him hire somebody, why don't you? Or

35

let him hire you. Ain't I convinced you that you deserve wages, anyway?"

Billy pondered and then raised his thoughtful face.

"I guess I do," he said. "I hadn't thought—but I guess I do deserve 'em, and I guess I'll get 'em!"

"You think so, eh? What sort of wages will you ask for?"

"Man wages!"

"Not half wages?"

"Half wages?" He drew himself up proudly. "I ain't very big," he admitted, "but I ain't so small, either. I can rope a cow as fast as most, ride as well as a few, handle a gun in a pinch, run a plough, milk a cow if they's a herd of milkers—not that I'm extra good at any of them things, but I do as well as most, I think."

"So you think you'd ought to get full-sized wages?"

"That kind or none at all."

"H-m-m," murmured the King. "Well, you go tell Shaw right now what you want. I'll wait here till you come back."

The boy frowned.

"But what makes you think that I'll come back?"

"When you get through telling Shaw what you want and he gets through telling you what he thinks of what you want, you'll be ready to come back here."

"Why should I come here?"

"Because I'll be waiting here with a pretty good idea of what you'd ought to do next."

The boy hesitated. Several times he seemed on the verge of speaking. Then without a word he turned and hurried towards the street.

As for the King, he settled himself philosophically in the sun—for it was now near evening, and in the approaching night-chill the yellow sunlight possessed a grateful warmth—and waited for the development of events.

He consulted his watch. Twenty minutes had passed, then half an hour, then forty minutes. He began to grow alarmed. Had the youngster lost his nerve at the last moment? He had not seemed of that kind. But then, one could never tell. Shaw might be a shrewd old fellow with a great hold over the imagination of the boy. And boys are all imagination.

What was happening?

A full hour ran out and the sun was a bulging disc of red balanced on top of a western hill when a shrill whistling came up the street, turned a corner, and behold! there stood Billy English in gun-belt, canteen, and a small roll of blankets thrown over his shoulder. Best of all, he was laughing.

What a trump the youngster was, thought the tramp.

"Well?" asked King Charlie.

"He sure had a lot to say," chuckled the boy. "He told me that it plumb busted his heart to hear of such ingratitude as mine—me having been reared tender and careful by him. He got so sorry for himself that the tears came up in his eyes. I was afraid that he was going to bust out crying. Well, I sort of weakened, but I kept saying that I thought I'd ought to get paid for my work.

"Then he tried a new line with me, just like a hoss that switches from fence-rowing to sun-fishing. He got dignified. You'd of thought that he was the minister.

" 'How much money a month d'you think you're worth?' he asks me.

" 'Forty dollars with board and keep,' says I.

"He lets out a yell at that.

" 'You young limb of Satan!' he hollers. 'Are you trying to hold me up and rob me?'

" 'Well,' says I, getting sort of mad, but leading him on, 'how much d'you think I *am* worth?'

" 'I hadn't ought to give you nothing,' says Shaw. 'But I suppose if you want to drag money out of a poor man's pocket I could afford to pay you five dollars a month.'

"Well, I laughed in his face at that, and he begun

to storm. I turned around and went up to my room. Pretty soon he come and followed me. I heard him and locked the door.

"He stood outside and started begging. It made me sick to hear him. I sure have been a fool, living with that old hound all these years and never guessing what sort of a gent he was when he bullied me and kept driving me to work.

"He started by offering me seven dollars and a half a month. And he said he couldn't afford that much and that I wasn't worth that much, but that he was so fond of me that something come over him at the idea of me going.

"I told him I knew what had come over him, and it was a terrible shock to think of what he'd have to pay in board and keep and wages to two full-growed men that he would have to hire to do the work that I'd been doing for nothing.

"At that he let out a yell and started in telling how hard he'd worked when *he* was a boy, but I let him yell and kept on looking around for the things that I owned, because I was plumb set on not taking with me anything that the old man had bought for me—"

"H-m-m," broke in King Charlie at this point. "That sounds sort of foolish to me, Billy."

"How could I keep anything when I was leaving him?" asked Billy.

The tramp waved to him to continue.

"Finally he worked up to the point where he was offering me thirty dollars a month and keep and Sundays off. The old scoundrel! Then I threw the door open and walked down on him and told him a few truths about himself and what a skunk he'd been to work the hide off of me all these years—just the way you told me how to talk.

"And Shaw? He just curled up, the yaller sneak!"

The boy burned with righteous indignation.

"When I was leaving, Shaw locked the door behind

me and then cussed me through the window and told me that he'd always hated the sight of me, but that he'd got a couple of thousand dollars' worth of work out of me, and that was the only reason he'd kept me. He wished me bad luck—yep, he's a sure enough bad one."

He added, seeing a curious expression in the face of the tramp: "And now what?"

"They's a gent here that seems to want to talk to me," said the King uneasily.

The boy turned.

"Why, that's the sheriff. Hello!" he called to the dusty rider.

The latter waved a cheerful greeting, or at least a greeting as near cheer as he ever could come. The wide disc of the sun was half down.

"You got half a minute," said the sheriff to King Charlie, "to start out of town."

The King bowed with vast dignity. He hated the sheriff with all his heart for having come at all, but above all for having arrived at this moment, of all moments the most inopportune.

"You got power on your side, sheriff," he said sadly. "I ain't got the strength to stand against you."

The sheriff frowned, then glanced quickly at Billy English. This speech was made for effect—that was plain. And therefore it must be made for its effect on Billy English.

"Why ain't you at home doing your chores?" he asked a little too sharply, as even the most kindly men will occasionally speak to a child.

But Billy English considered himself well past childhood, and though there was no conceit in his honest young head, he felt that his work of that afternoon entitled him to a good deal of extra consideration.

"I'm through doing chores for old Shaw," he said carelessly. "He's had enough charity work done for him."

"H-m-m," said the sheriff.

"Besides," went on the boy, "I'm kind of curious, sheriff, to find out what you got agin my friend Mr. Smith."

"Is that his name?" asked the sheriff, turning a grim eye on King Charlie.

The latter saw that he would have to fight for his prize before he carried it off.

"It is," said the boy, "and grinning won't change that name a mite—"

For the sheriff was faintly smiling.

"It won't?" echoed the sheriff in a tone which might be taken to imply many things.

"Nor it won't stop him from being my friend," said Billy stoutly, driven by the sheriff's recalcitrant attitude farther than he had intended to go.

"The name I know him by," said the sheriff at length, "is King Charlie."

"What's that nickname got to do with him?"

"You've never heard of him?"

"Never!"

"You're a bright kid, Billy, but they's a pile of things that you ain't never heard of yet. A million folks know King Charlie the Tramp!"

Billy turned like a flash on the stranger. In all his hard working young life he had come to know of nothing more detestable to him than the naked hint of a tramp, a professional idler, living on the labours of honest folk like himself.

"Is that true?" he asked bitterly. "Are you—what the sheriff says?"

King Charlie was fairly cornered. He could not fight his way out by dint of argument, but he must trust to evasion to extricate him from the contempt of Billy English. He took off his hat and bowed with ironic politeness to the sheriff.

"Him being the sheriff," he said, "he must be right."

"Don't say that," said Billy, "but tell me the truth!"

"No use," said King Charlie with affectation of vast sadness. "You'd take his word before you'd take mine."

"I wouldn't," cried Billy. "Your word means as much to me as the word of any man; until you've proved yourself something I can't trust."

It was such a copybook sentiment that King Charlie dared not meet the fierce eye of the sheriff. In spite of himself he shrank in shame. It was indeed cruel to persuade this youngster to go off with him. And yet the prize was great. He was, he had to admit, no longer as young as he had once been, and supposing that he could convert the boy to his way of living—as, with his superior mental training and powers of persuasion plus age, he should easily be able to do—he would be providing a "staff and a comforter" for himself in days to come. Besides, something within him yearned towards the brave youngster. Rascal that he was, he could not but love the fine honesty of the boy.

"Let the sheriff call me what he can," said the King. "I know myself. I ain't ashamed of what I am. Poor, yes. Homeless, yes. A wanderer, yes. But not without a good honest pride, I thank God. Not without that, I pray!"

Of course, it meant nothing in words; the tone was everything, and the tone threw a glitter into the eyes of Billy English.

"You hear that?" he demanded of the sheriff.

"I hear him making a fool of you, Billy. Are you going to believe such fool talk as that?"

"I'll be a judge of that," said Billy, dark with dignity. "Maybe I ain't a sheriff, but it don't follow that I'm a fool, I hope."

The King instantly seized the opening.

"He's a terrible wise man, your sheriff," said the King. "He sees right through you and me, Billy. He sees that we ain't no good, but he's sure got his nerve with him to stand up and talk about it the way he does! If I was a younger man—"

"You old villain!" cried the sheriff. "You sneaking rascal, Charlie! What are you planning to do with the kid here?"

Charlie turned to the boy with a gesture.

"Will you listen to that?" he asked. "As if I could do anything with you that I felt like doing! Is that sense?"

"Charlie!" cried the sheriff, "the sun is down. Get out of town, and get out quick!"

Again Charlie removed his hat and bowed as to tyrannous authority. He turned to Billy and extended his hand.

"So long, son," he said, "I only wish that I'd had a chance to know you better."

"You'll have that chance," said Billy, brushing the hand to one side and glaring at the sheriff. "You'll have that chance if you don't mind me going along with you."

The heart of the tramp leaped into his throat. Was he not carrying out his threat of taking from the town something from under the very nose of the sheriff?

"Come and welcome, son," he said in a voice shaken by triumph and a truly kindly emotion.

"Billy, you damned little fool!" roared the sheriff, "what you aiming to do? Go with that old buzzard?"

But Billy snapped his fingers.

"Seems to me," he said hotly, "that you're using an awful pile of strong words, sheriff, and the next time you call me a fool I'll be thanking you if you have your hand near your gun."

"Why, you young idiot," cried the sheriff, "you need a licking, that's what you need."

"Start giving it," said Billy, swinging a little from side to side in a very ecstasy of passion. "Start in! And I'll damn you to start you off!"

He stood there with his knees flexed a little, a lithe, taut figure that motionless suggested more speed than another in full action. The sheriff missed not a line of that body and attitude. He studied Billy English with curiosity and sadness commingled, for in his own harsh way he was a kindly man.

"You're going to go, then?" he said at length.

"D'you think that you can stop me?"

"No, Billy," said the sheriff; "but if you've set your mind on that, all I ask you to remember is that when we found you, a little four-year-old shaver, you was all dressed up fine, Billy. You looked like the son of a high-class folks, Billy. And you talked bright as a dollar, and used better English than I'm using right now. I'm asking you to remember them things when you step out with the King. Keep your hands clean!"

Billy English favoured him with a parting glare.

"I'll try to keep care of myself without your help," he declared. "Come along, Mr. Smith."

King Charlie turned and removed his hat to the sheriff for the third time, and a smile of commingled malice and triumph was curling his lips.

Chapter Six

Straight down the road went Billy English at a terrific clip, and since they were heading straight for the railroad the tramp allowed him to take his own way. They continued in this fashion for perhaps fifteen minutes, when finally Billy stopped short, and leaning against a fence post he took off his hat and wiped his face with a trembling hand.

"Does it cut you up as much as that, son?" asked the older man with a real sympathy. "Does leaving the town hurt you as bad as that?"

"As bad as what?"

"Why, your hand's shaking; matter of fact, you're shaking all over!"

"Because I was so tarnation mad at the sheriff," said the boy. "I was seeing him all in red—and it wasn't the sunset that made him look red, either."

"You still feel that way?"

"I'm getting over it. But for a minute, Mr. Smith—

well, for a minute, I just wanted to light into the sheriff."

"And knock him off his hoss, eh, with your fists?"

"Knock him off the hoss, yes—but with a slug out of the gun!"

It brought up the tramp with a start.

"No more of that, Billy," he said sternly. "No matter how you have to fight, never with a gun."

"Why not?"

The answer was beautiful in its simplicity:

"Because you shoot too straight!"

Upon this statement Billy English meditated for some time, and indeed he did not directly reply to it. But he began to feel that his companion knew a very great deal. Who else would have thought of cautioning him not to shoot simply because he shot too *straight?* Yet he could see the wisdom of the warning, and his respect for his companion increased inversely as his rage at the sheriff and all of the sheriff townsmen decreased. Indeed, he might have obeyed a certain hollowness at heart which bade him forget the foolish impulse that had driven him away from the Shaw house and urged him to go back among the familiar people who knew him and who valued him. But having started with this tall fellow who seemed to come from nowhere and to know everything he had not the moral grit to abandon the trail. In the meantime he noted the walking powers of his new acquaintance with admiration. Himself reared to a life in the saddle—the only flaw in his otherwise neatly made young body being the slight bow of his legs from constant riding—he knew nothing by progression in any other manner than in a saddle. But King Charlie swung along with a faultless roll from hip to heel and toe, fairly shooting himself along at such a pace that Billy English had to stretch to a semi-run from time to time.

They hurried up a long slope, and came close to the railroad in this fashion, and by the rails King

Charlie paused. Here he eyed his young friend askance. Billy English was panting so heavily that his chest was a veritable bellows; but he did not make a single murmur of complaint. And the King saw and understood. The test meant much to him. If the boy had complained of the rate of their walk, or spoken enviously of the long legs of his companion, or made an excuse about sore feet, the good opinion of the King would have been half destroyed on the instant. But instead, that resolute silence and the eyes which unflinchingly went up the steeper slope beyond the rails made the heart of the tramp leap again with pleasure.

Here was metal—here was certainly finest steel. Oh, to have the moulding of this youngster into a man, a destroyer of Society just as he, King Charlie, had been, but beginning younger and more perfectly trained, Billy English could be what he, the King, had never been. He sighed at the thought. How tractable the boy was, too, how gentle of spirit, and yet how indomitable!

"Here's where we get a lift, if you're coming along with me," said the King.

"Where?" asked the boy. "There's no road near here, that I see."

"Ain't there a railroad here?"

"But no station. Besides, I haven't a penny for a ticket."

The King rubbed his long, bony hands together. How strange to find a half-grown boy who did not know that the railroad was the great free highway on which the only tickets needed were courage and a certain measure of address.

He raised a hand. "Listen!"

"I can't hear nothing," said Billy English.

"Listen again. Hear that humming and whining, sort of beyond the edge of the sky?"

"Yes, yes."

"That's a train coming—a freight, too, I guess. If it

46

is, you and me take it, son."

He estimated the grade. Yes, the train would, if a loaded freight, be climbing this grade so slowly that they could take it, even though the leap might be a hard one to make.

So, having done enough to kindle the interest of the boy, he said not another word, and although Billy English was writhing with curiosity and impatience he immediately adopted the laconic attitude of his newfound friend, and maintained the same silence. So, as they sat in the screen of some bushes near the track, they saw the front of a tall engine rock around the curve below them, with a thin screen of steam and smoke dragging behind the chimney. That screen, as the fireman fed up to give the engine full power on the grade, turned into a coughing black that puffed up a dozen feet above the smoke stack, and then was caught by the wind of the engine's speed and snatched away in a line parallel with the earth.

"It sure ain't going to stop," said the boy, instinctively crouching a little and making himself smaller at the sight of that monster engine.

The King listened with keen ear. That heavy rumble meant a loaded string of twenty-five or thirty cars, and, if so, he would make an effort to board the train. Billy English must follow; for he could estimate, from the manner in which the engine grew out at them, that the train was not coming too swiftly for an expert to mount it.

It mattered not that Billy was not an expert, he told himself grimly. It mattered not that he was only a boy. For if he were to be capable of the great things which the King was already sketching dimly and in loose strokes for the future he must be capable of doing whatever within any reason was asked of him.

"There we are," said the King complacently. "There she comes, Billy. Does she look good enough to ride on, to you?"

"But—does she stop here?"

"Stop? Sure she doesn't. But you and me ain't going to worry about that. We'll jump for it, eh?"

Billy English looked to his companion with a wan smile, as though ready to appreciate the joke, but when he saw the King already looking with an earnest eye at the approaching train he turned white as a sheet. The King, noting with a side glance, was not entirely displeased; he was simply anxious. For he did not want any thick-skinned clod, unafraid because he did not know what fear was. He wanted a keenly sensitive and alert organism. Only such could prove worth the schooling which the King intended for the boy.

"Jump for it?" echoed Billy.

"Aim at one of the ladders, them iron ladders going up the side of the car," said the King negligently. "When you jump you bunch your feet and your hands together. You aim at one step with all four, because you can be pretty sure that your hands will hit above the one you aim at with your feet. If you do that way you got a good chance of swinging on. If one foot misses, the other will most likely land. If one hand misses, the other will be pretty apt to catch on. And there you are. Another thing: when you jump take a run as fast as you can go alongside the train the same way that the train is running, but when you jump turn in towards the train and jump straight at it just as if you was going to punch a hole clean through the box-car. Understand?"

He illustrated the manoeuvres with little brusque gestures, and Billy English listened with his teeth setting hard, although his face was colourless.

"Listen to 'em roar!" muttered the old tramp, half closing his eyes. "Listen to them cars come, lad. They got some empties in that string too. You can tell 'em by the sort of hollow ring they got—a whole lot higher than the rumble of a loaded car. Now she comes! Let 'er go—let 'er shoot—oh, beauty!"

King Charlie

The enthusiasm of King Charlie waxed to an epic intensity as he heard the train roar more and more loudly. Oh, sound so welcome after the hot silence of the desert and the endless sands!

"Watch me; then you do the trick, Billy!" cried the King, and so saying, he rolled to his feet with surprising quickness, and scurried down the line, several roads, under cover of the brush. He was at length at a considerable distance, and Billy English, watching with unspeakable concern, saw the King, as the monster freight panted past, dart out of his hiding place and race like the wind beside the train, then face sharply in and leap catlike, straight at the car, with feet and hands, as he had said, bunched closely together. When he struck on the iron rounds of the ladder up the side of an empty box-car the impetus of the train swung him far towards one side, so that only a faultless grip with his hands and his feet, and flexible wrists as well, enabled him to hang there without his grip being broken.

But in another moment he had righted himself and slipped catlike up the ladder. There he remained, with his head barely above the top of the car, waving towards him and making cheering signals.

Yet Billy English paused, panting hard. There was no reason for him to make this leap into the teeth of danger except to please a vagrant stranger who should mean nothing to him. There was, indeed, no reason at all. Besides, there was something dangerous in the tall stranger—something dangerously attractive. He had a manner too persuasive. It had seemed to Billy that if the tall man cared to exert himself he, Billy English, would be forced, by sheer weight of words, to act as his preceptor bade him act. He could not stand up against the subtle and fluid talk of the King. Better far to stay far away from him.

The big engine swayed past him, grinding up that rough road, dripping hot, stinking oil, and spurting steam from labouring pistons. Inside the cabin was the engineer with his black visor drawn aslant across his worn, care-stricken, young-old face. And behind him he saw, as the cab rolled past, the fireman, a gay-faced Irishman, with his mouth agape over a song, not a murmur of which was audible above the mighty groaning and rushing of the train.

On came the long line of the train, their noise of grinding and of clanking wheels a comparative silence the moment the engine was by. Each set of wheels had a different note; each clanked by with a diminishing racket as the distance to the engine increased.

And yonder was the figure—jaunty in spite of its age—of the King, clinging with only one hand and his weight resting on one foot while he waved his hat in gay invitation towards the boy.

Billy English groaned, averted his eyes, and through what seemed to him an age waited for that figure to pass. But when he looked up again with a guilty start—behold, the form was still not by him!

There seemed a fate in it. He could not be tried and found lacking by a man who should be far past the age of agility. Settling his strong, lithe young shoulders under his pack, jerking his belt and the dependent holster more snugly about his waist, Billy English gave a tug to his hat, and then turned out into the open and sprinted ahead faster than he had ever sprinted before.

But his speed was almost nothing. Still the line of freight cars strung out ahead of him, floating easily away, and as he raced so close beneath the train, he could the better estimate its surprising speed. One car went past him with a swish and short wink of open air and sunlight on the far side; another whisked past, and then he saw the King coming, shouting inaudible words.

Suppose he were to leap and fall short—or suppose missed his grip? It mattered not, for he would swing in—swing in and under, and the smoothly spinning wheels would shear him in two.

Yet he turned in with a sudden short cry of desperation and furious, determined mind. So, his face convulsed with effort, he hurled himself as high and as far into the air as he could, and to such a purpose that the next he knew he had crashed flat into the side of the car and received on face and breast a crushing blow. His feet slipped from the rung at which he had aimed them, and the velocity of the train's forward motion left him clinging by no more than one handgrip.

Chapter Seven

He trailed to one side, flung out like a flag by the speed of the train, and he felt his left hand, by which he clung, slipping, with a strain cast on the wrist that threatened to splinter the bones.

If he made another effort, in all probability he would wrench himself from his hold. But he had to freshen that grip or fall. Across the top of the freight car, racing at full speed with marvellous disregard of the uneasy, rocking footing to which he had entrusted himself, came the King, but in spite of his speed, he would come too late. Billy's destruction or salvation depended on himself.

He was swinging back now towards a normal hanging position, and as he swung he reached with his right arm. Naturally, it worked his numbed left hand loose and the fingers slipped entirely from their hold. With all his might he reached and gripped with his right hand, but he failed of his hold, and it was a rung lower where both left and right hand secured a lodging.

The wrench nearly tore his shoulders from his body, but the double grip supported him. All of this had happened in the space of five seconds from his leap. Now he dragged himself up on the ladder, found knee-hold and then foothold, and eventually clung to it, upright, with a dizzy feeling of sickness.

Here the hand of the King was reached to him, and he dragged himself up to the top. He himself was paralyzed still with the reaction from his fear, and he half expected to find the King laughing at his pale face. But, instead, he was surprised to see that the King himself was by no means ruddy. He clutched Billy and dragged him down on the top of the car.

"That gave me the worst scare I ever had in my life," he panted. "By God, Billy, I'm all in with it—all in!"

In fact, he looked it. The permanent patch of colour high in either cheek was now no more than a faded purple, and his breath still came in gasps, as though his had been the exertion and not Billy's. A brakeman presently found them. He balanced back on his heels as the train shot around a sharp turn, the wind making his hickory shirt cling to his body as though soaked in water.

"That was a close one," he said, grinning. "You won't come that close to your finish more'n once more, kid. Never hopped a train before, King?"

It amazed Billy English that the brakeman should know his companion, but when the fellow went on, the King took much credit to himself for this fact.

"They all know the old King," he said, leaning back on his elbows. "They all know me, eh, Billy? Took years to get as well known as I am along this road. Years and years and years! Some day maybe you'll have as big a rep. Would you like that?"

"Sort of," said Billy without enthusiasm. "I dunno but I could get along without it, though."

The older man cast a glance at him and decided that he must continually use caution in his words to the youth.

"Look yonder," he said, by way of diverting attention. "Look at the way we're flying into the west and into the sunset, Billy. I guess that this beats riding a hoss, eh?"

Billy English shook his head. "It's just different," he declared. "Just different—but better. These planks under you may be going fast—but they ain't thinning and feeling the same's you are thinning and feeling. These planks can go faster, but they ain't a hoss, sir. Nope!"

The King shrugged his shoulders. This absurd notion must be extracted from the mind of the kid when there was time for it. In the meanwhile, he looked about him and placidly regarded the flitting of the miles. All was going so easily, so swimmingly, as compared with the footsore miles of the desert, that it seemed an easy thing to tell the prodigious lie towards which he had been drifting ever since he had heard how Billy English was found in Carterville.

"Billy," he said, "what you remember about your father?"

"Nothing much," said Billy. "You see, I was only four when—well, the gent that I guess must of been my father was just sort of tall. But I ain't a bit sure about anything. Nothing about him, that is. I remember my mother; that's all."

"What you remember about her?"

"Things I don't talk about," said the boy with a blending of dignity and sadness that moved the hardened tramp in spite of himself. "Things," he added, "that I *couldn't* talk about."

Plainly, then, his past was a mist. That was all the King wanted to know.

"Would you like," he said, "to know more about your father?"

"Would I like to go to heaven?" said the boy, trembling with sudden eagerness. Then he whirled on the King and gripped him.

"By God," he said, "you knew him—or you know him now. He—he's still alive. He's sent you to find me! Is that why you followed me down the road? But why—"

"Listen," said the King, quivering with an emotion which was real, though it was not at all what it seemed to be. "When you met up with me, did you feel anything queer, Billy?"

"I dunno. Why?"

"I'll ask you a question right back. Why are you here?"

"Because—because I had a fight with Shaw."

"That any reason for you to swipe a ride on a train like this?"

"You told me to—"

He stopped short.

"That's it, Billy. I told you to. And why did you do what I told you to?"

Billy English frowned heavily.

"What you driving at?" he asked.

"When you first seen me," said King Charlie, playing his cards with care and swiftness combined for this great stake, "why was it that you started right in doing what I told you to do, and why was it that I was the only one on the field that knowed really just how you was feeling underneath your smile?"

Billy, who had regained some of his colour, now lost it again.

"D'you mean—I don't foller you, I guess!"

"You do, but you won't let yourself. Look hard at me, Billy. Look me straight in the eye."

The boy obeyed.

"Don't you recognize nothing, don't you feel nothing?" cried King Charlie, throwing into the voice all the feeling he could, and in his present state of mind that was not difficult. "Look hard at me, Billy, while I tell you my right name—I'm Charles English!"

Billy English winced and gaped at his companion.
"You mean—"

"Don't you see," cried the tramp, "that's why I'd
walked across the desert to find you? It was an instinct leading me back towards the place. And then
I seen you on the field riding the hoss and something
jumped in me: 'It's him!' says I to myself. 'No, he's
dead eleven black years ago,' says myself to me. Then
I ask about you, and they tell me how you come in
from the railroad tracks ten or eleven years ago saying that you was four years old and that your name
was Billy English. When I heard that name my head
started spinning. I near went out cold. I kept telling
myself that it couldn't be true."

As he spoke, the King watched the boy's face
shrewdly, and he saw that Billy was moved past in-
credulity and had been swept into the tide of the narrative.

"And then," went on the King, "I said to myself:
'Can I show myself to him? Can I let him see me the
way I am—without a home, without money, with
nothing but my self-respect left to me—that and my
freedom that they couldn't take away from me? Can
I show myself to him the way I am, and take him
away from a good home, maybe?' I says. And then I
start to find out, and pretty soon I know that you ain't
got a good home at all. No, because an old skinflint
that's working your hands to the bone has you. And
then I says, 'I'll go and see him and try if he likes to
live this life with me—of freedom that can't be
bought.' And so, Billy, here we are. After eleven
years, you and your father are joined together on the
train—on the same tracks where we lost each other
eleven years before."

He felt that his speech had trailed off into a most
ridiculously unemphatic conclusion, and he would
not have been at all surprised had Billy English burst
into ringing laughter and pointed a finger of derision
at him. But too many strange things had happened

to poor Billy that day. They had broken down the barriers of his caution, and now he had no power to stand back and criticize what he heard.

For a moment of bitter suspense he threw back his head and stared into the eyes of King Charlie, and then he caught the hands of the rascal in a strong grip.

"God a'mighty," he said, "how I've dreamed about this; how I've plumb ached for it!"

Chapter Eight

Into such a happy delirium had Billy English fallen that it was easy for the King to answer the babel of questions which now poured out on him.

The story he told was one which he had only loosely sketched to himself before, and which he now told with as little detail as possible, filling it in as he went along. He had been, he said, a prosperous man, happy with his wife and his child, until the tragedy overtook them. That tragedy occurred when little Billy disappeared from the train in which his wife was travelling. The train had slowed at a water-tank, and Billy had gone back to the platform to look out. There he must have climbed down, and when the conductor came inside and shut up the platform again, Billy must have been left on the ground outside.

This was what they guessed later. And this was what must have happened. Mrs. English had fallen asleep, and it was a matter of several hours before

58

she wakened and missed the boy. When he left her she could not say, and the train had made a dozen stops during the time she slept.

There was nothing for it but to advertise in the papers and send inquiries back to every station along the line. But since there was no station or station-agent at the tank where Billy had really escaped, no search was made into the surrounding country. That was the only manner in which he could explain the failure to find Billy. In the meantime, Mrs. English grew sick with anxiety, and a short time afterwards sunk under a slight malady and died. He himself would not give up the search, but abandoning his dry-goods business in St. Louis, he had taken to the road in search for the boy until, examining into the particulars of the run of the train on that division on the night of Billy's disappearance, he learned what had not been previously reported through the neg-ligence of the train crew—that when the train pulled into the next town, it was found that under the train there were bloodstains and evidences that someone had been crushed on the track. It was simply held that some tramp had fallen from the rods and no more attention was paid to the matter, but the King was convinced that this was the fate of his son.

After this he made a futile effort to run his busi-ness, but all went wrong, and when his business failed completely he took to the road again, drifting here and there, the life of a vagrant, with the power of society directed all against him. And so he had fought on, reckless as to how he lived, sent again and again to prison, usually for crimes which he had not committed, until at last he had come to be what the boy beheld him.

He painted the picture as black as possible, for now he was attributing all his guilt, indirectly, to the disappearance of Billy; he was placing the burden deftly on the shoulders of the boy, and though Billy winced and shrank, it was plain that he accepted the tale as the Gospel truth.

Darkness, in the meantime, had fallen, and the King was profoundly grateful to nature for veiling his face from the eyes of the boy as he concluded his invention.

After that a long silence fell between them, and in the end he felt the hand of the boy fall reverently and affectionately on his shoulder. There was little honesty or generosity left in the heart of the King, but at this touch he came close, indeed, to recanting his lie and telling Billy English that it was all a jest. But his tongue clove to the roof of his mouth when he attempted to speak, and the truth remained unspoken.

After that he listened to Billy's account of his own uneventful, work-tormented life, with all the story of his ambitions and hopes worked in towards the end. In conclusion, they spoke of the future, and in this the father took the guiding hand. They would settle down to an honest and industrious life very soon, and in the meantime it would be necessary for the King to complete one or two small affairs. He would, in short, have to mingle for a while with gentlemen of his own ilk along the road, and Billy must come with him.

Among the "jungles," he told Billy, they must never refer to each other as father and son. For a thousand reasons it would be better simply to treat each other as friends.

Their narratives and these plannings for the future occupied the time until close to midnight, when they approached the swirling and scattered lights, far ahead, of a small town, and when the freight took a siding here the tramp and Billy English swung down to the ground and King Charlie led the way to the far side of the village.

Weary from the long day and the hard work which he had crowded into part of it, exhausted by all the strange things that had happened to him, Billy En-

King Charlie

glish stumbled along behind the tall man who walked with such an elastic, untiring step—the man whom he was hereafter to think of as father. And strangely conflicting emotions swayed in the boy's heart as he walked. Vagabond and disreputable in many ways he knew that man to be, and, besides, that suspicion which most honest folk feel even subconsciously for the evaders of the law was still like a shadow in the back of his brain.

Yet he went on. He was far too tired to think out the tangled problem at this time of night. A fire now gleamed and winked afar off among the trees, momently growing in size and distinctness, until they broke into a small glade, and Billy English beheld for the first time in his life a tramp "jungle" where the wanderers of the earth put into port like unknown ships to cook their stews, brew their coffee made of ten-times boiled coffee grounds, perhaps, and wash their clothes—if they be nice in their habits—and then exchange tales with what company they may find in the resort.

On this night the fire was surrounded by a goodly assembly. A gaol in a town some fifty miles away had just disgorged a half-dozen vagrants who, having been arrested on the same day, were turned loose on the same day, and had come to the conclusion of their first day's journey after receiving liberty together.

These having received a few dollars for their work for the county on being liberated were now flush, and they had come to the jungle laden down with dainties dear to the heart of a hobo. Canned tomatoes, onions, potatoes, and chickens they had contributed to the contents of the enormous stew which now simmered in a big wash boiler, and over which stood the eldest and most trusted cook of the six stirring the mulligan from time to time with a long stick, one end of which had been whittled clean. In the meantime, the others of the company, men of all ages from the lean twenties to the grizzled fifties, sat around in a semicircle hugging their knees and with their heads thrown back while, like so many wolves, they inhaled the aroma of the coming feast.

They were not the only claimants of the camp-fire, however. On the other side of the blaze were three worn and tattered veterans of the road which had no ending. Unshaven for days, and uninterested in shaving, dressed in patched odds and ends of clothes, these blowed-in-the-glass-stiffs, permanent and unchangeable tramps, lounged at their ease, making themselves as comfortable as possible and attempting to show no interest in the mulligan of which they had not the money to buy a share, though they writhed as in pain when the changeable wind on occasion wafted the fragrance of the stew towards them.

The sight of these mangy rascals made Billy English shiver with aversion, and turning his glance sharply to one side he looked into the face of the last member of the camp-fire party. This was a wide-shouldered man who lay flat on his back with the heel of one foot based on the toe of the other, puffing at a half-finished cigar, with his hat drawn deep over his eyes. His clothes were of far better make than those of any other person in the glade, and his whole appearance was such that he might have passed easy muster as a respectable member of Society on a city street.

Towards him the King also had now turned his gaze, and the first sight of the man who lay prone caused him to start.

"Colytt!" he said. "By the Lord, it's Colytt! Ain't that luck for once in a year?"

So saying, he stepped out from the shadow of the trees where he had until this moment lingered, and striding to the man he had termed Colytt he kicked the uppermost foot of the latter sharply.

The result was as surprising as the release of a

tightly coiled watch-spring. Colytt came to his feet with a leap, and showed a dark, beady-featured face, now scowling with malignance. His hand was back to strike when he recognized the smiling face of Charlie.

It required a moment for him to let the snarl relax from his lips, and then, with a shamefaced smile, he extended his hand.

"Hello, King," he said. "Damned if you didn't give me a start. Hey, bos, here's the King! Here's King Charlie!"

That announcement operated like magic upon the rest of the tramps, who came to their feet of one accord, and sent a clamour towards the celebrity. In another moment he was among them, and they were busy shaking his hand. Only the three dyed-in-the-wool veterans made no move to approach him. He went around the fire and stood over them, his hand extended, and Billy English shuddered to see his father meet such vermin on their own level.

"Chicago Lou!" cried the King. "And here's old Whitey from York. Damned if it ain't good to lay eyes on you, boys."

At that signal, as though they had been holding back, not sure that recognition would be welcome to him, they started up and took his hand one by one, at the same time glancing proudly towards the others on the far side of the fire.

"Have you had chuck, yet?" asked the King.

They averred that they had not, and he stepped to the wash boiler and glanced at the contents.

"Enough for a dozen," he declared. "I'll pay for your share to-night. Hey, Billy!"

Billy English followed slowly into the firelight, and stood frowning on all sides.

"Here you are, pals," said the King. "I want to make you known to a sidestepper of mine, Billy English."

Chapter Nine

That was the introduction of Billy to a class of men among whom he was to spend so many years of life and with whom he would accomplish many adventures. He shook hands with them hesitantly, feeling that he must be at least as friendly towards them as his father was. But inside him there was something which revolted against them. They, for their part, were entirely cordial. The youngster had not that rat-look which they were accustomed to see in youthful recruits to their order, but if King Charlie introduced the lad he must be all right.

So they made poor Billy welcome, and gave him a good seat by the fire and furnished him a large and steaming portion of mulligan and "punk"—bread—in a big tomato can. He dipped into the provender cautiously, for the can had not seemed entirely clean, and the mulligan appeared to contain every variety of food of which he could think. For everything goes into mulligan—pieces of stale bread, tomatoes, po-

64

tatoes, vegetables of any kind, peppers, marrow-
bones, meat of any sort chopped up, pepper and salt
in reasonable quantities. But a vast hunger urged
him to taste the stew, and he found it delectable beyond words. It is, in fact, the best possible way to
prepare an appetizing ration out of cheap materials.

About him he heard slang which he could hardly
follow, so thickly was it used and so strange were the
words to him. When he heard one ragged gentleman,
for instance, speak of "getting a stretch for soaking
an elbow" it did not dawn on the untutored brain of
Billy that the man was simply saying that he had
been sentenced to a year's imprisonment for beating
a detective. Nor did he gather the meaning when he
learned that another man had "got an anchor when
he was due to go up Salt Creek," but later on Billy,
having enjoyed the fare, found those who had
cooked it better fellows than he had at first suspected.

When they had eaten, the tone of their conversation changed—grew considerably heightened—and
as they told yarns, disputed, jested with growing
abandon, Billy noticed that the King and the wide-
shouldered gentleman had drawn apart, and were
conversing softly together.

The purport of their conversation was somewhat
as follows:

"Where'd you pick up the kid?" asked Colytt. "He
don't look the right kind, King."

"He ain't the right kind, my boy," said the older
man. "Matter of fact, he ain't the right kind at all.
But if he's handled with gloves he may turn out to
be worth ten times as much as one of the 'right kind.'
Ever hear of any of the 'right kind' showing any gratitude to them that taught 'em everything they knew?
Or ever hear of 'em staying around and helping when
the gents that done the teaching go down on their
luck? No, you never heard nothing like that. But this
is a clean-bred 'un, Colytt, as they say on the Blue

Grass. He'll act different if I can keep a hold on him and learn him something."

Colytt cocked his big, ugly head to one side.

"You was always a smooth one, King," he said. "Well, go ahead with the kid, and I wish you luck. But I tell you this to start with—you can't change the colour of a cat."

"Croak if you want to," said the King; "but sit up and watch results when I'm through."

That prodigious lie about the fatherhood of the boy he dared not communicate to even so hardy a character as Colytt.

"What's up now?" he asked. "Working up a plant?"

"Got a plant all laid out," said Colytt mournfully, "but I got nobody to work it with me."

"What's the matter with me?" asked the King.

Colytt smiled.

"You with the shakes?" he said. "No hope, partner. You'd be meaning well in the thick of it, if something went wrong, but you might not be no good to me or yourself. You know that."

The King snapped his teeth together.

"Maybe not," he said; "but what about the kid?"

"Too young—you'd ought to know that."

"Why?"

"This work I got planned is risky stuff, King. If it comes to a pinch I got to have somebody along that I'll be sure has the nerve to shoot, and shoot straight."

"Listen to me, bo. I picked this kid up at a hoss-breaking contest that he lost because he'd absorbed all the punch that there was in the hoss and the other gent was just rocked in a cradle. And then I tried this boy out with his gat. I threw a can in the air—a little oyster can, half as big as your fist. I chuck it high and far, and told him to blaze away when it started dropping. His draw was as pretty as a picture, and he drilled that can clean through the centre before it had a chance to kiss the dust. How does that sound to you, Colytt?"

So excited had Colytt become during the recital that, as he was sitting cross-legged, he rocked far forward until his knees pressed against the ground.

"That's as neat as anything I ever heard tell about even you, King."

"Maybe. But how does he sound to you now, Colytt?"

Colytt looked critically towards the boy, and the King sat back to wait. Colytt had been a safe-blower in the East before the country became too hot for him, and he had moved West to become one of those cold-nerved adventurers who roamed up and down the length and the breadth of the mountain desert striking their blows here and there, and escaping with their loot as best they could, depending for their safety upon the speed and endurance of their horses, the knowledge of the country, which they studied until every mile of it was mapped in their memories, and their friends among the small ranchers, nesters, and trappers, whom they cultivated with small donations of money when they were flush. But even in spite of all that they could do their lives were a continual and desperate hazard, as their class title of "long-riders" signified. Colytt was a type of them, if there could be a type. Fierce, fearless, incapable of fatigue, cunning as a wolverene and as strong, never fighting save when it was absolutely necessary, and then always fighting to kill, he had lived, perhaps, seven years on the ranges, and into that space of time he had crammed the deeds of seven wicked lifetimes.

It was for these reasons that the evil mind of the King hung in suspense as he waited for Colytt to pronounce judgment.

"He looks good to me," said Colytt at last in his deep voice. "He looks damn good. He ain't one of these talky kids. He ain't told them bums a thing about himself. But how could you persuade a clean-set kid like that to go ousting peters, King?"

"There's ways of doing everything," said the King. "I'll do the persuading. But tell me what your lay is?"

"There's a runt of a bank down at Yorkville, a little town over the hill. It's easy to get the safe, but it ain't going to be any too easy to get out of town after we start the racket. They's been a couple of stick-ups around there."

"Could we get hosses?"

"Sure. I got a friend out the way, here. He's got a couple of good skates. I got a couple myself over behind the bushes yonder. You go talk to the kid, will you?"

The King, accordingly, went to Billy English, who was nodding in the heat of the fire and only half hearing what the hoboes around him said. The King called him away, and put his point with a directness that should be convincing if anything was.

"Billy," he said, "you seen me talking to Colytt?"

The boy nodded.

"He's been telling me about some dirty work that a bank down in Yorkville done a rancher friend of his. Seems that this bank got his pal into a close corner with a mortgage and then closed in on him and grabbed everything he had. Understand?"

"Not quite," said Billy. "But—"

"They do terrible things to a gent that has a mortgage agin him," said the King sadly. "I know—because it's been done to me. In this case they just cleaned the poor fellow out of house and home, and put his wife and four kiddies out from under a roof—three little girls and two curly-headed boys. Ain't that a rotten thing to hear, Billy?"

Billy clicked his teeth.

"Something had sure ought to be done about it," he snapped.

"That's what Colytt has been thinking," said the King. "That's what made him so darned thoughtful and quiet when we first seen him here. He was wondering how he could help that friend of his. Understand?"

"He must be a good man," said simple Billy English with warmth. "He must be a fine sort of a gent, sir. I didn't think he was when I first looked at him."

That "sir" rang to the very heart of the old rascal as he watched the boy, and once again, for the hundredth time, he wavered in his purpose. But no—this youthful Billy English must serve as the King's meal ticket when the latter grew old.

"But what can he do?" asked Billy.

"He's going to get that money back for his friend," said the King sternly. "He's going down and blow open the safe that the money is kept in and take as much as belongs to his friend, and then get away and—"

"But that—" gasped Billy. "What would happen if he was caught breaking into the bank?"

"Penitentiary," said the King darkly. "Think what he's risking for his friend!"

Billy caught his breath again.

"All alone?" he asked.

"No, Billy; I'm going to go along and do what little I can, though I'm not much account in such affairs."

The boy caught his arm.

"Could I go along and do what I can?" he asked. "D'you think he'd trust me that far?"

It was so ridiculously easy that the King could have laughed aloud had he not been a trifle concerned to see the boy so gullible. But, after all, he decided that it was not so strange, considering the fact that Billy English felt that his own father was telling him these things.

"I dunno," said the King with great gravity. "We'll go back and ask him if you can come along."

Chapter Ten

Twenty minutes later, Colytt on one horse and Billy English on the other—for the King vowed he'd rather walk than ride, at least for a short distance—they proceeded away from the jungle at a brisk walk for the King and a jogging trot for the horses, from time to time, to keep up with the swing of those long legs.

Considering the gravity of the work before them, there was astonishingly little talk, it seemed to Billy. The main theme of conversation was introduced by the King after they had been going for only a short distance, and it was a strange topic to start on such a trip—keeping in mind their destination. He held forth at length, in the first place, upon the difficulty of such a thing as a bank robbery and the great probability that the robbers, if they showed the slightest weakness, would fall a prey to the vigorous pursuit, even if they were so lucky as to get away from the town itself. Many a man had been so captured; whereas those bandits who rushed boldly upon a town, galloped to their selected bank, blew open the safe or called on the cashier for the money, and then rode off shooting in all directions—those men went safe time and again.

The inference was plain—that this was the preferable method. Unfortunately, they did not have enough men to act in this manner. He went on to tell what happened to those who were captured. Usually they were instantly hanged on the nearest trees by the infuriated townsfolk. Or if they did not act with such immediate violence a destiny even more terrible awaited the robber. He was sent off to prison, and there he was treated with particular brutality. Bread and water became his portion, and he was made to labour with terrible assiduity all day, while at night he slept in a dark cell to which little air entered. His imprisonment was for a term of twenty-five or thirty years, it appeared, according to the King.

"But," cried poor Billy English, "I heard about a gent taken for bank robbery that was pardoned after he'd been in only five years. I read about that in the papers."

"You read lots of queerer things than that in the papers," said the King wisely. "Besides, a couple of exceptions only go to prove the rule. Am I right, Colytt?"

There was a grunt from Colytt, and Billy fell into a brown study which led him to exactly the conclusion that the King wished to carry him to—namely, that rather than be captured in the robbery of a bank, it was far preferable to be killed, and obviously, therefore, it was better to shoot to kill in turn. With all his might poor Billy wished that the unnamed friend of Colytt might have been served in some other manner, but he dared not ask questions, and he was ashamed to show the white feather.

But when the crisis came, what would he do in case there were a close pursuit? Would he shoot to kill rather than risk the miserable fate of prison or the shameful death on the end of a rope hanging from the nearest tree?

In this dire dilemma he felt his opinion sway back and forth. To hang or die in prison was horrible; to kill in self-defense was yet more horrible; and most shameful of all was it to draw out of an enterprise in which his own father adventured so fearlessly.

They reached a house, at the door of which Colytt knocked, and held consultation with the man who answered the summons, lantern in hand. Then he went out to a small shed behind the house, saddled a horse which he found there, and returned leading this to the King. So, all three mounted, they now scurried ahead at a more rapid pace, and the King swung in beside Billy English for a time and drew for him the long and quiet content of the life that was to be theirs—once this disagreeable and necessary job of the night were finished. He, the King, would have new courage to carve out an honest and honourable career, he avowed, now that he had his boy again.

And he proved his good spirits by breaking into a ringing song a moment later, which was harshly cut short by the voice of Colytt.

"Stop that damn noise, will you?" cried the yegg. "You think I want to have everybody in the county know that we're on the road tonight?"

The King made no protest, but stopped singing, and as he did so they came over the top of a hill and in sight of a town spilled out in a long, loose chain of lights, the scattering nature of which was ample indication that the majority of the people in Yorkville were asleep. Billy English vaguely and wretchedly traced the outline of the town. It was like Carterville—grouped entirely around one long street or road.

The orders were issued briefly by Colytt on the way down the hill. There was one watchman on guard, but he had previously "fixed" that watchman, and as

King Charlie

soon as he appeared and gave the signal the watchman would receive a hurry call to go on some pressing errand down the street—for the bank was not the only place he watched. But the chief watch must be held against chance passers-by, for the windows of the bank were glass, the safe was mortally near the front of the store, and it was very possible that anyone who came by might see the shadow of Colytt through that uncurtained glass. The King was to stay at the rear of the bank, therefore, to watch for anyone who might come in that direction, which some official of the bank might possibly do to finish up some work, since it was not much more than ten-thirty. But the main danger would be guarded against by Billy English in front of the bank, where he was to take his stand by the side of his horse, and having first spent some time fumbling at his reins, which he could claim had come unbraided should anyone come near, he could then go on to examine the hoofs of his horse as though it had picked up a pebble, and in this fashion kill the time until the explosion was heard. In that case he was to swing into the saddle and rein his horse between the bank and the next building, and so guard the rear, and open fire on all who came near until the whistle of the two in the rear of the bank announced that Colytt was clear with the loot. In the meantime, should someone come down the street, Billy was to commence whistling "Auld Lang Syne," and Colytt would desist in his work or keep safely out of view until the danger passed.

Fifteen minutes later Billy found himself in the designated post, standing at the side of his horse and working foolishly, without purpose, at his reins. But the village street was perfectly dark, and no one came in view through what seemed an eternity, though all the time he could see forms pass and repass across the lighted shade of a window in a house not fifty yards away.

Every moment he expected to hear the explosion, though, as a matter of fact, Colytt would need far more time. But seconds dragged past like minutes with Billy. And now came a new alarm and added danger. The night, which had been thick as a fog in the beginning, now rapidly thinned away, so that he could look the length of the street, and next he saw a slowly ascending fire drift up through the trees on a distant hill and take shape at the top as a round, yellow moon at the full.

The devil was indeed in it to take away the kindly dark which had shielded them.

And here, a moment later, came a singing fellow who sauntered idly down the street, not hurrying like a man who wishes to get somewhere, but ambling on as though he were merely out to enjoy the night. The heart of Billy climbed into his throat.

Busily he began prodding at the hoof of his horse which he had lifted up. He was aware that the stranger had paused, and, turning to the other side of the horse with a muffled "Hello," he picked up that hoof in turn and began to examine it.

But the stranger did not pass on. He stayed.

"What's wrong?" he asked.

Billy turned and faced a strongly built man of perhaps thirty-five, a solid form as suggestive of muscular power as the form of Colytt himself.

"Picked up a pebble, I guess," said Billy. "He started limping on me, so I got off to take a look."

The other chuckled.

"Well," he said, "you ain't much of a hand with hosses, son, if you can't tell which foot a hoss is limping on. Where you come from?"

And he dropped a conversationally careless hand on the top of the nearest post of the hitching rack. Sweat rolled out on the forehead of Billy English though the night was cold. Suppose that this talkative fool were to stay here until the explosion went off? At his side he wore a big forty-five in a most workmanlike fashion, low on his thigh. And if ever a man looked the part of an alert fighter this was he. When he heard that noise, things would begin to happen in this street, and they would happen with great precision.

Would this fellow shoot him down, or was he doomed to shoot down the stranger?

"Where you come from?" repeated the other, more aggressively. "Didn't you hear me, kid?"

"Over yonder," said Billy, waving his hand vaguely.

"What's that mean? Troyton?"

"Yep, beyond Troyton."

"You mean on the other side of the river, eh?"

"That's right."

The other laughed softly.

"There ain't any river beyond Troyton, kid. Now tell me, what you doing here?"

Bill leaned back against the shoulder of the horse. He was very sick and cold in the pit of the stomach.

"I dunno what you mean," he murmured.

"Don't you?" said the other. "Look here, son, you run away from home to join the gold rush up in—"

The sentence was split away to nothing by a dull and muffled sound like the dropping of an immensely heavy weight, wrapped in thick mufflings, upon an immensely strong floor. The big man turned like a flash towards the bank.

"By God!" he cried, as the meaning dawned on him, and his gun whipped from its holster.

He was late, however, far too late, for the practised hand of Billy had automatically slipped out his gun the instant he heard the explosion, and now his finger curled around the trigger and held the life of the stranger in a balance.

The latter whirled, and Billy stepped in with the sudden energy of a desperate man and struck with the long, heavy barrel of the gun. The blow landed squarely along the head of the other, and he toppled back into the thick dust, sending a bullet at the heart of the sky.

Over him leaned Billy. Had he killed the man? No, there was life in that sturdy body, though Billy could have sworn that he had felt the skull sag under the blow.

But the explosion of the gun had roused a score of human echoes near by. Doors banged and voices ran out upon porches. Men began calling to one another until one dominant throat called: "The bank—look yonder! Hey, there, who are you?"

Billy was already swinging into the saddle. He did not wait to reply, but, leaving the dark, sprawled figure against the white of the moonlit dust behind him—a damning accusation—he spurred his horse around the corner of the bank.

Two bullets chipped the bricks as he whirled to safety, and voices roared directions as to how they should cut off his retreat, but that retreat was not the immediate object in the eyes of Billy. Panic had him by the throat, but still he remembered the orders of the King.

Under the shelter of the wall of the bank he whirled his horse around, and riding back to the verge of the street he fired—at such an angle into the air that he could not strike anyone—up, down, and across, with a result that the pursuers, who had been rushing gun in hand out to do battle, now scattered for shelter with yells, only sending a desultory fire behind them as they gave way.

At the same moment there was a sharp whistle, immediately broken off and reinforced with curses, from the rear of the bank, and Billy twitched his neat-footed horse around and spurred for safety.

He had not too much time. They were swarming like hornets behind him, and bullets were smashing against the wall of the bank from a dozen different directions. He brought the horse swerving into the open stretch behind the bank and saw two dark forms darting away across the open fields.

After these he loosed his rein and came rapidly upon them. At the edge of a small grove of scrub oak he caught up with them, but they gave him neither glance nor word until they had topped the next rise, and from that point of vantage had looked down upon the moonlit plain and seen the posse streaming in pursuit.

Then: "Damn all the luck this side of hell!" roared Colytt.

"You didn't have time enough," said Billy. "I guess I didn't give you time enough to get what you wanted?"

"You? Time enough? Good God, you gave me time enough to carry the whole bank away; you done noble, kid! The old King there couldn't have bested what you done in his palmiest days, but the safe"— here a torrid explosion of oaths followed—"the safe was double. Me, like a fool—I thought it was just a tin can, but inside that rusty old piece of junk they was a brand new outfit."

All that danger, and not a cent had been taken. But Billy English, for some strange reason, merely tilted back his head and broke into shrill musical laughter, while they turned the heads of their horses to the left and glided away under the cover of the hills.

Chapter Eleven

The slant, warm sunshine falling on the face of the King the next morning wakened him. He shifted himself slowly to one side along the floor of the shanty to which he and Billy English and Colytt had come at the end of their flight, so far from any sign of a pursuit that they had decided to risk sleeping here.

For a time, as the sunshine dropped in on the rest of his body, he lay luxuriating in the warmth which thawed the night chill out of his limbs, and which, it seemed, was likewise thawing his mind and permitting the disastrous events of the evening before to filter into his recollection.

It was very bad in one respect, and very good in another.

It was bad in that the stroke had fallen and had not brought to them the rich returns with which he had promised himself to corrupt the mind of the boy for ever. With gold he would buy him to the easy life

78

of yegg and long rider. It was very good, however, in that the youngster had shown such dauntless grit.

On the way up the hills he had told them about his attack on the stranger, and they for themselves had heard the barkings of his gun in reply to the entire village, holding the avengers back and giving them a chance for the flying start which had meant their safety. Yes, Billy English certainly had the nerve for the work, the coolness and the address. To be sure, he had seemed a little shaky on the way into York-ville, but the important thing was that he had daunt-lessly stood watch while the deft Colytt was running the mould of soft soap around the door of the safe. He had stood guard, and he had fought for the general good of the three in the time of need.

So much did the thought of this warm the heart of the King that he closed his eyes again and lay for a long time dreaming of the good time to come, when the power of this boy, trained by his own skill and the brain of Colytt, would begin to crack safes. Then they would live on the fat of the land indeed. What a series of hauls that would be!

He could no longer contain himself, so great had grown his self-content. He sat up. There lay Colytt, his face buried in his arms, breathing heavily. But Billy was gone. No doubt he was busy somewhere in that bright sunshine fishing for trout in the stream they had heard running the night before.

"Colytt!" he called.

Colytt opened one eye.

"It's morning."

"Damned if I care if it's night. We missed the loot and—"

"Hush u-p—easy! Don't let the kid hear you talk none too frequent about 'loot.' We're doing all this for the good of your friend, you know."

"Damn my friend," replied Colytt, but he neverthe-less softened his voice as he sat up. He rubbed the sleep out of his eyes and then turned his ugly face towards the King. "A game kid, that. He sure is the grit, King."

"Ain't he? I told you I could pick 'em."

"And he said he was game to stay with us and try again, didn't he?"

"That's right. I'd almost forgotten about that, Colytt."

"A good kid, I say. I'll have to take him in hand and begin teaching him things. He'll take to it like a duck to water. Hello, what's that?"

A piece of wrapping-paper fluttered from the wall, to which it was attached with a splinter.

"Covered with writing," said Colytt, and scooped the paper from the wall, started to read, and then roared: "Hell, he's gone!"

The King, with a cry that was half groan, half whine, leaped up, caught the paper and read aloud in his turn:

" '*DEAR KING CHARLIE AND COLYTT,*

" '*I hate to sneak off like this in the middle of the night, but I got to do it.*

" '*This is why. You two are going to get some money to help a friend, which is all very fine and right. But you're going to get it by busting into the bank. Well, I can't stand it.*

" '*I'll tell you why. When I was on guard in the front of the bank last night, I was plumb scared to start with, but after a while I began to get over it. And then came the explosion and the guns going off all around me, and I thought that I ought to be scared to within an inch of my life, but I wasn't.*

" '*Matter of fact, I liked it. That sounds queer, but it's true. It was more fun than anything I've ever done in my whole life.*' "

The King paused.

"*Can you beat that?*" muttered Colytt.

"*You can't,*" said the King, and continued at once with the reading:

King Charlie

" 'And when we got away I felt like singing. So when we reached the shack and you two went to sleep right away, I couldn't sleep. I lay awake seeing everything all over again, and I wanted to go right down and do it once more.

" 'Well, after a while I saw where that was leading to. If I didn't watch out I'd begin doing things like that, not to help out anybody that had been treated bad and lost money, but simply to get the excitement again.

" 'That thought scared me, and I saw what I had to do. I had to get away before you wake up, because when you wake up we'd go and try this thing again. And if I did it once more I'd get a regular hunger for it fixed in me.

" 'That's why I'm sneaking off this way all quiet.

" 'I'd sure like to see you both again.

" 'King, if you'd drop around to Carterville inside a year, say just a year from to-day, I'll be there to meet you; but I sure can't trust myself now. I got to try myself out!' "

Here the letter ended with the postscript:

"I ain't taking a hoss. I'm going to start over to the railroad and start travelling the way you showed me, King. I'm aiming back for hosses and cows. That's where I belong."

The King lowered the paper, dazed, and he barely heard the torrid curses of Colytt.

"I thought you knowed this kid?" cried Colytt. "I thought you knowed what he'd do? I thought he'd stay with you?"

"Don't talk to me," said the King.

"He'll come back, though," said Colytt.

"Not for a year," said the King sadly. "Not for a whole year. And then when he comes back I won't have no hold on him. He'll know all the truth about me then. Why, right now he thinks that I'm an honest man, or pretty near honest. And—he thinks a lot of

81

other things about me. A year from now he'd laugh in my face."

"Well," said Colytt, "don't take it so hard. He was your insurance against old age, but you'll get along, anyway. You got the brains to get along."

"Brains don't give you lots of things."

"What?"

"Well, a family, for instance—a son!"

"What you talking about?" cried Colytt.

"Nothing," sighed the King.

PART II

Chapter One

King Charlie looked above the trees, and with dolorous eye marked where the bald, bare mountains shot up against the moonlit sky. To him this cattle country of the Western mountains was all that was gloomily forbidding. He could see no reason why any man—ay, or any beast other than vipers and gila monsters and starveling coyotes—should wish to remain in its precincts. The great silences were to him a weight upon the soul. They bore him down and crushed him with a sense of his own insignificance. The wide horizons were more terrible still, for they gave him the assurance that here was a land where man could not hide from man. Yes, and man could not hide himself away from the consciousness of the pale blue sky and the stern God above it. So it came about that he, a lover of freedom, loathed the freest country of all.

Only a quest of the most vital importance, a need which had haunted him during the past year, made him return. And now he sat in what he told himself would prove the last comfortable "jungle" between that point and the coast. In between there was a vast expanse of hardy country and scarcely less hardy towns. In the place of hoboes ranging swiftly hither and yon on the railroads, there were dauntless "long riders," as they were called, which simply meant men who covered great distance in the saddle, striking here and there at widely separated points just as travelling yeggs will do, with this difference—that the yegg melts back into the obscurity of the drift life of the railroads and finds safety in swiftly stirring numbers, whereas the long rider drops back into the wide silence of the desert and finds safety in the solitude.

That solitude to King Charlie, veteran of many a year, and still dauntless tramp royal, ready to go blind baggage on the fastest express—to hardy King Charlie that solitude was as bad as a levelled gun. With all his soul he yearned to turn from the waste places and herd back with the crowd which had here washed out to the very boundaries of trampdom. The mountain desert they often crossed, to be sure, but they crossed it in strides as huge as long railroad divisions could take them, but before King Charlie lay the unenviable task of living in that bare region and hunting up and down through it for the one human being who meant much to his sardonic, self-centred soul.

He looked back, with a shiver of apprehension, to the fire where the mulligan had been cooked. It had been a very good mulligan. The tramps who had ventured into this outlying territory were one and all good rustlers, able to "throw their feet" (collect supplies) with the best. Most of them were, like Charlie, tramp royals, blowed-in-the-glass stiffs, who disdained to carry a roll of bedding or to lift a hand in honest labour at any time. They had fixed this jungle for the night so that it represented the maximum of comfort.

King Charlie

A steady wind came piercingly out of the north, weaving through the shrubbery and piercing through the stoutest clothes like knife-points through soft butter. Against it the fellowship, under the direction of King Charlie—who, of course, never did more than direct—had erected a barrier of dead branches broken from the trees or picked up from the ground, and upon this framework, in turn, they builded a thick thatching of shrubs, whose more dense foliage, thus arranged in several layers, sufficed to turn the wind and leave them comfortable behind their shield. The fire had then been built, and in a great wash boiler the stew was made for a dozen men, and each of the dozen—except King Charlie again—had contributed his share. What the King did was to pay for what he ate.

That was his inevitable custom, and it had in no small measure contributed, along with his fifty-odd years of age and dignified demeanour, to give him his title of "King." For where others were lucky to be turned from a door with a dry crust, the King could get a "set-down" and usually a little money when he left. This was due to the fact that the "gloss" was still left on him. The "gloss" is that aspect, or aroma, it might be called, of respectability which a certain amount of elbowing through the underworld will usually wear away. But the King had never quite lost it. He never took favours for granted. He had about him an air of sad dignity and humility as he accepted, with bowed head, the gifts which were pushed into his hand. Like Milton's fallen hero, he seemed not yet "less than archangel ruined." In fact, he seemed a worthy man, a man of a family, perhaps, who had encountered unmerited trouble and had been crushed by force of circumstance. And with this atmosphere surrounding him and never lost it was no wonder that doors flew open at his coming.

Now he sat with his bony hands extended to the blaze of the fire, gradually dying since the cooking had been accomplished. In his eyes there was the far-off look of one reviewing past glories. And, in fact, he was thinking back to those halcyon days when his nerve was still like chilled steel, impenetrable by fear. Long since the "prison shake" had gripped him, and the many years behind the bars had left their shadow printed on him. But in the other times—ah, then he had had power indeed! Then his coming to a "jungle" such as this had been a sign for rejoicing while the hoboes flocked around eager to do his bidding, and feeling rewarded for all their efforts by the least of his anecdotes and the smallest of his glances. For which one among them might not be remembered and enrolled in the good graces of the safe-blower, to be used in one of his jobs sooner or later and rewarded with some share of the profit.

But those days were ended, alas! Never again could he do more than lay the "plant" and watch on the outside while some others operated with soap and "soup" on the inside. Poor King Charlie! Was it any wonder that he sighed?

He wrested himself away from such melancholy reflections, and brought into his attention the talk which was going on around him. They were laying their plans to defend one of their number from danger of attack by another hobo called "the Kid." He who was threatened was a formidable fellow, lank-jawed, lank-limbed, with the ferocity of a mink in his little reddish eyes. But he sat with his great hands locked around his knees, and drank in with insatiable greed the assurances of his comrades that they would stand by him if the Kid should come. One had a knife handy to tickle the ribs of the Kid. Another had a trusty club. Another, in case of final need, would draw his gat and pump a shower of lead into the Kid's vitals.

"But who," interrupted King Charlie, turning his handsome though rather harsh featured face towards the rest, "who is the Kid? What's the rest of his monniker? Denver Kid? or the Blondy Kid from Chi? What's his whole monniker, bos?"

"Don't you know the Kid?" they responded in chorus.

"Sure. I know a thousand Kids," answered King Charlie. "But what about this one? What's his particular label?"

All eyes turned to the lanky man who had been receiving the promises of immunity from the terrible Kid. But he, with a shudder, passed the interrogation on to another.

"The King ain't been out in the West lately," he said, "or he'd know. But let Little Steve tell him. Stevie has met up with the Kid since I had dealings with him!"

Little Steve, so called because his immense and shapeless feet supported a burden of some two hundred and forty pounds of bone and bulging muscles, turned towards the speaker a head of the type called "bullet" and amazingly and disproportionately small for the compass of his shoulders.

"Sure I met up with him," said Little Steve. "I'd just done a little job, and blew West to get out of a cooling. I had a hundred and fifty berries when I bumped into the Kid. He rolled me for the whole wad," he sighed. "He was shaking dice like a flash. Going like a crazy comet, he was! I stayed with him three flops, and then I was through. I was cleaned. I had to take a freight out half an hour later. I struck him for a fiver before I blew. 'Sure,' says the Kid, 'here's fifty, and more if you need it.' And he started to get out his wallet. I thought he was jollying me when he started that talk about fifty. It made me mad. I told him so too. Why not? I'd never seen him before. Far as I knew, he might be just a gay-cat on a streak of luck. Didn't look more'n eighteen or nineteen, if he's that old. Well, I didn't get more'n half way warmed up when he sloughs me along the jaw a wallop that made me see stars. Mind you, he ain't half my size, hardly. I stepped, give him a laugh, and then tell him to hold off or I'll eat him. His way of answering was to step in and hit me twice in the stomach before I could think. And every punch he landed was packed full of lead. I put him down for a pug right off by the way he glided around and wobbled his head out of the way of punches and let me have it with short-arm punches that didn't travel more'n six inches apiece. He sure is a sharp shooter, at that! But pugs, take 'em by and large, don't mean much to me if I have a chance to get my hands on 'em!" He spread out, as he spoke, his immense hands, made to seize and crush. "I made a jump at him and ploughed through thin air, while he gives me this." He touched an eye which was still partially discoloured. "Then I dived for him again, roaring for blood. I was mad enough to eat him alive. Soon as he seen what I wanted, he stopped dancing and hitting and dived in under my hands pretty as you please. I reached for him and got my hands on him, and I just nacherally picked the clothes right off his back; but all I got was handfuls of clothes, not the Kid. He was like an oiled pig. He squeezed and wriggled right out of my fingertips, and before I knew it he was around behind me and had me in about ten holds, one after the other, and the last of 'em was a full Nelson. When he got that I quit, and the minute I hollered he was off me. When I sat up I seen the boys standing around giving me the laugh good and hard. Well, I hung around that jungle until I got wised up to what the Kid was."

"Tell me what you found out?" asked the King, greatly interested in the account of this young and epic hero.

"I found out," said Little Steve, "that there was just one and only Kid, and that was why they didn't hang another monniker on him. If he's on the trail of Skinny here, most likely you'll have a chance to see him before the night's out." Here Skinny groaned.

King Charlie

"But what I found out was that he hadn't been on the road very long. He plays the blind baggage and the rods some; but mostly he hangs right close to the mountains and does his travelling by hossback. Among the long-riders he's a big gun. Some say he ain't been on the road more'n a year and that he ain't more'n sixteen right now, though he looks three years older. But he's all boiled down wild-cat, you see, King? He's spent six months of his year in the pen, and there he got hardened up and learned a whole pile. When he come out he started to use what he'd learned. Anything from train stick-up to cracking a peter is nuts for him. He's a genius, that's what he is, and if it wasn't for the fact that he'll be dead before he's twenty he'd be a credit to anybody's bringing up. Eh, Skinny?"

Skinny responded with another groan.

"What was the bust between you and the Kid, Skinny?" asked King Charlie.

"I was batty with moonshine, and I rolled a pal of his for a goal," said Skinny sadly. "We had a mix up on top of a train, and his pal done a tumble off the top. He didn't die, but he got both legs busted, and now the Kid is paying his doctor bills. Also he's out to get me; but the boys will give him his hands full, the young hell-cat!"

"But does he fight fair?" asked the King.

"Is a tornado fair?" growled Skinny in response. "You see it coming, but that doesn't let you know how to keep it from tearing the roof off your house, does it?"

Chapter Two

But when an hour had elapsed the exciting topic of the Kid was quite forgotten, and the King had relapsed into his former melancholy broodings. For he was fast growing old. In his hard-skinned cheek there was fixed an unalterable flush of false youth, but in his body there was a growing sense of feebleness as time went on. Not only could he no longer work as a safe-blower, but he was even of little value as an assistant. He was simply becoming a "worthless" hobo in his own eyes; the heroic qualities which had once distinguished him were fast fading. Before long the "gloss" would begin to go also, and then he would sink at once into the muck. He would become one of those wretched creatures who live in the slums of great cities in barrels in the night and crawl about to sheltered, sunny corners in the day. He would beg no longer for dollars, but for quarters, and lower than that, he would ask for five cents. The proud erectness of his shoulders would be exchanged for the miserable stoop which is necessary when the beggar begs from the poor. He would have to assume sufficient squalor to appear wretched and pitiable even to the wretched and pitied.

Rather death before he reached that point! And yet he knew, as he reflected, that he would not have the courage to slay himself. For he would drift to the bottom by imperceptible degrees. And when he aroused himself to the truth, he would be already irreclaimably lost. Out of this dismal brooding he was recalled again by a sharp scuffle of rising forms and a short cry of fear. He looked up, and saw that Skinny had bounded from the ground and stood now cowering near the wind-brake with the light of the dying fire adrop from the long blade of his knife. Others of the tramps were also rising to form a bulwark for Skinny against the intruder.

The latter stood in the middle of the clearing with the wind flapping up the brim of his sombrero. He was a young fellow under twenty, with strongly made shoulders and a body, not over tall, tapering rapidly towards the ground. He stood now with his feet braced well apart, and his bearing that of one ready to enter into any sort of action. His garb was that of a cowpuncher, the bandana fluttering behind his neck, and the cartridge-belt drawn sagging about his hips by the weight of the heavy Colt which it supported. But what was most of all noticeable was the glittering of the wild blue eyes. He looked wild-cat and bulldog combined. It was no wonder that the hoboes shrank away from him, and that, although they drew back towards Skinny as though ready to defend him, there was an uncertainty in the attitude of each man that promised the whole band would scatter if the youngster charged them. For this very act he was teetering forward upon his toes when King Charlie, with a harsh cry of joy and strange sorrow combined, sprang to his feet, darted through the ranks of the tramps, and confronted the Kid.

"Billy!" he cried. "Billy English!"

The fire died from the eyes of the boy.

"God a'mighty," he gasped. "How come you here? You!"

"I'm here hunting for you. I couldn't stay away any longer, lad. And here I've found you just when I thought that the hunt was starting."

He drew close. As though by mutual agreement the two fell back, so that their cautiously lowered voices were out of earshot of the staring, gaping tramps.

"King Charlie," said Billy English, "I got one thing to ask you before you go any farther. I got to know. Tell me the straight of it. Were you just bluffing when you told me that you're my father? Was that just a bluff to get me started? Was that just part of the frame that you worked on me?"

King Charlie hesitated.

It was, he felt, the one unforgivable sin of his life that he had told the boy that he was his son, and had created out of thin air that fiction to explain how Billy had been deserted and allowed to grow up from childhood in the village, unclaimed by father or mother. But as he recalled the baseness of that lie, he recalled also the circumstances under which the lie was inspired—the bright hot sunshine, the crowd gathered around the fence, and the fighting, wildly pitching horse with the boy in the saddle, fearless and gay and generous of heart. And the old rising of the spirit that had made King Charlie yearn towards the boy overtook now, also, as he looked into the steady blue eyes which were studying him.

"If you were bluffing now," the Kid was saying, "take a good think before you lie to me again. Because sooner or later I'd be sure to find out the truth and I'd go about a thousand miles out of my way and swim a whole flock of rivers to get even with you, King, if it *ain't* the truth!"

Hastily the King reviewed the facts about Billy English as he had learned them at the village where he

King Charlie

first found him: at five years he had wandered in from the railroad track, and since then he had not been applied for by man or woman claiming to be his parent. How could he dig back to such an obscure past? Those who had abandoned him so long ago would never care to claim him now if they could ever recognize him. Shame would keep them silent.

Therefore, the King threw back his shoulders and shook his head as he met the eye of Billy: "Son," he said, "I've brought no good into your life—yet—and I don't blame you for having your doubts of me. But look me in the face, Billy! Don't you see the likeness? Don't you see that we're kin?"

He even threw out his arms a little, inviting the inspection, and the effect was irresistible.

The word was wrung from the lips of Billy English: "Dad, I believe that you're telling me true. If you ain't, God help you some day when I find it out!"

He ground his teeth at the thought and then sobered suddenly.

"I've got something to do here," he said. "Wait over yonder a minute and I'll come back."

He slipped past King Charlie as he spoke and started towards the hoboes, but the "father" caught him suddenly by the arm.

"I've got to do it," said Billy English. "I've been promising it to myself for a month."

"You've got to do nothing of the kind," said King Charlie softly. "They're all laying for you, Billy. They'll shoot you to pieces if you start anything. Wait till you get him alone. Wait till you have a chance!"

Billy English writhed with distress.

But the solid front which the tramps now presented to him was a convincing argument, and he at length turned with a sigh towards King Charlie.

"Sooner or later I got to get him," he said.

"All right," said King Charlie. "And I'll tell you this right now, son: this old world ain't so big but that you meet everybody twice that you meet once. You

95

can tie to that idea because it never fails. I dodged Slippy Joe of Kansas for twenty years because I owed him twenty dollars, but just last month, when I thought he must sure be dead and buried, he up and struck me for the two tens. It knocked me stiff. But come on, Billy."

Billy obediently followed until they stood among the trees on the far side of the clearing, with the wind whistling shrill about them, for it was the middle of winter.

"We'll get out of here," said King Charlie. "It ain't none too healthful for you, son, even with me here to look out for you now. Best thing we can do is to shift along. They tell me that you're doing most of your travelling on horses. Are you coming that way tonight?"

"I am," said Billy English. "But you can ride the hoss, dad. I'll walk. We can slide over to Cornwall City inside of an hour. Will that do you?"

"Fine," answered the "father," "except that I'll do the walking."

And on this he insisted when they reached Billy's horse on the lee of a sand-hill. Despite all that Billy could say, King Charlie refused the saddle and swung away across the desert at his swinging stride, taking the smooth-going heel and toe at a rate that started Billy gasping in amazement. Athlete though he was, he could not hope to match that sweeping pace. And his horse broke into a steady jog-trot.

They went on as men do in the cold of a night, hardly speaking a word, though it was a year since they had seen each other. When King Charlie spoke, it was only because he had been warmed by his exercise.

"D'you ever regret leaving us that morning, son?" he asked.

"No," answered Billy English truthfully, though a little brutally. "I sure never was sorry for that." And he added with a bitter laugh: "A hell of a lot of good

it done me, though. I had it in my blood all right. I
got it straight from you, dad. When I asked you a
while back if you'd been telling me the straight of it,
when you said a year ago that you was my father,
d'you think I really had any hope? Nope, I didn't. I
knew I had your blood in me. Why, that one night
was all I needed to get me going. I tried to go straight,
but I couldn't. I lived a year in' a day fighting away
the temptation, and with all my fighting it was no
good. I had to buckle under. And pretty soon I was
drifting off the ranch and sloping into town and
hanging out around the railroad station and listen-
ing to the bos when they dropped off the train and
got to yarning about what they'd done and where
they'd been. And then—well, I just started at a fever
heat. Inside of a week I'd busted the law six ways
wide open and had a wad of coins that would have
choked a bull."

King Charlie sighed.

Oh to have the direction of this wonderful young
fighting-machine, cool nerved, quick of eye and
hand. There would be a fortune both for Billy English and his manager.

"After that," went on Billy English, "I was rolled
for my wad and I hunted around, found the bird that
rolled me, and beat him to a pulp. I went too far with
him, and beat him so close to dying that they
grabbed me for it and shoved me in the can. I was
there six months. And what I didn't learn inside the
can you won't find in no book, bo, you can take it
from me."

And his harsh laughter rang into the night wind.
King Charlie shrank. He, after all, was the source of
that hardness of heart. The winter wind had long
been as cold as snow, and now it blew a crisp flake
into his face. But he was glad to bend and fight the
approaching storm. It gave a vent to his feelings and
allowed him to work off his self-hatred. oIt was he
who had started Billy English on the down road, no

matter how swiftly he had gone.

"Sometimes," went on Billy, "I tried to take a brace and get back on my feet—my honest feet, you see? But then I remembered that you were my father, and I decided that it wasn't no good. The stuff was in my blood, dad, the stuff was in my blood! Sooner or later it had to show, anyway. So I went on."

"And what have you got out of it?" asked his "father."

"Nothing," said Billy. "When I'm flush I spend it like a fool. But maybe I got that from you, too."

"Never!"

"No? Then how much have *you* got?"

King Charlie was silenced for a moment, but he went on again: "Billy, what you need is some managing. You can't keep up with the game for ever. Sooner or later you're going to be pinched and stuck in the cooler so long that your nerve will get as brittle as ice. and you'll break in pieces when you try to take a chance. I *know!*" He shivered as he said it. "But with me handling you, son, and getting you in line for a few big jobs, we ought to be able to retire in a couple of years.''

"We?" said Billy.

"Well, ain't I your father, son?"

"Hell," said Billy. "Don't play on that string. It's worn all thin already. What kind of a father have you been, eh? But come along. I can't ditch you now that I've found you."

"It don't mean nothing to you—finding me again?" asked King Charlie, as sadly as he could.

"Nothing means much to me," replied Billy English. "I've got nothing out of the world, and the world ain't going to get anything out of me."

Chapter Three

Prison and a year's life in yeggdom had certainly made a great difference. In a year of actual time, Billy English had added five years of apparent age. He had been a frolicsome boy at fifteen, only a man in his strength of arm and his trained agility and courage. At sixteen he was a man in his cold suspicions, his venomous hatreds, his contempt for everything and everybody, including himself. And all of these things could be traced back to the influence of King Charlie's lies which had set Billy adrift from his home village and an honest life.

The tramp shrugged such thoughts away for the time being and looked about him. There had been a rift in the massed dull grey of the clouds which sheeted the sky, and for a few instants the moon looked through, her visage blurred continually by whirling rain mists. That light was sufficient to show, however, the country through which they were walking. The moment they left the tree-shaded hollowed by the flag station, they had stepped on to a barren plain, over which the wind swept in full career. This plain presently broke into naked hills. It was unfenced range. Before them drifted a number of odd-shaped silhouettes; cattle were moving restlessly, helplessly, down wind. If the wind kept up and the snow continued to give an edge to its blasts, those cows might continue to move until they huddled under the hills which, in the distance, were a smudge beneath the skyline.

They went on, Billy English keeping his pony to a jog-trot still, to match the swift walking of the tramp. Something else passed before them in the night—a blur of lightning motion rather than a form. It was a lofer wolf racing with the wind and venturing near to man with a boldness of which no other creature in the mountain desert could be capable. But he, like a bold and cunning gambler, knew how completely night and his own matchless speed served to render him safe. He had gambled close indeed in this case, for as he shot past, Billy English wrenched a long-barrelled Winchester from its case beneath his left leg and pumped shot after shot towards the fugitive. Just before he vanished in the moonhaze, the creature leaped high into the air, sure token that it had been severely wounded at least. But it landed running at a rate which made its former progress seem slow. Billy English pursued it with curses.

"Nice shooting, son," said King Charlie, with as much paternal pride and real admiration as he could muster. "Nice shooting. If you'd had clean moonshine and no dirty wind, you'd of dropped him sure!"

"If there'd been clean moonshine," said Billy English, ramming the rifle home in its case with another oath, "the lofer wouldn't have showed up within a quarter of a mile of that close. They got the brains of a man, damn their hides!"

"But what good is it to try to kill him?"

"What good? Why, I hate a lofer the way I hate

poison. And didn't you see them cows wind-drifting a ways back?"

"What of 'em?"

"Ask Mr. Lofer that! He'll dine off of one of them before morning, that's all!"

"What of it? They ain't your cows, are they? But the ammunition *is* yours."

Billy English grunted his disgust. "If you'd ever rode herd," he said, "you wouldn't talk that way. I got an interest in every cow on the range, because I've seen the like of 'em born and grow up and die. I've seen 'em fight screw-worm and heel-flies; and I've watched 'em die in blizzards and die in droughts. A cow is game. You can lay to that. She's a plumb fool, but she's game. And a lofer has the brains. That's why I hate a wolf. He doesn't take on them that have a fighting chance."

"You like the mountains and the range," said King Charlie. "That's because you ain't had a chance to see what's what in the East where—"

"Haven't I?" sneered Billy. "I've been flush in Chi and I've been flush in New York. I've been busted in New Orleans and in gaol in Philie."

"You've crammed all of that into one year?" asked King Charlie.

"Blind baggage takes a gent over the road pretty fast," said Billy.

"True and right—true and right!" murmured the King. "But how you managed to do so much travelling and work up such a rep around here is more'n I see. But I'll catch on after a while. When you going East again?"

"Never," answered Billy English. "The mountains suit me. I get hungry for 'em if I'm away too long. I'd rather be quiet for five minutes of a desert night than listen to all the swell music in a city."

Again King Charlie noted the differences which gaped between their habits of thought. But he would take time and patience to wean the brilliant and terrible boy away from the country he loved and take him East for "real money."

And as he came to this decision they arrived in view of a rambling little town tossed down without plan or reason among the hills. This was Cornwall City, though there was nothing about it to justify the second word of its title. The railroad did not tap it. It was a relic of the older days when men built without reference to the possible direction which the iron rails might take through a vicinity. Now it would never grow to a greater size. It lived on such mining and cattle and timber industries as flourished in the surrounding highlands, and continued its bleak existence in monotony, broken at not infrequent intervals by the incursions of joyous cowboys hell-bent, which being translated means simply bent on a good time.

Down to Cornwall City they came, with the town suddenly blotted out by the coming of snow. For the wind died, allowed an immensely thick curtain of flakes to commence falling, and then leaped up again from the horizon and hurled that mass of snow into the faces of the blinded travellers. With numb hands and chattering teeth, the King looked on while Billy English led through the main street and around a big building to a barn behind, where he stabled the horse. He lighted a lantern which hung from a peg near the door, and by that light, as he passed down in the rear of the stalls, King Charlie caught glimpses of the finest group of horses he had ever seen. There was an instant differentiation between these, for instance, and the little cowpony from which Billy English had just dismounted, and the old tramp could not help noting it aloud.

"Looks to me," he said, "like some of the boys who lived at this hotel travelled in style, eh? Who owns these horses?"

"Which ones?" asked Billy, returning from giving his pony a feed of grain and hay.

"The grey and the chestnut beside him."

"Mine," said Billy.

"Both of 'em?"

He stepped nearer. No, they were not shams, but long-legged, narrow creatures meant for speed. There was much good blood in them, to be sure.

"*Your* horses?" echoed the amazed King, as he stepped back.

Billy English looked at him quietly, and finally shrugged his shoulders as though he did not care to reveal the whole truth even to one with whom a confidence could be placed in entire safety.

"I have to travel long stages sometimes," he said. "That's why I need 'em."

"And the other horses?" asked the King. "What about that big black?"

"That belongs to Hoyt. When you see him you'll understand why the black has to be big. Joe weighs a ton, pretty near, and he needs a hoss made the same way."

"And the brown horse at the end?"

"Belongs to Dean. Now d'you know enough?"

"And the three of you all work—"

"Shut up!" snarled Billy English.

He stepped up to his "father" with the quick, gliding step of a pugilist. And his face was an ugly one to watch.

"You mind your tongue when you're around with me," said Billy English. "Ask all the questions you want to, but don't ask 'em loud. Understand?"

"Anything you say," answered the King calmly. But in his heart he wondered. This young savage was certainly not the boy he had first drawn astray the year before. In twelve months he had been thoroughly brutalized.

"Now come on with me," said Billy English.

He led the way to the rear door of the house, and there he paused again, and waited in the snowstorm while he delivered himself of another ultimatum.

"Look here," he said. "When you get inside the hotel you may have a lot of folks asking you questions. Well, you don't know nothing, you see?"

"I see."

"Don't forget it! I'm going to take care of you, if I can. But I ain't going to be bothered more 'n I have to. You let me grow up anyway that looked good to me. And now when you come around you can use me for a meal-ticket, but you can't use me no other way. Have you got that straight?"

King Charlie, no matter what anger he may have felt, simply nodded. There were too many possibilities ahead of him, and he did not wish to destroy them before they had been well examined.

Chapter Four

It was never intended for use in such a climate as that of Cornwall City. Those thin pine boards had been warped loose by the fires of summer, and then soaked and rotted and wrenched at by the snows and winds of winter, until now every gust was split into a myriad small voices which ran whispering through the building. The clothes of King Charlie were plucked at softly by the draughts as he climbed up the groaning stairs behind Billy English, lighted on the way by the flame which fluttered in the throat of a smoky chimney, where the lamp was placed at the landing.

In the upper hall, having passed one or two doors, Billy English struck the next heavily with his fist by way of announcement that he was about to enter, and then turned the knob and kicked the door open.

The scene within revealed animal comfort to such a degree that King Charlie, drawing the door to behind him, was amazed. A fairly thick rug lay upon the floor. Heavy curtains on the inside of the door and the window minimized the draughts which worked in around these major openings. Upon the table stood two bottles of bootleg whisky with glasses handy. A stove glowed red-hot in a corner of the room with a pan of water simmering on the top in case anyone should desire to make, with hot water and sugar and lemons, which were spread in quantity on the little kitchen-table adjoining, a hot punch. Moreover, there was a coffee-pot on a corner of the table and a can of coffee beside it. Not that the room gave the appearance of a housekeeping apartment. It was simply equipped with such conveniences as would be most appreciated on a cold winter's day. The two cots at the sides of the room were made up with plenty of soft, thick blankets, and there was an extra supply of cushions in case the lodgers desired to lounge there.

As for the other appointments of the room, they were chiefly guns of all varieties in racks and hanging in holsters along the wall together with all manner of clothes, most of them muddy. An open door hinted that there was another room to the suite which Billy English and his associates occupied.

These associates, in the meantime, were sitting at the main table in the exact centre of the room engaged in a friendly little game of poker. The hungry eyes of King Charlie fixed instantly on the heaps of greenbacks, which were the stakes, and even as he entered he heard a low voice say: "Bet fifty!"

What manner of men were these who could afford to bet fifty dollars at a throw?

It needed only a glance to tell him. Yonder tall, long-faced, sad-eyed fellow with the pathetic and many-wrinkled smile—that was the Dean, an expert "dauber," and otherwise a gambler of parts, who was also possessed of a variety of talents, so that he could turn his attention to almost anything and acquit himself well. It amazed King Charlie to see such a celebrity in such company. For Billy English was only a child, comparatively speaking.

The second player was a sharp contrast with the tall man. This, unquestionably, must be Joe Hoyt, of whom Billy had said that he weighed a ton. His great shoulders pressed back so that the top of the chair was almost buried in the overhang of relaxed muscles. His big head was set, without the use of a neck, apparently, squarely in the middle of the vast shoulders. Below the shoulders he did not taper to the waistline. He was straight up and down from the armpits to the floor, where his bulk was distributed upon two large, shapeless feet.

This man now rose and whirled to his feet, because his back was to the door, and the King found himself looking into a thick featured but rather handsome face, which at once smiled cordial greeting on Billy and turned to the King himself with a frank scowl of question.

Billy English sailed his hat across the room, and flung himself down on a couch.

"Hoyt," he growled, "and Dean, meet my father. This is King Charlie. I think I've heard you talk about him, Dean."

The Dean nodded gravely to King Charlie.

"How are you?" he inquired politely, as he shook hands. "Of course I remember you, King. But I never was wised up about you being a family man. Shake hands with Joe Hoyt. Hoyt, this is King Charlie. Maybe you've never bumped into him because he don't often come out as far West as you do. But Charlie *is* the king of them all?"

"Yes?" drawled Hoyt, unconvinced.

"The chief reason," said the Dean, "is because he never looks any older."

In the meantime Billy English had rolled from the couch to his feet and sauntered into the next room. Instantly the expression on the face of the Dean was changed.

"Look here!" he whispered to the King. "What's the play? The kid is ours. Where do you expect to horn in, Charlie?"

"My own flesh and blood," said King Charlie. "You can't expect a man to give up that, can you?"

"Flesh and—Charlie, do I look that much of a simp? There ain't a sign of you in him."

"No; he's his mother's son, there's no doubt of that," sighed the old rascal.

"You're going to try to make your play with him, eh?" asked the Dean darkly.

"It ain't anything that you boys can stop," cautioned the King, speaking as guardedly as they in his reply. "Now, watch out. He's coming back. Only lay to this—that I ain't trying to spoil anything you birds have planned."

So saying, he raised his voice to a hearty greeting for Hoyt just as Billy English returned. He crossed the room to the table, poured out a drink of whisky, and shoved it towards King Charlie. But King Charlie refused it, and Billy English tossed off the drink at a swallow, and began to pace up and down the room. The Dean and Joe Hoyt paused to look anxiously after him, and then they forced themselves to continue their game, but it could be easily seen that their interest was entirely perfunctory.

The boy, turning again on his father, seemed to remember something, hastily shoved a chair near the stove, and pointed to it.

"Sit down," he commanded, "and get warmed up."

"I'd rather get thawed out gradual," said King Charlie. "Don't worry about me. I'll take care of myself, son."

"Lay off of that 'son' talk too," barked Billy English. "Maybe I am, but nothing is bought by telling the world about it."

He stopped at the table in his hurried pacing and swigged off another big portion of the whisky.

"You're hitting it up pretty hard, kid," said the

Dean. "You better watch that stuff."

"Never mind me," said Billy English. "I'll handle my own liquor without no little helping words from you gents. Now—what's planted?"

The other two started and flashed glances at King Charlie. These glances plainly said: "You fool! Do you expect us to talk before a stranger?"

"I told you he was my father," said Billy. "Anything you can say to me you can say to him. I ask you agin, what you got planted?"

Hoyt, whose back was turned to Billy, winked at the Dean as one who had no solution for the problem himself, and bade the Dean talk or remain silent as he felt best. The Dean decided on silence.

"Haven't anything certain," he said. "Nothing worth talking about. Besides, what's the good? Can't ride on a night like this."

"Can't ride on a night like this?" cried Billy English, sneering. "Why not? Because they's a little snow in the air, will that hurt you? And ain't Warnerville dead ahead down the wind? We could hit it before morning."

"Wait a minute!" exclaimed the Dean. "You ain't in earnest, Billy?"

"Why not? The snow and the cold and the wind that makes you gents think that we can't make the play in Warnerville is just the reasons that the boys in Warnerville won't think that we'll come, if they got suspicions about it. And so we drop in, clean up, and make a getaway in the falling snow, that covers up our tracks as fast as we make 'em. Ain't that easy?"

"Billy, what makes you so hot on this trail? Ain't you fixed easy enough? Why, you could lay off for a year on what you've made lately."

"You're wrong," answered Billy. "I ain't got enough to pay for one gambling lesson from the Dean."

Here he stepped a little forward, and looked at the Dean so narrowly that the latter changed colour.

"Billy," he hastened to protest, "you know as well

as I do that I was only jollying you when I kept that money I won from you the other day. I don't want it. I told you right off that I didn't want it, and I say it again to-day. You can have it—"

"Bah!" sneered Billy. "I ain't a welcher, and you know I ain't. Shut up the windy talk, Dean. You can't work it with me. I'm tired of it."

The Dean flushed, looked down, and hesitated. Plainly he would rather have teeth pulled than force this issue, but his self-respect forced him ahead.

"Billy," he said gently, "I can't let you talk to me like that. I've done nothing to deserve it, and I can't sit here and let you talk that way. Not if you was as old as this bird that calls himself your father."

"You can't stand for it?" scoffed Billy. "You got to stand for it! Oh, I know the pair of you. I know how you're playing your dirty game. But I let it go. I know that I'm the door-opener for you. I get you inside the safe and then you and Hoyt pull down the loot, and you let me off with anything you think is enough to pay me for my trouble."

Accumulated anger seemed to be boiling in him. He effervesced with rage.

"When we got away from Glenn Lake, who was it that pulled the posse down the wrong trail, while you and Hoyt got off slick and easy, and you with a lame hoss, Dean? But out of that job you held out on me. You held out a whole handful of big greenbacks that—"

"That's not true!" cried the Dean, white faced with anger and nervousness as he saw the crisis approaching. "Billy, for God's sake don't let that murdering temper of yours run away with you. Let me tell you the straight of it. What we got out of that—"

"Don't talk!" cried Billy.

And yet every word had been spoken softly, with all the accents of rage conveyed in voices often no louder than strong whispers.

"Don't talk!" he commanded. "It—it makes me want to tear your hearts out. I know the coin that you've been sending away—and what have I got left? A measly thousand! A rotten thousand!"

"Because you throw your money away. Every bum that asks for a hand out you give half of what you've got. Is that—"

"That's different from what you gents do, ain't it? Yes, I'll tell a man that it's a lot different. You got not a cent to waste on the unlucky ones. But I been making up my mind that I've travelled the same trail with you boys far enough. It seems to me that you two fit in too pretty together to need me with you. I'm quitting."

He scowled at them with such unreasoning and sullen rage that King Charlie gaspcd. The last speech had stirred both the Dean and huge Hoyt from speech to action. They came threateningly close to the boy.

"You aim to draw out on us?" they said hotly. "After everything is set and planned for—"

They stopped, flashed a vicious glance at King Charlie, whose presence kept them from mentioning names, and roared in unison at Billy English, forgetting the thin walls of the house: "We'll see you in hell before we let you pull out on us!"

Their near approach had driven Billy back until his shoulders were pressed against the wall, and from this point his bright blue eyes glittered at the two big men. He was not in the least afraid, but plainly he was in a fighting rage, and wanted to merely balance accounts before he attacked them. And though King Charlie trembled for what might happen, he was tongue-tied in admiration of the dauntless courage of the boy. There was a touch of horror, too, in the eyes with which he watched. For it seemed to him that Billy English had been so far brutalized by his single year among the enemies of the law that now he would fight for the sheer love of battle and destruction.

"If you see me to hell," said Billy, "you'll, both of you, follow me! I'll take you both along, you damned thick-heads! Start something, Dean! Go for your gat, Hoyt! I'm waiting!"

Their answer was an inarticulate growl of rage, and the three men hung trembling on the balance of fierce action. King Charlie, cold blooded as a fish when it came to a fight, saw that his previous quietness had taken him out of their attention and that they were not guarding against him. Accordingly he glided to the nearest gun-rack and secured a revolver. It had hardly touched his palm, however, when there was a loud rattle at the door knob, the door was opened, and a sharp, small voice called: "I wish you please wouldn't make so much noise in here!"

Hoyt and the Dean glanced over their shoulders and saw in the open doorway a little five-year-old girl with a tumble of bright hair about a pale, pale face. And they staggered back from Billy English as though he had suddenly pointed two guns at them.

Chapter Five

Billy English was the last to see her, but when he did the effect upon him was even more startling. He brushed out of his eyes the bristle of hair which had fallen across them, and he ground his knuckles across his forehead as though he would banish a dream which afflicted him.

"How come the kid here?" he gasped. And he repeated: "Who brought her here?"

Here King Charlie, through the power of greater age, became the controlling factor in the room. He went to the little girl.

"Who are you?" he asked.

"Louise Alison Dora Young," said the child, rolling up her eyes with adorable gravity. "And my mother says you should ought to be quiet."

King Charlie, glad of the interruption which promised to prolong the life of his protégé, sat down on the nearest chair and lifted Louise Alison Dora

Young to his knee. He uttered an exclamation of dismay as he did so.

"Darned if she ain't all skin and bones!" he cried at his companions.

The girl shook her head at him in serious disapproval.

"You shouldn't ought to say 'ain't,' " she told him.

"I won't," said the King obediently. "I'll keep inside the fences you put up. But where's your mother, honey?"

"She's right over across the hall," said Louise. "She's sick and she can't go to sleep when you make so much noise."

"Oh!" exclaimed Hoyt, "your mother is *her*, eh?"

And he exchanged significant glances with the Dean.

"I guess she *is* sick," said Hoyt. "Can we do anything for her?"

"No," answered Louise Alison Dora Young. "All she wants is to be left alone. She wants quiet. She just cries when there's noise."

She conveyed that strange information with another shake of her head.

"Look at her neck," said King Charlie, grown suddenly husky with horror and rage. "She ain't had enough to eat, this baby. D'you live in the same house with—"

He checked himself out of respect for the big questioning eyes which flashed up to him. But, still staring at the others, he pointed out the starved small throat of Louise. The three men gathered about in a stunned and stupid semicircle and gaped at her.

"What'll we do?" they asked the King.

She became a little frightened under this steady scrutiny, and swept their faces in dismay until her eyes rested on the younger and more handsome face of Billy English. And a smile wavered into life on her pale lips. Suddenly she put out her arms towards him and Billy English gasped.

"What'll I do?" he asked of the King.

And the King laughed heartily.

"That means she's looked the rest of us over," he declared, "and decided that you're the one that she picks out. Take her up in your arms. That's what she wants. She's tired of me."

Billy English flushed to the eyes with pleasure and then awkwardly obeyed. He raised her in his strong young arms and suddenly tossed her up and caught her as she came down, a manoeuvre that brought a peal of laughter from Louise. And the laugh was echoed by three deep, pleased chuckles from the onlookers.

But Billy English had grown dark of brow again.

"You're right, King," he said, "she's all skin and bones. And—"

He broke short off, turned and went hastily to the table: there, from a covered little tin can, he took out a piece of bread. It had been cut the evening before, and the close proximity of the stove's heat had warped and withered it. This he raised, but no sooner was it in sight than Louise Young uttered a faint shrill cry and tore it from his hands. The next instant she was tearing it to pieces with an animal greed.

Hoyt and the Dean bowed their heads in mute shame and horror. And King Charlie watched agape. As for Billy English, he had turned livid with conflicting emotions.

"And her mother?" asked Billy suddenly. "Maybe that's why she—"

"Don't talk that way," cried the Dean, answering before the accusation was completed. "You talk like a fool, Billy. But—"

"We're going to go, see," said Billy. "And if it's happened the way I think it's happened, we'll all of us burn in hell-fire, boys."

And he led the way through the door with the others behind him. On the way, King Charlie hastily

115

made his inquiries. And he learned from Joe Hoyt that they had several times during the past three or four days noticed a woman who lodged across the hall from them and who seemed excessively thin and wan and languid, moving slowly, with great, dark-shadowed eyes fixed always down.

In the meantime they had reached the door of the bedroom across the way, and here Billy English lowered the child to the floor, where she at once opened the door and stepped on tiptoe inside, turning her head to warn them, with her finger pressed to her lips, that they must preserve silence.

She disappeared and came back after a moment to say: "She's sound asleep. She's tried a long, long time to go to sleep and couldn't."

"Why not?" whispered Billy English, and the others leaned closer to hear the answer.

"Because something hurt her inside," said Louise.

"Starvation," said King Charlie slowly. "That's it. If a woman'll let her baby get as thin as this kid is, you can bet that she is a wreck herself. How long has it been since your mother ate anything, Louise?"

"She doesn't eat any more," said Louise. "She stopped days and days ago, because she says that it makes her sick to eat. Isn't that a queer way to be?"

"And us throwing away coin drinking and—you go into the room again," said Hoyt, "and wake up your mother and tell her that you got a friend out in the hall that wants to see her. Will you do that?"

She nodded, slipped through the door, and presently they could hear her calling, first softly and then more loudly. And all at once, with a sort of stifled scream, she ran back to the door and sprang among them, huddling close to Billy English.

"I'm afraid," she cried. "I'm afraid. Oh, why won't she talk to me?"

The four strong men were turned to stone. At length the tramp stepped slowly to the door and paused there to look back, in case any of the others might have the courage to accompany him. But they merely gaped at him with frozen dismay.

So he faced the interior of the room again, dragged off his hat, and with a slow and uncertain step disappeared.

They heard his footsteps cease. They waited in mortal silence. And then they heard a hurrying footfall come back towards the door.

King Charlie came shuddering back and looked at them, and one glance was enough.

"Your mother wants to sleep, honey," he managed to say to Louise. "We'll take you in and keep you warm by the fire for a while."

He took her hand, but his own was shaking so much that she withdrew her fingers and Billy English had to pick her up again. In the rooms of the three long-riders they deposited her. And King Charlie gave orders.

"Billy," he said, "you stay here and keep Louise happy. Dean, come with me. I'll have to use you, Hoyt, too."

They followed him reluctantly into the hall. There, in hushed voices, they conferred.

"We never guessed," protested big Hoyt to the old tramp, as though King Charlie were judge and jury with power of giving and taking life. "How could we of ever guessed that she was really down and out and—"

"Never mind telling *me* about it," said King Charlie coldly. "I ain't the one to blame you. It's everybody else in the world that'll do the talking when they hear about gents that let a woman starve to death in the same house that they're drinking in. But you go down and tell the landlady, or whoever runs this place. Hoyt, you go down and tell her. Dean, you come in with me."

The Dean stalked slowly behind him, while big Hoyt shambled off down the hall.

The two, in the meantime, entered the death-chamber, and there the Dean saw a still form on the bed. He, like the tramp, dragged the hat automatically from his head as he approached. A single glance at her face was sufficient to suggest in what manner she had passed away. The eyes were still open and gazing wearily at eternity. The Dean closed them.

After that he was able to speak.

"What are we going to do next?" he asked.

"Maybe this lady will know," answered King Charlie, and as he spoke steps came hurriedly up the hall and approached the room, and they could hear a woman's sharp voice chattering busily to Joe Hoyt, while the yegg ventured only mumbled replies. At the door of the room King Charlie saw a virago appear. She planted her fists upon her hips and glowered at the form on the bed.

"I might of knowed," she moaned, "I might of knowed what was going to happen when she put off paying me, but I always let my soft heart make a fool out of me. I always do."

"Maybe you do," said the King, "but the important thing now is, where are her friends?"

"If I knew that, d'you think I'd be worrying?"

"Where did she come from?"

"From the camp down the road. She's been cooking for the logging camp. She's been there since fall."

"Well?"

"Well, she got fired, that's all. She come to town and got sick and spent all her money and—there she is now left on my hands when—"

"Wait a minute," said King Charlie. "You ain't going to be made to pay for nothing. We'll tend to all that. Only thing you can contribute is a little free information."

She was immensely relieved by the prospect.

"You don't know nothing about where she come from or who her folks might be?"

"Nothing, except that she calls herself Mrs. Young."

King Charlie

"That's rock-bottom all you know?"

"Yes."

"Then we're going to go through her things in that trunk over yonder. Know where the key is?"

"In the top bureau drawer."

They found it and unlocked the big trunk which stood close to the window on the far side of the room, but when the heavy top was lifted they stared down into stark emptiness. There was not even a rag within.

And here the landlady cried: "See what's happened? She's burned everything! Look around the stove!"

And they could see on the floor around the stove a handful of bits of papers, odd corners and margins which had blown out, perhaps, when the door of the stove was opened to shove more in. She had felt that death was near her, and she had destroyed the clues to her backtrail before she left the earth.

"And the brat!" cried the landlady. "Who's going to take care of her?"

Chapter Six

Here the Dean wrinkled his long face in disapproving anger. "Don't call her a brat," he said sternly. "The care of her ain't going to fall on you, ma'am, and you can start betting on that right now."

A bitter life had made her what she was, hardened to perfect distrust of all things, and particularly of all people. But the scorn and the anger in the voice of the Dean and the sick disgust in the face of Hoyt and King Charlie wakened shame in her.

"And who else is there to take in the poor forlorn kiddie?" she asked, whining.

"I'll take her," cried King Charlie magnificently. "I'll take her and give her a home."

As he spoke, a picture of his own "home" darted in a thousand images across his mind's eye. He saw the inside of an "empty," noisy as a madhouse, bumping along at fifty an hour. He saw a stray corner in a cellar. He saw an open fire in the "jungle." No wonder that King Charlie blinked as he thought of these things, and yet he maintained a dauntless front to the others. His statement had roused them to admiration of such reckless self-sacrifice. Not one of them had had a true dependent, and they were amazed by the King.

"As for this poor woman," said the King, stepping to the bed, "I dunno but she's a millionaire's wife that's run off because of trouble to home. Nobody can tell. Leastwise, none of *us* can tell."

"That's damned true," said big Hoyt. "She had the look of a high stepper even when she was—"

He choked over the word "starving" and became silent, staring gloomily at the floor.

"All right, Hoyt," said King Charlie. "Suppose you go out and make arrangements to take care of the body?"

Hoyt nodded and hurried out to find the undertaker. Meantime the landlady, feeling that she was no longer needed, slipped away without a sound, and King Charlie and the Dean went towards the room where they had left Billy English and the little girl.

"Partner," said the Dean slowly, halting his companion in the hall, "do you mind telling me what you figure on gaining by putting up the bluff about being the father of Billy English?"

"Bluff?" said the tramp. "That ain't a bluff, son. Not a bit of a bluff. That's the painful facts."

The Dean growled. "I ain't aiming to start no sort of trouble with you on a day like this," he said, "but I got to say that Hoyt and me ain't fools. We know your game. You've sicked him on to us with a lot of talk about how much money he could make with you and how damned little he's making with us. But we ain't going to let you get away with it. Don't forget!" He added, with a growing fury: "Otherwise, what should have sent him home ready to eat raw meat like this?"

"Dean," said the tramp, "it means nothing to me, that sort of a game. I'm not trying to get him to go away with me. If you doubt it, wait and see. He came here raving partly because you gents *have* been using him pretty cheap, and mostly because he went out on a trail tonight and instead of getting his man he ran into a dozen hoboes all ready to fight at once. So he came away without licking his man. That's what put him off his feed."

"Was that why he went out?" murmured the Dean. And he shook his head. "We saw him go out late this afternoon, but he didn't have no idea where he was bound. Guess he must have got some tip that his man was pretty close. That's the straight of it, eh? He's just crazy with disappointment, not up to any hell that you've put into him?"

"Not a bit," the King assured him. "Listen now to that."

From the room they could hear, in a lull of the wind, the voice of Billy English, softened, and singing one of those eerie melodies with which the cowpunchers, riding night herd, lull the cattle.

"She's plumb knocked him off his feet," said the Dean, grinning broadly, as though that song had put him out of all thought of the hostile intentions which he had just been cherishing against the tramp.

And so saying, he jerked the door open and exposed Billy English seated near the stove with Louise Young cradled in his arms, and singing blissfully to her sleepy ears and to the ceiling. He stopped his song and flushed a little, scowling at the intruders. Then he managed to raise one finger to warn them into silence. The child slept.

So they tiptoed awkwardly in, and Billy English carried the girl into the next room and deposited her on the couch there. He returned, closed the door, and announced in triumph that he had been able to put her down and cover her without wakening her.

"It's the bread and the warmth of the stove," said King Charlie. "She's apt to sleep quite a little while, and when she wakes up we'll have the other thing finished, I hope."

He indicated his meaning still further by a gesture over his shoulder, and the others went slowly to their chairs and sat down.

"After all," said the Dean at length, "it ain't *our* fault, is it? Ain't there other people in the house besides us?"

"She was right across the hall from us," said Billy English, "and we was in here drinking and wasting more 'n enough chuck to have kept her and the baby. How old might she be, King?"

"About five. She's got name enough for fifty. What is it? Louise Alison Dora Young. Take her quite a spell to write even her initials."

The others were thoughtful for an instant, and then Billy exclaimed: "D'you know what those initials make?"

"Well?" they queried.

"Lady is what they spell. L.A.D.Y. as plain as day. And maybe that's what her mother was—and what she's going to be—a lady! Notice how she talks. Just like a little book, by God!"

"You can't be talking like that around her," said the King.

"There won't be much chance to talk around her," said Billy. "Soon as she wakes up I suppose she'll be gone some place to find her relatives?"

"She ain't got none," the King assured him.

And they told him briefly how they had examined the room and found nothing in it which could serve as a clue to the identity of the dead woman and her child. The Dean even concluded the account with King Charlie's avowal that he would take care of the little girl and the landlady's willingness to hand over the child to him. To all of this Billy English listened with the greatest interest until the end, when he turned on King Charlie with a growl, his ugly quick temper changing his face.

"And what right in the name of God," he cried, "have *you* got to say that you'll take care of a kid like her—a *lady* like she's going to be—when you can't even take care of yourself?"

"If a gent has the heart he'll find the way," declared the King, undaunted. "Besides, Billy, you got to find a better way than that to talk to your own father."

"Show me a reason," snapped Billy, "why I should talk soft to you."

"So's you'll keep from spoiling the manners of the kid," said King Charlie with great calm.

"Damn the kid and the rest of you!" answered Billy with a black look, and in such a loud voice that there was a faint cry from the next room. Billy English, with a gasp, glided to the door of the room, opened it softly, and disappeared within. A moment later they could hear him talking softly to soothe the child.

The Dean swore in muffled astonishment as soon as the door had closed.

"Who'd ever think of a young bulldog like him being so careful with a baby?" he demanded. "Who'd ever think of it? He's been like a starved wolf ever since we've knowned him, so far as temper goes!"

"It's his mother working out in him," replied King Charlie. "Me, I'm a rough one. I don't try to hide that. But his mother was fine as silk. And look how it sticks out in Billy. Birds of a feather, you know? That's what makes him and the girl so thick. She picked him out of the lot of us, and held out her arms to him. And he sticks around her like he was her real father. You can't explain things like that away."

"I won't try to," answered the Dean slowly, and going to the table he picked up the pack of cards and began to shuffle, slipping the halves of the pack into each other with such oiled dexterity that King Charlie's eye glistened with approval. He could tell the master gambler at a glance.

But his skill with the cards did not appease the gloom which was rising in the Dean, and presently he tossed the pack from him, rose, and took from beneath one of the beds a case, out of which he drew a violin. He tuned it hastily, tucked it at length into place under his chin, and tilting far back in his chair until his shoulders touched the wall and his head was cramped forward, he closed his eyes and drew out sweet and melancholy strains. So light was his muted touch that each note was no louder than a whisper, but so deft was the bowing that every note was, in that thin compass, rounded and true. Of such matters the King was no good critic, but he knew enough to admire again. And he began to set the Dean down as no common man. For his own part, a scheme which promised him at least some days of peace and rest was growing in his mind.

So he sat back and said not a word until big Hoyt came into the room, shook the snow from his shoulders, and with a glance at each of them announced more plainly than words that the business was completed and the body removed from the house. Here Billy English returned to the room, shutting the door behind him deftly and noiselessly.

"She's sleeping again," he announced in a triumphant whisper to them.

He crossed to the stove and warmed his hands at it. Then he turned, still smiling.

"She's a lady, right enough," he swore. "All I did was tell her everything was all right and she needn't worry about nothing. She wanted her mother at first, but pretty soon she tucked her hand inside of mine, give me a smile, and went off sound to sleep."

He chuckled contentedly at the thought, and King Charlie decided that this was the most opportune possible moment to make his proposal. He rose, and thereby drew their attention.

"Boys," he said, "it looks to me that the only end that lady is coming to is an orphan asylum, pretty soon."

This announcement was greeted with a groan.

"There's only one way to stop it," said King Charlie.

They wanted to know, in one voice, what it might be.

"She might be adopted," said King Charlie.

"By who?"

"By us," said the King.

They gaped at him.

"I mean it," he went on, developing his thought. "If one man can adopt a son or a daughter, why couldn't the four of us shake hands all around and agree that we'd adopt her? Why not?"

They blinked at the suggestion.

"You're out of your head," said the Dean at last. "What's the average life of a—of them that live the way we do? How long would she have any adopted fathers?"

"That's the beauty of it," said King Charlie. "Any one of us ain't apt to last long, but out of the four of us, one is pretty sure to keep going. Besides, boys, if we should take Lady with us, we'd have something that would tie us all together and make us strong. What was it that smoothed out all the wrinkles a while back when Billy and you two was having words? Well, it was Lady coming to the door of the room and giving us a call. That means something, pals. That was more 'n an accident. If we had her to work for, we'd all stick and work for each other. Ain't that logic?"

"You mean," corrected Joe Hoyt sarcastically, "that we'd do the working and that you'd stay around at home with Lady?"

But here Billy English interrupted:

"Gents, if we could try that, you'd sure see me working all day every day and never asking no questions."

The Dean had been about to shake his head, but here he paused to consider, and finally he became serious, and his eye brightened. Many and many a thousand dollars could be made by that association

King Charlie

with Billy English if the lad were manageable, and the presence of Louise Alison Dora Young promised to make him entirely amenable to reason.

"Well, boys," said the Dean, "I think King Charlie has an idea. If you and me, Hoyt, stay to business, and if Billy English stops running off every now and then to hunt down some bo that's bothered him, if all them things was to happen, we could afford to keep King Charlie staked out somewhere keeping a home for us, and Lady could be in that home. King, is that your idea?"

"You take the words right out of my mouth, Dean."

"Shake on it," cried Billy English, and in his enthusiasm he ran about the room wringing their hands one after the other.

"You might say," said Joe Hoyt, who seemed the least joyous of the lot, "that we're a bunch of damn fools organizing a company for the sake of a kid we ain't knowed for more 'n a couple of hours. But—it's something new, boys, anyway."

Chapter Seven

"What," asked King Charlie, "are we going to do about telling Lady what—"

"You do *no* telling," said Billy English. "I've fixed that already. Her mother went on a little trip, and'll be back for Lady later on. I've told her all that, and she's happy."

This fragment of conversation occurred later in the evening before the supper hour. And when they descended to the dining-room Louise Young, so newly named "Lady," was carried on the broad shoulder of Hoyt, while a trail of silver-thin laughter floated up the stairs behind her. Many a time, during that meal, the four grew gloomy when they watched the smiling face and heard the piping voice of the little girl and thought, in contrast, of the dead mother. But they agreed that it was better thus. On the next day the body would be buried, and "Lady" should know nothing of what had happened. Far better that she should never connect her mother with the thought of death.

After supper there was a gay party in the rooms upstairs. The Dean played his gayest tunes on his fiddle, to the immense delight of Lady, and when she was bundled off to bed they sat down to another consultation as to her future. Funds were in the first place put in the hands of the King to buy her clothes in such quantities as might be advised by some woman of the village. After that they argued long and earnestly as to the best location for their permanent headquarters, where King Charlie was to establish their home while the three struck out here and there through the country and brought back what plunder they might gather. Of course, there was one great added danger in any such plan. Even in this town they felt that they had stayed too long for safety. But if they settled down permanently with Lady and King Charlie their home might sooner or later prove a trap in which the law could bag them all.

In the midst of this discussion there was a knock at the door, which was immediately opened by Hoyt, and exposed a youth with one of those faces which can only be described as crime-battered. For he was in his early twenties, handsome, smiling. But half a dozen scars seamed his features, his eyes, in moments of relaxation, were dull, and his walk was somewhat halting. Every bone in his body, they said, had been broken at one time or another.

They greeted him with acclaim. Everyone saving Billy English knew him of old, and Billy himself was quickly made acquainted with—"Here's Billy English, Jack. Here's Jack Turner, Billy. You boys must have heard of each other. He started a shade later than you, Jack. But he's sure used his first year in great shape, when it comes to making a name for himself."

They shook hands, at the same time estimating one another's force with sharp glances.

"Yep," said Jack, "I've heard a good deal about you, Billy. Matter of fact, that's one of the big reasons that I've dropped in on you boys. Because there's something ahead that needs doing, and I figure you fellows have the layout to suit me. Can I use you?"

"If we can use you," said the Dean, "we got nothing against being used."

"Hell," said Jack Turner. "You know me. I ain't the kind that tries to grab everything for himself. You can trust me, I guess."

They agreed, in chorus, that they could.

"But you, Charlie," said Turner to the veteran tramp, "don't have to listen in on this."

"Don't you trust me?" asked King Charlie, something offended.

"I trust nobody," said Jack Turner. "I don't aim that at you, Charlie. Everybody knows that you're as straight as they come. But I ain't throwing no talk that'll be useful to you, so why should you sidetrack near a temptation?"

King Charlie waved his hand in agreement and left the room for that in which Lady slept, only to drop on his knees and press his ear against the keyhole to such effect that he was able to hear enough fragments of the talk to get its general purport.

He heard Jack Turner quickly outline his plan to the others. He knew of a large shipment of money which was heading West, and he had determined to stop the train and blow the safe for the money. He himself was an expert all round, but he would be glad to have such a professional as Joe Hoyt to lend a hand. The Dean would be welcome in many details, such as holding back the train crew and keeping the passengers herded back inside the train. As for the stopping of the train, that would be best undertaken by someone who had never before been connected with a robbery of that character. For he understood that the train would be literally loaded down with guards.

King Charlie

No doubt one of these guards would be riding the blind baggage as the train struck the mountains to make sure that no one swung up on to that platform, from which it was a simple matter for an armed man to climb over the tender and down into the cab and hold up the engineer and fireman. But this was exactly what must be dared, and what must be accomplished in order to stop the train.

If there were two guards riding the blind baggage, as the closed end of the first baggage car is termed, it simply meant that the man who attempted to climb on there would be either kicked off to his death as a mere hobo, or else captured and held as a more dangerous possibility.

If there was only one guard riding the blind baggage, it was barely possible that an expert, fearless and quick of movement, might be able to climb on to the platform in spite of him. At least the odds would give him one chance in ten.

If there was no guard at all, the only hazard to begin with would be the dangers of leaping for the handrail when the train was in rapid motion.

In short, this was a task for which the crippled Turner would have immediately chosen himself in the old days, but now, unfortunately, he was far too stiff and slow for such work. The Dean and Joe Hoyt were possibilities, to be sure, but best of all would be one who united practised agility and the nimble feet of youth with perfect courage and uncommon coolness and strength.

This man, to be plain, was Billy English. To get him Jack Turner had travelled several hundred miles by train and by horseback. For the sake of swinging Billy into the deal, it seemed that Jack had given the cold shoulder to a dozen old pals, men who had ridden the length and the breadth of the mountain desert with him on one sort of an errand or another.

"Because," said Jack Turner, leaning over and talking out of the side of his mouth after the fashion of men who have learned the ways of the prisons through bitter years of experience, "because, kid, I've tried 'em all out, and though I know a bunch that are good, I've got to get one now that's a dead sure thing!"

But Billy English shook his head and rose.

"I ought to have told you sooner," he said, "but it's just been growing up in my mind while I heard you talking, partner. In that other room—which you can't be expected to know things that you ain't seen—there's a little girl that I've got to look after. No matter what I might be *wanting* to do, the thing that I *have* to do is to look after Lady. Well, Jack, I'm going to do that by getting a steady job and working as a puncher on some layout."

The news dazed the others.

Finally the Dean cried: "Good God, Billy, what d'you mean? D'you know what a puncher's wages are?"

"I know that they're mighty small," said Billy. "But they're mighty sure."

Joe Hoyt started to his feet. "Billy," he began, "if you—"

"Shut up, boys," said Jack Turner. "I got something more to say that'll sound to him. Listen!"

He leaned over and tapped the words into the palm of one hand with the stiff fingers of the other.

"In that safe on that train, d'you think there's some small time bunch of lunch money, Billy? D'you think that I've come all this way to get next to you with any little stake hanging in the air? Listen to me, son. There's going to be seventy-five thousand dollars soaked away in that safe. Seventy-five thousand— understand? And it's going to be ours. You're going to start to-night and ride like hell till you get to Williamstown, and then you're going to wait there till tomorrow night. Tomorrow night you're going to grab the blind baggage when she comes through on the express; and you're going to climb on to the tender and drop down into the cab when the engine begins to snake along into Jeffrey Pass. Understand?"

But Billy shook his head.

"It sounds good," he said, "and I'd like to work it with you. But not for me, Jack."

"Lost your nerve?"

"Don't say that," said Billy. "You get me nervous when you begin to talk that way to me, Jack. I'm staying behind for the little girl. That's why."

"Then you're a fool. How many of us are there? Four. Four ain't many to hold up a train, but every man here is the right stuff, and I'd rather have four good ones than forty common bos. But four into seventy-five makes something pretty fat. One-third goes out to them that tipped the shipment to me. That leaves fifty. Divide that by four. Leaves you twelve thousand five hundred apiece. And after you've got that wadded down in your jeans, you can *afford* to resign. Take this chance, and afterwards you and the kid are on Easy Street. Does that sound to you, Billy? Twelve thousand five hundred! Out of that you can fix her up. You can send her away to school. You can raise her like a lady."

At the last word, Billy English started and groaned.

"She *is* a lady," he said. "And how could I raise her the way she ought to be raised unless I got the coin? Suppose Hoyt and Dean were scooped in—that'd leave me alone with only thirty or forty a month riding herd and—"

He turned sharply upon Jack Turner.

"I'm with you!" he said. "Tell me the rest!"

Chapter Eight

It was cold midnight when he saddled, not the cowpony on which the King had seen him mounted earlier in the evening, but one of those tall, leggy horses which King Charlie had wondered at. At the same time the other three were making their own mounts ready and agreeing with King Charlie on the rendezvous. No sooner were they under way than he was to gather their effects in their rooms and make ready for a departure early the next morning, rain or hail or snow. They directed him towards what spot in the mountains he should aim with the buckboard and horses belonging to the three. There they would attempt to meet him and Lady on their return from the hold-up.

With these agreements completed, Billy English waited for no more, but, since his was the greatest distance to be covered to reach the railroad, he spurred off into the whirling snow, bending his head to the storm.

King Charlie

"Will he make it?" asked Jack Turner anxiously.

"He's got one chance in four, I figure," said the Dean, "of getting there and find that there ain't a guard riding on that platform."

"And if there's a guard that finishes it."

"If there's a guard he's got one chance in a thousand."

"Well," said Jack Turner, "all my life I've been betting on long chances, and I ain't going to stop now. We'll start for Jeffrey Pass."

But already Billy English had forgotten about the work before him and the men behind him. He was entirely occupied in the battle with the storm, with the snow sometimes hurtling into his face in semi-solid drifts, half choking him.

An hour later the wind abated, and the fall of snow with it. He continued over a country where the snow was swept nearly clean from all level places, but where it had banked and slipped on every slope of any size. Sometimes he was able to swing along at a round gallop. Again, he was forced to slacken his pace to a jog, or even to a walk as he floundered through deep drifts.

In the grey of the dawn he reached a small house almost buried in snow. Here he knocked at the door, and the sole occupant, a trapper, hunter, and small rancher, answered the knock. He recognized Billy English at once. For this was one of the stations which the long-riders maintained on the mountain desert, keeping a following by a judicious distribution of money here and there. And sometimes they maintained posts where they were dreaded and where the houseowner would have gladly supported the law, but where they inspired such fear that men dared not deny them.

It happened that this lonely out-dweller was only too glad to see one of the daring rovers approach. His season had been bad indeed, and the stay of Billy English meant both money and news.

Accordingly, he put up the fine horse from which Billy dismounted, and allowed the rider to stretch on the bunk for an hour's unbroken rest. After that, Billy rose, shook the sleep out of his head and body, drank the coffee, and ate the corn pone and bacon offered to him, and swung into the saddle on the trapper's own horse. A liberal donation followed, and leaving his host grinning and waving behind him, Billy shot away on the fresh mount into the storm.

It was much abated by this time. The sky was as grey as ever, but very little snow was flying in the wind. All the day Billy drove south and east on his journey, and in the dusk he arrived, saddle-cramped and half dead with continual exposure and the beating of the storm.

He stabled the horse at once, told a simple story to the livery-keeper to explain the fact that the horse would be left for several days, and that another man would call for it, and then paid the man to let him sleep another hour on his bunk.

That hour's rest worked wonders with him, and brought him out into the night, at last, with only a faint ringing in his ears to remind him of the arduous labours of that long grind through the storm.

There was still a full twenty minutes left before the train was due, and he spent this time in warming himself up and unlimbering the muscles of arms and legs with exercise in the cold night.

Finally, the blood was boiling through his body, his eye was clear, and his hand steady. It was the perfect state of mind and body for the work which lay before him, and now, far down the track, the whistle of the train was caught up by the face of the hill and echoed faintly down the wind.

Billy stayed back from the busy little lighted station as the great headlight poured down the track, caught the station house in a glowing circle, and then, as the engine turned a slight curve, wavered away and plunged down the gleaming rails. It roared closer, stopped, panting steam, instinct with strength; for nothing made by man is so nearly living as a railroad locomotive.

The brief stop was already terminated, and the "shack" (brakeman) had swung on to the blind baggage with his lantern. Plainly they were guarding carefully against hoboes, at least. The train began to move, the engine snorting like a horse at the grade and the load it was required to set in motion.

In the meantime Billy had backed down the track. He must get a sufficient distance ahead, and yet he must not go so far that the spreading circle of the headlight would glow on him. With enough ground between him and the engine, he must wait until, as the train gathered headway, the "shack" swung down from the blind baggage and swung on to the train again farther down.

And all the time Billy blessed his lucky stars that no guard was riding that same blind baggage. For certainly the "shack" would not be wasting his time in this fashion if the blind baggage platform were already occupied.

All that could prevent him from getting on, it seemed, would be the ability of the brakeman to stay on that platform for so long, while the train gathered headway, that Billy could not catch the step and handrail as the car flashed past. But this was made the less likely because the shack had to dismount from the platform himself and swing on to the train farther down the line unless he wished a long and cold ride to the next stopping point.

Accordingly, Billy jogged backward, looking over his shoulder as the train gathered headway, and waiting for that moment when he should see the descending arc of light, which meant that the shack was swinging down with his lantern.

Presently that light showed, hung a moment as the brakie waited on the lowest step, scanning the track ahead and letting the ground skim beneath his dangling foot. Then he dropped off, the yellow spot of lantern-light staggered, and presently it hooked up into the train farther down as the brakie swung aboard.

Exultation began to rise in the breast of Billy. That shack, he told himself, was a "simp." In the meantime the train was advancing at a good round gait, but it was as nothing to him. Taught in the first place by the celebrated King Charlie himself, and so initiated into many fine points of the game, he had improved his opportunities to learn during the past year—or, rather, during his six months of liberty of the past year—and now he was as active and daring in his manipulations around a train as the most expert shack or experienced hobo that ever lived.

He increased his run to a sprint as the engine thundered past him. Then he faced in and leaped for the handrail of the blind baggage, bunching his feet well up towards his hands to strike out for the step in the darkness, as a well-trained hobo always does.

Fair and true both hands and feet struck. The resulting wrench to the side would have torn a less experienced hand away, but Billy English had allowed himself to sway in, jerking himself close to the car.

He slipped his hand higher on the handrail, and a heavy blow descended on the fingers, crushing them against the iron. His fingers, numbed by that blow, slid helplessly from the rail, and he lurched to the side, falling, and such a fall meant perhaps a roll under the wheels and horrible mangling, at least a broken neck as he struck the gravel road-bed.

And in the split part of a second which that lurch occupied he nevertheless had ample time to think of both possibilities. With his right hand he clutched. It struck the rail with stinging impact as he shot to the side. And his grip slipped—held. At the same time he hooked his right foot in, and it caught on the lowest portion of the rail.

King Charlie

In the meantime, the sweep of the train had flattened him against the side of the car, and the only parts of him which even touched the rail or the steps were the extended right hand and the foot. No wonder, then, that the man who had delivered the blow, now looking down, saw nothing and shouted fiercely into the night:

"One damned hobo less in the world!"

The words shrieked with inhuman loudness in the ear of Billy.

So the platform, after all, was guarded. If he swung back on to the steps he would be beaten off them by an armed man—for, no doubt, that blow had been delivered with a revolver-butt. To be sure, if he swung back quickly enough, he might be able to get into his place on the steps, jerk out his revolver, and kill the shadowy form above him.

But Billy English had never yet shot to kill, and that thought was impossible for him. Nevertheless, he could not hang there indefinitely, with the wind tugging at him. He held on until the blood began to course through his injured hand and the fingers commenced to ache.

Then he drew himself back, cringing down and making himself small on the lowest step and peering up in an anguish, half expectant of seeing the dull glimmer of naked steel in the night above him.

But now? He could see the vague shadow of the brakeman's body as the fellow stood guard there, but apparently there was no motion. He had dismissed all thought of Billy from his mind. To him it was impossible that Billy should be alive. His thoughts must be picturing the tramp crushed beneath the whirring wheels of the long train, or else smashed on the road-bed where he might have fallen.

What a malignantly cruel trap it had been! To have the brakeman swing on and off and all the time with a guarded platform.

Hot rage mastered Billy English and made him

139

shake for an instant. That was his greatest enemy, that blind rage which leaped on him and blurred his eyes with red. He shook the passion off instantly, and, cold and ready for action, gripping his smashed and bleeding left hand, in spite of the pain, around the handrail, he slipped up, changed his footing, and then dived over the top of the steps and at the knees of the guard, shooting himself in with the full strength of his arms and with a lucky sway of the train to drive him all the faster.

He succeeded so very well that he nearly rolled them both to horrible death on the far side. For the shack went down like lead, too stunned by surprise to even shriek, and he and Billy tumbled to the very verge of the far steps. Both clutched for safety in the nick of time. But as they scrambled back, Billy chopped down with his clenched right hand, and the hard knuckles thudded home just under the ear of his enemy. The shack stretched out limp, without a murmur, and Billy set about calmly binding the hands and feet of the victim. After that he went through the pockets of his man, extracted and re-stored the wallet—there was none of the petty thief in Billy—and finally wound up by taking the fellow's gun and knife and tossing them into the darkness.

Chapter Nine

As the train lurched forward, still gaining speed on the grade, Billy English settled back, crouching on his heels, and attempted to examine his injured hand, but in the darkness that was impossible. And there arose in him a singular feeling of fierce triumph. Since that blow which the shack had given him by surprise he felt that whatever he might do would be simply an act of retaliation. Behind him the long train was thundering, each car loaded with life, gaiety, unconcern. Before him the engine laboured swiftly up the rails. And all of this power and the cargo it was transporting might be stopped and held still by his sole command. No wonder that it set him breathing deeply.

But suppose, when he climbed over the tender, that the engineer and his fireman showed fight. They were a hardy lot these trainmen, used to danger and the taking of chances, and trained to consider their own lives as nothing, compared with the comfort and safety of the passengers in their charge. Suppose they were to attack him in spite of the drawn revolver which he levelled at them. The warm blood was dripping down his fingers. And when they saw this blood they might be the more encouraged to attack him. In that case, what could he do?

The resolution which was so deeply implanted in him—that he would never shoot to kill, least of all a harmless law-abiding citizen—was become worse than a gun pointed at his head. What was the taking of a common chance to other bandits became a mortal peril to him. But he drew his revolver and felt some consolation as the roughened butt pressed up into the palm of his hand.

In the meantime the shack was wakening. He had been badly laid out by that blow beneath the ear, driven home with such cruel force, now he roused himself with a groan, and there was a fierce and silent struggle as he strove to free himself from the bonds. Billy English watched and listened without a word, for he enjoyed the spectacle immensely, there on that black-shadowed blind baggage. There is no love wasted between the brakeman and any of the criminal class who are forced to travel by stealth on the railroads. They hate one another heartily and take advantage of any opening to inflict pain on their enemies. If there is an occasional friendly shack, the root of his friendliness is usually found in his belief that he can extract a few dollars from the hobo for the passage on that division.

These two, therefore, glared at one another through the darkness. The shack was only astonished to find that he had not been tumbled from the platform to die wretchedly on the road-bed as he fell. He decided, therefore, that he was being reserved for some finer torture. And he began to shout as soon as his wrestling had revealed the fact that he was securely tied hand and foot. Strips of his own clothes had been used to make those bonds.

King Charlie

The shouting was stopped by a hand which shot under his chin and secured a strong grip on his throat.

He heard a voice mutter: "You damned shack, I'll tear your head off if you let out another yap!"

And he lay still. In the first place, the voice was convincing in intonation. In the second place, the fingertips which had gripped at his throat were like tearing steel. He saw that it would be well to consider this game concluded. Now the cold muzzle of a revolver was shoved into his face.

"I'd blow you to hell, shack," said Billy English, "if it wasn't easier and quicker, almost, to just roll you off the train and let the ground hit you. That'd be sure enough the way we're shooting. But you lie still and maybe you'll come through this yet. I ain't *promising.* Understand? But I won't bump you off unless you get to really bothering me."

The brakeman lay still as death. He was a brave man. He had been picked for the cold duty of guarding the blind baggage for that reason and for his relentless hatred of tramps. But now he realized that a life which he had really lost was being restored to him, and he neither stirred nor spoke. "When in doubt keep your mouth shut." That is a great law of the road.

And Billy English settled back again and watched the mountains growing up on either hand. For the wind had whisked the heavens clean of clouds, and now the sky was mottled with points of fire, a stippled background against which the dark peaks were in relief. They rose higher and higher. They crowded closer until it seemed that at last they would close above the rushing train. And Billy English knew that they were nearing Jeffrey Pass.

He began to grow tense as the time for action approached. He slipped down on the steps and swung out. He could mark the place well. Straight ahead

143

rose the great sugar-loaf mountain which was to be his milestone.

He clambered back, went up the back of the tender with great agility in spite of his crippled, aching hand, and from the top turned and snarled a warning back at the shack, who was cursing softly in the realization that his conqueror was something more than an ordinary tramp.

"If you open your head," snapped Billy English, "I'll stop what I'm doing and come back here and slice your throat, you rat! Keep thinking about that."

The shack was silenced. Billy turned and resumed his progress. A second later he was peering at the engineer's back as he leaned against the side of the cab to stare down the tracks. And the heart of Billy smote him. There was so much weariness and yet honest purpose combined in the grease-marked, overall-clad back of the engineer that Billy almost relented.

Above him the sugar-loaf was thrusting higher and higher into the heaven, a monstrosity. Somewhere on the far side of it, Jack Turner—the great Jack Turner himself—and the Dean and Joe Hoyt, everyone of them a man among a million, crouched in waiting. They had made out the roar of the train, in this narrow pass, long before they saw the headlight, but now it must be playing down the rails as it turned the last curve. And those men who waited were wondering if he, Billy English, would play his part.

It was no little thing. To have stopped such a train would entitle him to deathless consideration among their ranks. He would become a known man, one of those the mention of whose name caused the other dwellers in the underworld to lift their brows in attention and respect.

And yet such a consideration was no consideration at all. But yonder in the mountains, somewhere, King Charlie had driven with his buckboard and carried the girl to the new refuge. Yonder in the mountains they were waiting for the return.

"This is the last time," panted Billy to himself. "After this there won't be no call for such things. I can put her up like the little lady she is. I can fix her so that she can live in style. I can give her everything that *I* missed."

And his big, generous boy's heart swelled with the resolve.

An instant later he was in the cab with his wounded hand doubled to conceal the blood from the two. His levelled revolver was as steady as though rested upon a rock.

"All right, boys," he said quietly. "You don't have to shove your hands up. Just watch that you don't make any *fast* move. Understand? I ain't going to wait to see *where* you move your hands. But as soon as you let a hand jump I'm going to shoot."

He had learned the greatest lesson that any criminal can learn, and that is, when confronting a victim, to keep on thinking not to attempt to bluff the other, but to let him become aware of a coldly sure and active brain at work. And as he had slipped on his mask before climbing on to the tender, he had steadied himself for the part which he must play. Now he was instantly at home in it.

The fireman was a boy of twenty-five, with the red hair and the fighting blue eyes of an Irishman. He leaned against the side of the cab and glared at Billy with deathless hate. As for the engineer, he seemed dazed. He even forgot himself so far as to make one of the quick motions against which Billy had cautioned him, but the movement was up, a flicker of the hand across his face. He seemed to be brushing a mist from his eyes.

Billy would have thought him drunk had he not seen him at his post. He was not drunk. He was simply dazed at the catastrophe which was befalling, not him, but the train which was under his charge.

"You'll stop up yonder the minute you get past the

sugar-loaf, friend," said Billy English.

He was hoping that the young fireman with the fighting face had not noticed that he was allowing the move of the man's hand to go for nothing. Once either of them decided that there was the slightest element of a bluff about this hold-up, Billy knew that he would have them both at his throat in deadly earnest.

"You'd better begin easing up on this train," said Billy.

The engineer merely stared, his forehead wrinkling as though there was no comprehension in his brain. And then he lurched at Billy with arms outspread.

He was a big man—a full two hundred pounds. And though he must have been well past forty, he was still strong with muscle under the outer layer of fat. Billy English saw the Irishman, with a hoarse shout of battle-rage, gather himself to leap in to the assistance of his comrade, regardless of the fact that the revolver was pointed full in his face.

And even in that crisis Billy admired their courage with all his boyish, quick heart. He had six deaths there under his trigger finger. But he could not shoot any more than if his hand had been paralyzed. Instead, he jerked back the revolver and struck sideways with it, cuffing the engineer along the head with the long, heavy barrel of the gun. There was a thud of the steel sinking into the bone, and the big man went down while the fireman was stopped, with his hands at the very throat of Billy, by the feel of the revolver muzzle as it was jabbed into his belly. For an instant he hesitated. Then he gave way to the inevitable and fell back.

"He ain't dead," said Billy, answering the despairing look which the fireman cast at his late chief. "He's just knocked cold. Now, damn you, stop this train or I'll stop you first and the train afterwards."

The fireman turned with a groan. The fall of the

engineer had had some weight with him. He worked for a moment, then Billy saw a small cloud of steam roll into the cab, and an instant later the engine stopped chugging and the brakes began to grind, catching on the whole length of the train.

To the right the great sugar-loaf drifted past with diminishing speed. But what if he stopped the train too soon? What if, when it halted and the train crew poured out to find out the reason for the halt, his comrades were not present? In that case he would be immediately swamped. But for that he could only trust to chance. Jack Turner would not be apt to let his share of such a bargain fall through unaccomplished.

The engine rocked, halted with a jar, and Billy backed down on to the step, hooking his left arm through the rail to steady himself, because his left hand was now so swollen and painful that he could not grip with it.

There he waited. Down the train he heard voices, and the noise of traps being jerked up. And then, like a blessing to his straining ears, the voice of Joe Hoyt booming from the darkness just at his side: "Good work! Good work, pal! Make 'em flood the firebox now."

He heard a man running past with another behind. Hoyt and another were taking that side of the train. He heard the voice of the Dean shouting on the far side of the train: "Keep inside, folks. We ain't aiming to harm nobody. Just keep inside them cars, that's all."

Here the engineer heaved himself to his elbow with a groan.

"Oh, God," he was muttering, "I'd rather of died. It's the first accident in twenty years. It's the first time, Mike, that my train has been stopped by—"

"Shut up!" cut in Billy, as much to stop the progress of his own sympathy for the man as to get action. "Shut up! This firebox has to be flooded. Get busy, boys."

For unless this were done, the train would thunder on out of the pass, and in a few minutes, from the nearest station, the telegraph wires would be charged with messages rousing the whole district against the outlaws. The levelled revolver forced both the engineer and the Irishman to do as Billy English commanded. Those other voices in the night made Billy seem a more important figure. Hoyt and Jack Turner and the Dean were shouting back and forth with loud clamours. The Dean, in particular, was running back and forth, so that at one instant he was shouting from one end of the train and at another from a quite different section. The air was filled with voices. Had not he known the actual number, Billy would have thought that a score were engaged in the hold-up. He caught other noises—the shrill cry of a terrified woman, and then two sharp reports of a revolver, followed by the heavy roar of what Billy knew must be a sawed-off shot-gun.

What had happened there? He had no chance to think. The roar of the steam as the water was turned into the firebox drowned his very capacity for thought and emotion.

Then he stepped back from the engine. There was no longer need to watch the engine crew since the engine was dead. There was a greater need for him to see if his companions did not require his aid farther down the train. Either one of them was dead or wounded, or one of the train crew was down. Or had that roar of the shot-gun proved to be simply a blind effort at resistance?

The latter proved to be the case. The men who were guarding the money shipment had been routed out of their stronghold by the roared threat of Jack Turner that he would use enough "soup" to blow both the car and its contents to the devil unless they opened the door. They had taken him at his word, and opening the door they had leaped out, both of them, with shotguns ready. But before they could locate their enemies Joe Hoyt from the side had brought them both down with snapshots aimed low. Wounded through the legs, they had dropped to the ground, and there one of them in pain and despair had fired both barrels of his gun blindly.

No harm was done to the robbers, and an instant later Jack Turner was in the car and at work on the safe.

These facts were briefly communicated to Billy by Joe Hoyt as the two guards sat up and worked bandaging their wounds and strewing curses through the air.

"What can I do now?" asked Billy.

"Start praying, kid," muttered Hoyt. "Just start praying that these blockheads don't find out that there ain't about a million of us. I wish that there was ten Turners in there working to blow the safe. Every second counts for us. Here he comes!"

Jack Turner swung out of the black doorway of the car and ran towards them.

"Get these out of the way!" commanded Turner.

The two guards were seized and dragged several paces before Turner commanded: "Now get down on the ground—flat!"

They dropped, and hardly had they done so when there was the sound of the explosion, not like thunder, but like an immense puff of air, if such a thing can be imagined, multiplied a thousandfold. At the same time there was a sort of soft blow that shook Billy from head to foot. Looking sideways he saw the long top of the car lift as though on hinges and settle back with a great crash.

Jack Turner was on his feet already and running with peculiar speed, in spite of his limp. Into the car he leaped. And then suddenly they heard a wail of rage from him. He jumped down at once, stamping and raving and beating his hands together like one possessed.

"What's up?" cried Hoyt. "Was it an empty?"

"It's a double safe!" cried Turner. "I peeled the outside off like a shell, but—"

His voice died in curses.

He was able to gasp at last: "And there ain't a damned drop of soup left! I've used it all up in the first try!"

Chapter Ten

By simple processes the minds of the great bring about the defeat of their enemies; and by simple neglect of little things they themselves are destroyed. Napoleon is beaten at Waterloo by indigestion, not by the red-coated squares against which the French cavalry ground itself to pieces. And yet the mind of Billy English grasped at, but could not comprehend, the fact that the great Jack Turner, of whom he had heard in his very childhood, should have played so amateur a prank as to use up all of his "soup" in blasting the outer jacket off the safe.

But the realization of what had happened was now brought home to them sharply. Far down the length of the train a number of men poured out from a car, and there was a sudden fusillade of shots that hummed and whirred around the heads of the robbers. They could stand their ground and drive these fellows back, perhaps, with a few well-directed shots, but what was there to be gained by fighting?

Jack Turner whistled loud and shrill, and set the example by turning about and bolting for the brush. Joe Hoyt did likewise. But what of the Dean, left unsuccoured on the far side of the train?

Billy English called to his companions to stay and hold back the crowd until the Dean had secured his retreat. But they made no answer.

Billy dropped to the ground, and tried the effect of a few well-directed shots sent into the air, but close enough to the heads of the passengers for them to hear the whine of the bullets. The result was magic. Down dropped the advancing line of half a dozen bold spirits. They sent a fierce fusillade which whirred above the spot where Billy lay breast high. He was amusing himself with shooting out the windows of the cars, with a resultant crash of glass that kept back the armed men of several other cars.

But suddenly the whole train seemed to waken to the fact that yonder in the dimness there was only a single man opposing them. Wild yells of rage tore the night, and men bolted out from every car.

As for Billy, he had accomplished his purpose. In the interim the Dean had raced for the head of the train on the farther side. Now Billy saw what he had been straining his eyes to observe—a tall, spare figure leaping around the front of the engine and breaking for the dense woods. And Billy followed with all speed.

The others had delayed not a second for the sake of the Dean. And even for Billy they were waiting only a moment. They were just urging their horses away when he burst upon them and leaped without a word upon the back of the spare horse. Well he knew the feel of the good chestnut's barrel between his knees. He flung himself forward along the neck of the horse, like the others, and instantly they were shooting ahead parallel with the railroad, but screened from it, for a hundred yards, by the narrow row of trees.

King Charlie

The shots of the enraged men from the train combed the trees above their heads, but when they emerged from shelter, far down the pass, they were effectually screened by the darkness, and began to draw their horses down to a more moderate gait.

Here the Dean pulled his horse in to the side of Billy.

"Waiting for me like that was a pretty white thing to do, son," he said. "I'll remember."

"Aw, hell," growled Billy. "Don't talk about it. You'd do the same for me."

And through the night they rode on, with never a word spoken concerning their disappointment. They climbed through the first range of the mountains, and when they had circled down into easier ground beyond Jack Turner drew in his rein.

"I'm going to leave you boys here. I'll have to owe you this hoss, though."

"Keep him, Jack," they told him. "You're welcome."

"Because I'm broke," he persisted. "But I'll be flush again one of these days, and I'll have another idea. Then I'll come and hunt you boys up. Unless you've decided that you don't like the kind of luck that I bring."

They laughed such a thought away. They would try luck with him any day, they declared. Then he came closer to Billy English and said:

"Billy, you done a fine bit of work in stopping that train. I'll tell you something man to man: I knowed that that train was going to be guarded. But I sent you after the job, anyway. The reason was that I wanted to see what sort of stuff was in you. Well, son, I sure know now what you can do, and you're going to hear from me again, one of these days. So long!"

"So long," said Billy, and watched the outlaw turn and ride into the night.

He himself rode downheaded with his compan-

153

ions down the trail which led to their place of rendezvous with King Charlie and Lady.

"That was rare talk to hear from Jack Turner," said the Dean, after a time. "He's got about as much warm blood in him as a fish. I remember four years back at the Cranston job. Bud Sendal dropped the Chink when the yaller hound was about to knife Jack. He dropped on Jack and covered him with blood. Jack gets up as cool as you please. 'Damned unclean, killing these Chinks,' he says. And that was all. Never ever said a word to Sendal about it, but the reason that Sendal got pardoned when he was sent up, they say, was because of the coin that Jack Turner spent on his case. They say that Turner went busted hiring swell lawyers to fight for poor old Sendal. And finally he got him clean off! That's the kind of a gent Turner is, Billy. He'd rather a thousand times do a thing than talk about it. So you can write down this day in red."

Billy grunted, as his way was, and continued in his brown study. The dawn found them far away in the foothills with six hours more to ride before they would reach the rendezvous. And still there was no sign of a pursuit behind them. Long before this the telegraph must have been humming with news of their attempt. It had failed, but they had stopped the mails, and they had wounded two law-abiding citizens. Moreover, there was something which particularly struck the imagination in a crime which had to do with the stopping of a great train in the mountains by a mere handful of men. No doubt the hills were buzzing with news of them and every village was sending out its quota to hunt for them.

They were favoured by one thing alone. The storm had started again with the first blur of daylight, and now the wind was howling through the hills, bearing thick drifts of the snow before it. Men were not apt to hunt with much zest in this impracticable and discouraging weather. More than that, they would be most likely to have a hard time in discovering any trail of the fugitives.

The last hours of the journey were weary ones. They did not speak at all. They merely swayed with the labouring, leg-weary horses until, at last, they came on the welcome smell of wood smoke blowing down the wind. And in the throat of the narrow gorge, where they had told him to go, they found King Charlie ensconced with Lady.

The little shack had been busily repaired by the old tramp during the day. Now it was fairly storm-tight. On the great, clumsily built hearth on the end of the room there was a big fire of logs blazing, and over this fire simmered various scraps of broken pots and pans which Charlie had found, scoured out, and now had filled with various sorts of food. And when they had put up their horses in the shed behind the house and come in, they found Louise Alison Dora Young sitting in the middle of the floor profoundly engaged with a doll which consisted of a potato with matches stuck into it for arms and legs.

She leaped up with a shout, and came running to greet them. And Billy English, entering last and closing the door behind him, chuckled as he saw the two big men, stern from their hazardous and profitless adventure, shrug away their gloom and scoop her up into their arms with laughter.

Last of all, she insisted on sitting on the knee of Billy and superintending the job when King Charlie set about cleansing and binding up the battered hand which the brakeman had struck with a pistol-butt.

In the meantime the food was served, and they ate as men who had laboured without the comfort of food for eighteen hours can eat. But more than the food, more than the drowsy, pleasant warmth in the room, more than the kindly face and the soothing voice of the man whom he thought was his father,

Billy English centred his attention on the bright head of Lady.

Afterwards he drew King Charlie to one side and consulted him seriously in murmurs.

"What would you think," he said, "of doing what I suggested the other day—cutting loose from your trains and your rod-riding and settling down somewhere where I can look after you and you can look after Lady?"

The old man refilled his pipe and lighted it before he answered.

"That sounds pretty well," he said, "and it might *work* pretty well until some gent like Turner come along with a good proposition to break your neck and make a million. Then you'd go off with him just the way you went off this time. Nope, I couldn't put no sort of reliance on you, Billy. And I'd have to be able to put reliance in you before I could think of settling down."

"What's the harm in an experiment?" asked Billy sadly.

"I'll tell you what's the harm. A travelling gent like me needs to have a pretty thick skin and a hard skin. I've got both them things by just rolling along and never stopping. But if I was to settle down it would only be a day or two before I lost all my callouses, so to speak. And then where would I be when you left me again? I'd be just as helpless as if I'd never learned nothing about how to take care of myself."

Billy English shook his head.

"I'll never leave again," he said solemnly.

"Make me believe that."

"I can. Look at the girl."

"I been looking at nothing else for the whole day, until you boys come in."

"Well, look again. She's worth it. And when I look at her I understand that she *is* a lady, and that the only way I can hope to take care of her is to be a

156

gentleman. Understand? So I'm going to make myself over."

"H-m-m," said King Charlie. "Seems to me that I've heard long-riders talk like that before."

"This time," said Billy, "you're hearing one that means it. Why, look at her, and tell me if she *ain't* a lady! And if she is, how am I ever going to give her the proper sort of a bringing up unless I make myself decent? Look at her, King!"

And King Charlie looked, and looked, and finally removed his pipe and stared with dim sad eyes at the child.

PART III

Join the Western Book Club
and GET 4 FREE* BOOKS NOW!
A $19.96 VALUE!

Yes! I want to subscribe to the Western Book Club.

Please send me my **4 FREE* BOOKS**. I have enclosed $2.00 for shipping/handling. Each month I'll receive the four newest Leisure Western selections to preview for 10 days. If I decide to keep them, I will pay the Special Members Only discounted price of just $3.36 each, a total of $13.44, plus $2.00 shipping/handling ($19.50 US in Canada). This is a **SAVINGS OF AT LEAST $6.00** off the bookstore price. There is no minimum number of books I must buy, and I may cancel the program at any time. In any case, the **4 FREE* BOOKS** are mine to keep.

*In Canada, add $5.00 shipping/handling per order for the first shipment. For all future shipments to Canada, the cost of membership is $16.25 US, which includes shipping and handling.
(All payments must be made in US dollars.)

NAME: _____	
ADDRESS: _____	
CITY: _____	**STATE:** _____
COUNTRY: _____	**ZIP:** _____
TELEPHONE: _____	
E-MAIL: _____	
SIGNATURE: _____	

If under 18, Parent or Guardian must sign. Terms, prices, and conditions subject to change. Subscription subject to acceptance. Dorchester Publishing reserves the right to reject any order or cancel any subscription.

Chapter One

Pangs of hunger beset King Charlie, and there was an odd weakness just behind each knee, the sure sign that he had fasted long. Yet he maintained his dignity as he strolled down the street, even as befitted one with his nickname of royalty. He cast no furtive and hunted glances from side to side. There was no half-cringing and half-snarling appeal in his manner. Instead, he walked on slowly, and with the easy air of a man of leisure, now and again pausing to glance in at the windows, for he was on the main street of the little town of Culver Crossing, and the chief stores lay compactly within the next two blocks.

Of course, when he faced in he was not looking at the contents of the windows. He was merely studying the reflections of faces in the heavy plate glass. He was noting a score of people at a glance, perhaps, and striving to select a victim. For if King Charlie was to eat, someone must proffer the means out of his pocket-book.

As for getting a meal by "battering doors," there was no hope. For a day and a half he had fondly nursed the delusion that somewhere in Culver Crossing he would be able to find a soft heart and a well-stocked kitchen. But not long before some "tramp royals" with smiling faces and fine "fronts" had blown through that little Western town and had robbed by night the houses from which they begged meals during the day. Accordingly, the King found hard looks from the women and threatening fists from the husbands. And there were no meals. Even the perpetual colour which flared in the midst of his weather-tinted cheeks, and which no danger, no fatigue, could greatly dim, was now beginning to wane. It was like the dying flame of a candle. It showed how close the high spirits of the tramp were to dark extinction. And though he still carried his sixty odd years with as light a step and as casual a demeanour as ever, King Charlie was rapidly growing desperate.

It was just at this moment, when he turned from the window of Culver Crossing's leading haberdashery, that he saw his first good opening. And this opening was more than good. It was a Godsend, he felt. It was a glimpse of square meals for an indefinite period.

What he saw was a wallet which had been drawn from an inside coat pocket by a wide-shouldered man just ahead of him, and which, after a glance at the contents, accompanied by the crisp rustling of the wind down the edges of many bills, was dropped into a deep outside overcoat pocket.

King Charlie reached for the surface of the plate glass window and supported himself. It was like having a fortune placed in his hand by the will of a dead relative, so secure would this be.

Instantly he froze to the man of the wallet. The fellow was well dressed, though rather flashy in his choice of clothes. He even sported a cane, which gave him a foreign and, it seemed to King Charlie, a

King Charlie

rather distinguished air. He was very tall. He was as lean as he was tall. And the gloved hand which swung at his side showed fingers of amazing length. Altogether, there was something entirely strange and yet something oddly familiar about his make-up. And King Charlie did his best to place in his mind the recollection of the man which was knocking at the door of his memory, though never quite admitted. Since the other never turned, however, the King did not succeed in his effort, and he gave up that effort at once when he saw the hand which had dropped into the overcoat pocket with the wallet come out without it.

Truly the fellow must be a foreigner. It was bad enough to swing a cane and wear gloves, and thereby focus all eyes upon him as he strode down the street of Culver Crossing. It was still worse to leave a wallet in an outside overcoat pocket on this windy, chill October day.

King Charlie slipped close, waited until the tall man was merged in a knot of pedestrians waiting for a hay waggon to pass at a street-crossing, and then, when all the eyes in the crowd were drawn up as the driver of the waggon on his lofty seat made some remark, King Charlie dipped his hand into the pocket.

Once that hand had been famous for its skill. Even now that he was an old man he could do certain things with a delicate deftness which a youth with the sensitive fingers of a musician might have envied. Down inside the flap of the coat the fingers stole. They glided down with equal caution and speed. They encountered the upstanding stem of a pipe which had been placed in the pocket. They passed this and the tips rubbed over the rough surface of the old leather wallet.

Down hooked the little finger until it was under the lowest part of the wallet, and then he began to withdraw the prize slowly, slowly, making sure that a sudden diminution of the weight in his pocket should not attract the attention of the tall, slender victim.

And at length the wallet was near the top of the pocket, then, with a movement of consummate speed and smoothness, the wallet was transferred from the pocket of the victim to his own inside breast pocket.

The whole operation had been a single deft insertion and withdrawal of the hand occupying in actual time less than a second.

Now the King drew back and stepped to the side, working through the knot of people towards the side street, while the little group, released by the passing of the waggon and its load of baled hay, surged on across the crossing.

The King turned back to the right and paused at the side window of the store he had just passed. In the first place he did not wish to draw attention to himself by hurry. In the second place he did not wish to isolate himself from the rest of the pedestrians along the main street by going down this alley. A crowd meant safety.

Moreover, in the reflection in that window he could dimly follow the movements of the tall man. The latter crossed the street with the rest, but when he reached the opposite kerb, he paused and whirled sharply, and as he whirled, even in the wavering and uncertain reflection in the window, the King recognized his man indeed.

Blockhead, treble fool that he had been! There were revealed to him the long face and the many-wrinkled features of the Dean, that famous gambler and terrible gun-fighter. The Dean! Had he not chummed with that man in the long distant past? Had he not known the Dean as fellow-trencherman at the same table? Had they not entered upon the same exploits together? Were they not mutual friends of Billy English, of strange and wonderful

King Charlie

memory? Yes, this was the man, and hardly changed by the ten years which had elapsed since the King last saw him. He was, perhaps, a little leaner and a little paler, but that was all. He carried his forty years as well as he had ever carried his thirty.

Why under the wide blue heavens had not King Charlie recognized him? If he had struck the Dean while flush, as he was now, the Dean at the least would fork over twenty dollars, and that meant comparative comfort until he had beaten his way out of the West, where only labourers flourished, and back to the East, where a died-in-the-wool one would be given a chance. But, like a fool, he had, instead, helped himself, and now the chances were even that he would draw a grim vengeance upon his head. Or should he simply go back to the Dean and tell him what had happened, and apologize for having taken the wallet of a man whom he did not recognize? No, that would be a thin excuse to so sharp a fellow as the tall gambler.

But while the King paused, full of an agony of doubts, the Dean began striding back across the street, searching every face with eyes as glittering and keen as the eyes of a snake. His right hand was dropped inside the breast of his coat. And well the King knew that the long, bony fingers of his former companion were wrapped around the handle of a revolver, and if that revolver were drawn it would probably lodge a bullet in flesh—his own poor flesh.

Should he await the nearer approach of the tall man? In spite of the fact that he knew it would be much the wisest thing to simply stand there and stare through the window at the display he could not help flinching. With his best air of nonchalance he thrust his hands into his trouser pockets, and, turning down the alley, he began to saunter away.

Instantly he saw that he had done wrong. To thrust hands into his pockets was far too youthful a means of showing an idle disposition for a man of his years.

Moreover, who would wish to saunter down the alley? He should rather have stepped out at a brisk pace.

A footfall crunched on the gravel of the walk behind him, and panic struck through the soul of the King. He started forward at a quickened pace. Then, in spite of his endeavour, he could not help throwing a glance over his shoulder, and that glance showed him that the Dean had not stirred in pursuit.

No, he was standing irresolute on the corner. It was a young boy who had come a few paces down to look in the window. But the moment the Dean caught sight of that furtive glance he was hot on the trail. With a brief, deep shout he snatched the revolver from its hiding-place in his coat.

"Stop, thief!" he thundered.

King Charlie lunged forward as though about to take to his heels. But his second step was a spring to the side which flattened him against the wall of the house. At the same instant the revolver exploded, and the bullet literally brushed past his face. His manoeuvre had saved him by a hair's breadth from the first aimed shot, which, as is known, is apt to be the most accurate shot fired from a revolver; just as the first broadside of a ship, in the old sailing days, would quite probably do more damage than all the other shots which it fired during the entire course of an engagement. The instant that shot whirred past him the King was off again, racing like a youngster of twenty years.

He kept dodging as he ran, and that veering course was enough to save him from the four shots which the tall man pumped down the alley, the noise of one crowding the echoes of the preceding. Then, with a yell, the Dean raced in pursuit, and behind him a dozen quickly gathered recruits hurried.

That race could not last long, the King well knew. He was old. Terror had, to be sure, poured a false strength into his limbs, but that strength was already

King Charlie

ebbing, and leaving him his original age-numbed muscles. Inside of three minutes at the most the powerful hand of the Dean would fasten upon him, unless the latter chose to shoot him down at short range as he came up.

All of this was in the quick-working brain of King Charlie as he swerved out on to the narrow street beyond. And there good fortune once more stood him in stead, for at that moment he saw a buggy driven up the street with a boy in the seat.

King Charlie, with a moan of joy, flew for the rig, and, as the boy drew up the reins with a startled exclamation, King Charlie flung himself into the seat and tore the strips of leather from the hands of the driver. The latter showed fight, but he was deterred by the sight of the blue-nosed revolver which the King shoved into his ribs.

"Get out that whip," said the King, "and start flogging that hoss. We got to be travelling, son, and we need a fast start."

Now the pursuit, headed by the flying form of the Dean, plunged out of the alley and started up a babel in the street. A yell of rage and despair came from the lips of the tall gambler as he saw the position of the thief. Then the whip descended with a loud crash along the back of the horse, which spurted ahead at a full gallop.

It was not a very fast horse, nor a very young one, but that first detour to the side of the main street gave the King a priceless handicap, for it led the pursuers away from their horses. They had to stop and turn back for the means of carrying on the pursuit, and in the meantime the King had made hay while the perilous sun shone.

The buggy bumped out at the lower end of the town, and the King found himself driving among the hills.

Far behind a gathering roar of horses' hoofs and shouting men's voices told that the impromptu posse had formed and was spurring to get on his traces.

"Where's the main line railroad, kid?" he asked the trembling boy.

"Two mile ahead."

"Good! Now you jump."

"While the rig's going like this? Why, it'll kill me, mister."

"Get up!" He prodded the boy up with the muzzle of his gun. He dared not slow down for the sake of the boy, but at the same time he must not let the youngster follow him and his plans. And the absence of his weight from the buggy might make a vital difference before the race was over. "Jump!"

The boy threw up his arms with a wail of dismay and leaped into the air. He landed, luckily, in thick, deep dust, which had the effect of muffling his shout at once. But at the end of his roll he came to his feet unhurt, a white form, and shouted hatred and defiance after the King.

Chapter Two

The latter had put the whip to the horse, and was rollicking up the road at a terrific gait, the buggy flying up at every bump they crossed. Looking back, as he neared the top of the rise, he saw the horsemen issuing from the town in a dense group which rapidly lengthened out as the fleetest horses took the lead and began to draw away from the rest.

And, conspicuous among the rest, he saw the Dean. By the length of that gaunt body he could tell him. From some cowpuncher in the town the gambler had borrowed a speedy mount. He had thrown away his overcoat. His hat had been blown from his head. He rode with his revolver naked and flashing in his hand, and he yelled like a madman at the very head of the procession.

Plainly he meant business. And the King knew perfectly well what the Dean, in a serious mood, was capable of. No Indian could be more cruel. No giant could show greater strength.

Again he turned to the whipping of the horse. The ground from this high point sloped rapidly down, and so they gained impetus at every leap. And ahead of him he saw a streak of dim light, the tracks of the railroad, a scant mile away now. Not only the tracks of the railroad, but the murmur of a train was rumbling nearer and nearer among the hills. Oh, to be on that train and hurtling away.

But the pace of his horse was growing perceptibly slower now, and the poor nag was showing a lameness in the right forefoot. The King, with a yell of despair, stood up to apply the whip with the greater effect, and as he did so the tall form of the Dean loomed above the hill-top behind him and exploded his revolver and sent a rambling bullet whistling after the fugitive merely by way of showing him that the chase would be a hot one.

And hot and short it certainly promised to be. Desperately the King turned over chances in his mind. But even if he were to throw away that well-stuffed wallet, it made no difference. He would be arrested for carrying a concealed weapon, for stealing a horse, which was worse than murder, wellnigh, in this part of the country, and for various and sundry other offences.

The horsemen were naturally gaining—gaining fast. All he could do was to keep on at the best speed he could make, and trust to luck that something would happen.

But what could happen? They would have run down the horse and buggy within a few minutes. And they were too close for him to attempt to leave the buggy and hide himself in some gulley among the hills.

Then, startlingly near, he saw a misty cloud of smoke rising and sweeping closer and closer. It was the smoke and vapour from an engine labouring up the grade through the hills. And as he rounded another hill-shoulder the King saw the train itself, the engine sweeping grandly about a curve as it thundered into view. King Charlie's heart went out to it. There was his kingdom, there was his country—the land of the metal rails that twine together in the dwindling distance, the land of freight and passenger expresses, of the rods, the blind baggages, and the empty boxcars. Oh, to be on it! The stately freight was empty. Even at this distance he could tell that by the sound of rattling which the cars made as they poured up the track. If he were on that train he would wish for only one thing—that the train were going East instead of West.

But could he not reach the train? At least, it was his only hope, to reach that train and so be drawn away from the pursuit, for, if he knew trainmen well, no engineer would stop his train on such a slope and break up his running schedule for the sake of a mere thief.

He stood up in the buggy again and called aloud upon the poor horse which laboured between the shafts, pounding its forefeet to ruin as it galloped down the slope, and the wretched animal seemed to know the need and responded to it with a greater burst of speed. Instinctively the King knew that the whip could not draw from the horse more than it was already giving, so he dropped it, and looked back to see what progress the Dean and the others were making.

They were coming up fast enough, but they could have come faster. He could see the face of the Dean quite clearly now, and it was no longer the face of a man in a frenzy. No doubt he had seen that the chase could have only one ending, and he was in no hurry to bring about that conclusion. He would rather draw out the misery of the fugitive somewhat. So he had put away his revolver, and he was drawing up his horse and letting the rest of the posse catch up with him.

King Charlie, with a groan, turned to look towards

the train. It was running slowly, comparatively speaking, but no horse could keep up for any distance with even the speed which it maintained upon the grade. And it seemed to the King that he had at least the ghost of a chance. At least, he could thank heaven that the Dean did not see and understand his purpose. Otherwise, the tall gambler would have spurred in upon him and the chase would even now be over.

But the latter still held back. It was only when the train was passing across the road not a furlong away that the Dean saw and understood. And as he saw he yelled to his mount and leaned forward to bring it again to its full speed.

The distance was too short, however, to make up much vital ground. The old horse whipped the buggy forward at a flying pace, and now the King turned aside from the road and, close to the speeding train, he was whipping up the track beside the box-cars.

They drifted rapidly past him. The engine was gaining speed with every instant as, reaching a level stretch, the drain of the up grade diminished. Then the King saw the thing for which he had been praying—a smooth stretch where he could swing the buggy in close, close to the edge of the ties.

He yelled to the horse, and gave a final cut to rouse that poor animal to yet more frantic efforts. Then he climbed back over the seat and stood up on the edge of the side board. The side of the box-car was like a lofty wall hurtling past him.

A wild yell and the explosion of firearms caused him to glance to the side, and there he saw the Dean flogging his horse with a quirt in his left hand while he blazed away with the revolver in his right.

Then King Charlie picked out the first iron ladder that whirled past him and leaped for it. Fair and true his feet and his hands struck the rails. A moment later he lay flat on the top of the car, gasping and panting for breath, while the bullets purred over his head. But he could look back and see the Dean spurring his horse down the track.

Just too late the tall fellow had solved the plan of the King, and had taken to the pursuit, and he had swung off the road and on to the road-bed of the train just as the last car of the train drew past.

For a minute he raced his horse after the train and gained a trifle on it, but at the end of a hundred yards the pace told and the mustang began to fall back, while the train gathered more and more speed. It was then that King Charlie rose to his feet. He took off the hat which had not been displaced in spite of all of his gymnastic endeavours of the past few minutes, and he waved that hat at the Dean and gave him a rousing shout of mockery and farewell.

At the same minute a hand fell on his shoulder. He turned quickly, and he found himself looking into the face of a hardy young brakeman, athletic of build, solid of shoulder, red of hair. On the whole he was exactly the sort of "shack" that even the hardiest of tramps would not care to have trouble with. But now the youngster grinned and nodded at him.

"By God," he said, "you sure swing a neat pair of heels for an old boy your age. How the hell old *are* you, bo?"

"Old enough to know better than to lead the sort of a life that I lead," said the King with a mock sadness.

The youthful shack laughed with great good nature.

"What were they after you for?" he asked.

"Just for nothing, if you ask me," said the King with a shrug of the shoulder. "All I did was to look into a gent's coat and lift out a bit of spare paper that was littering up his pocket. And here it is."

He had folded his arms and one hand had dipped inside his breast coat pocket and extracted a bill, which he then dropped into his side pocket, and this was what he now exposed under the eyes of the shack. The latter exploded a single great curse.

"Did they raise all that hullabaloo on account of *that?*"

It was a one dollar bill which fluttered in the stream of air.

"Son, you don't know Culver Crossing," said the King sadly. "They started after me not on account of that one dollar, but because of the principle of the thing. That's the kind of a town it is. I been battering doors for two days trying to get a handout, and nary a bit of food have I had."

The brakeman swore again in sympathy.

"Well," he said, "you keep that dollar. I've got the change for it, but I guess you're old enough to need all of the loot that you can get."

Chapter Three

Afterwards the King smiled sourly as the brakeman passed on. It was plain that he was over young and, for a shack, endowed with too trusting a nature. Any other brakeman would have insisted upon searching the refugee and then splitting the loot fifty-fifty with him, unless he chose to take the lion's share for himself.

Left to himself, he took the first opportunity of going over his prize, and when he had counted it hastily, he gasped with pleasure and surprise. For the one dollar bill was one of only a thin sheaf of that small denomination and the rest of the tightly wadded money consisted of fives and tens. He counted no less than fifty tens and forty-eight fives—seven hundred and forty dollars at a single stroke—and seven hundred and forty dollars taken from no less a person than the terrible Dean himself.

The King rubbed his hands together. He felt that the warmth of youth had returned and made a spring-time in his blood. To be sure, it was quite probable that he had not been taking himself seriously enough of late and that he might have wasted his time. He might return to the ways of his golden period of prosperity and—

As that thought entered his mind, however, a strong shudder passed suddenly through his body. And his face altered at the same moment, the jaw dropping, his cheeks falling, and the perennial colour fading until his cheeks were a dusty grey. He clasped his right wrist with his left hand as strongly as he could, but in spite of that the tremor continued, shaking his hands violently. He cast himself back at length and lay flat along the top of the box-car gasping and mumbling to himself, and praying that he might not start rolling towards one side while this shuddering helplessness was upon him.

Then it passed as it had come—in a breath. And he sat up slowly, weak of body, weak of soul. It was a long time since the prison tremble had seized upon him, because it was a long time since he had grossly violated the law. But now he felt as though that one long moment of agony had been sufficient payment for the entire seven hundred dollars.

His spirits revived again later on. And when, in the early dusk, he dropped off the train at the division end he was strong-hearted once more. For he had in his possession now the sinews of war which would enable him to go East. He could, if he wished, actually ride the cushions. But he quivered with disdain at the thought of a railroad fare passing from his hands into the hands of a railroad company. No, he would ride the rods back, since he was no longer nimble enough to ride the blind baggage. Or, better still, he would take his leisurely time and ride the slow freights, pausing at such towns as he came to to rest and enjoy himself, and going on again when he was in the mood. For until this seven hundred was spent, he would not feel the great urge to start off for unknown quarters of the world again.

Full of this resolution, he stepped into a cheap restaurant near the station, while the whistle of a fast West-bound passenger train screamed in the distance. He ordered a huge meal. Like all of his kind, King Charlie was a huge eater when occasion served. He could lay aboard, like the camel, enough solid food to last him for days. Yes, so long as there were edibles in sight it was strange indeed if the King could not find a nook or a cranny to stow away the remnants. Now he had a long fast to make up for. His accurate nose was distinguishing, one by one, the odours which floated from the kitchen of the restaurant, and he was ordering rather by sense of smell than by the menu.

He began, of course, with ham and eggs. The large platterful disappeared under his dexterous knife and fork work as though by magic. It faded as a morning mist fades when the sun appears. After that he drained a great bowl of oyster stew and downed a capacious mug of coffee and hot milk. When this point had been reached he sat back in his chair and settled down to the serious study of the menu in the mood to do his real ordering of the occasion.

He had just ordered a steak with half a dozen eggs on top when he heard a low and strangely familiar voice saying: "Never mind that. I'll sit down over here with my friend."

And then a long, lean hand was laid upon the back of the chair opposite him.

King Charlie's eyes rose slowly along the bony outlines of those fingers and up the prodigious length of arm, which seemed an affair of bones only, under the loosely flapping sleeve of the coat, and thence up to the skinny neck, and then the lean, sombre face of the Dean.

King Charlie grew sick at heart and white of face. And then he smiled in answer to the terrible smile of the Dean.

"Ain't you going to ask me to sit down, partner?" the Dean was saying.

"Why, sure," said the King. "Sit down, pal. Sit down and give your order."

"Thanks," said the Dean.

He eased himself into the chair, considered the menu with a detached air, as of one to whom eating is a habit rather than a necessity, and then, having given his order, folded his big hands on the edge of the table and regarded the King.

"A long time since I seen you all right," he said mildly.

King Charlie studied him with a frantic interest. When the Dean was explosive he was bad enough. But when he was polite he was absolutely deadly. He drew out the wallet and pushed it across the table.

"There's everything in it except one dollar," he said. "I met a shack that wouldn't take a dollar and it surprised me so much that I swore on the spot that I'd give that dollar to the first person I seen when I got off the train. And the first person I seen was a dirty-faced kid. He's still hugging himself and looking at that money, I reckon."

This astonishing piece of news was too much for even the grim-minded Dean. He pocketed the wallet without so much as a peep at the contents.

"A shack that wouldn't take a dollar?" he gasped.

"I know," said Charlie. "It don't sound reasonable. But it's a fact, son. You see, he figured that I was so old that I needed the money morn'n he did. And the truth is, Dean, I ain't as young as I once was."

So saying, he passed his hand over his grey head and looked appealingly at the other. But the face of the Dean was entirely disinterested.

"A gent as old as you," he said, "sure ought to figure things out before he does something that gets him into trouble, eh?"

A cold silence ensued.

At length King Charlie could stand it no longer.

King Charlie

"You got—the passenger, eh?"

"I nabbed it the same place." A shade of wonder passed over the face of the Dean. "What's the matter with you, King? Did you think that you could get away with the stuff as easy as this? Didn't you credit me for enough brains to trail you this far? Did you think I was plumb batty?"

King Charlie shook his grey locks.

"Nope. I'm just getting old. I forget. Old and forgetful and pretty near the end of the trail."

"Right," snapped the Dean, and his voice was as cold as winter wind. "Pretty near the end of the trail by my way of figuring!"

"Do you mean that?"

"You damned skunk!" said the Dean. "Why you and me had been partners, and now you turn me down cold! You try to trim me and pass me up like a sucker."

"Dean, I didn't know you. I swear to God—"

"Bah!"

That exclamation sealed the talk for the time being. King Charlie looked down. Sadly he raised the knife and fork as the vast platter with its load of steak and eggs was placed before him.

"Dean," he ventured timidly, "might you be interested in a little of this steak and egg? I've sort of lost interest in it."

The Dean smiled joylessly.

"You'd better eat it," he said. "I'm thinking. I'm thinking about something that might save your rotten old hide after all. Understand? Does that give you back your appetite?"

At this King Charlie fastened upon his companion a wistful and faintly hopeful gaze, like one who knows that there is inevitable ruin ahead and who yet hopes, in spite of sure knowledge, that something may be done. The sardonic, pursed face of the Dean revealed nothing. He might have been thinking of Christmas—or murder. And his long fingers were

179

clasped together on the edge of the table, and they were coiling and uncoiling ceaselessly, so that King Charlie was reminded of a spider writhing over the body of a victim.

But suddenly the keen eyes of the Dean lifted and looked through and through him.

"Charlie!" he said.

The King choked on the morsel which he was attempting to swallow at that moment. Then he answered: "Well, Dean?"

"For what you've done or tried to do I sure ought to get you bad, King."

He was relenting. Such an opening sentence could mean nothing else. So the King instantly assented.

"It was sure a bad trick, Dean. I was starving—that was—"

"I know. Now, King, suppose I show you a way to pay me back. Suppose I show you how you can fix this up and make everything square, and all it will cost you is a little talk. Are you willing to talk to make this up?"

The King drew a great breath. It was like receiving a pardon on the verge of execution. "I'll talk for you," he panted.

"But if you don't talk well enough," said the savage Dean, "we come right back to the starting-point. Is that square?"

"Yes," said the King with a little less enthusiasm.

"The whole game is this: I was trimmed last month. I was trimmed bad!"

"You don't look it," said the King. "Not with the front you're sporting now, son. And not with that seven hundred kicking around loose in your pocket."

The Dean shook his head. "Seven hundred?" he said with unspeakable sadness. "Seven hundred? What's that? Nothing! I'm going to tell you a story about how I had a thousand times that much in my pocket. A thousand times, King Charlie."

Chapter Four

"Seven hundred thousand dollars?" gasped the King. "You mean to say—"

"More than that," insisted the Dean with a doleful calm. "Fifty thousand more than that. Yes, sir, I had three-quarters of a million in my hands and I was done out of it by damned crooked work!"

At the first part of this speech, marvel, and then a chilly fear for the sanity of his former friend, passed through the mind of the King. It had been close to insanity for such a man as the Dean to put a wallet in an outside overcoat pocket, for instance. But the last part of the remark changed the trend of Charlie's thoughts. Crooked work? He hardly restrained a laugh when he thought of the consummate knavery at cards by which the Dean had worked his way through the world.

"It was down in San Tone," said the melancholy Dean. "It was down in old San Tone that I met up with my good luck. God a'mighty, it seems close on to ten years ago, but, matter of fact, it wasn't much more 'n ten days. But down yonder I met up with my good luck. You know, Charlie, that I always used to say that I never had no fair chances and that the reason I didn't make no progress was just because I didn't meet up with the right sort of gents?"

"I recollect many times when you've said that," said the King soothingly. "I sure enough remember you saying that often. All you needed was to sit down to a table where there was a million dollars, and if they was willing to play high you'd walk away with the most part of the coin."

"I said it and I meant it," said the Dean proudly. "I been held down all my life by having to play with pikers, King. But all my life I was waiting for a change in the luck. Well, that change come, and one day down in San Tone I found myself sitting with four gents that could of bet at least half a million each and paid in cash the same day.

"Everyone of them was playing crooked, and everyone of them was as good as a professional at the cards. But I beat 'em, son. I sure trimmed 'em neat. They played me for a fall guy, but all the time I was double-crossing them, and when they thought they was leading me on, I was only plucking them proper. Big mistake that I made was that I didn't get all that I could that first day. But I thought that that was a come-on game, and that if I got 'em worked up good the first night, they'd come back the second day and I could sink the hook good and deep. So all I got away with that first evening was fifty thousand—"

"Fifty thousand!" cried the King.

"Shut up, you old fool!" snarled the Dean, treading heavily on the toes of his table mate. "Don't you know that some of the boys in this place have ears and know how to use 'em?"

King Charlie murmured an apology, and the Dean went on.

King Charlie

"Fifty thousand was what I picked up that first day. But it looked like nothing to me. It was twenty times as much as I'd ever cleaned up before, but I was looking for enough to retire on and get respectable. I was a fool, too. Because the next day those boys put their heads together and decided that I was too much for them. They all sent me notes regretting that they had business that kept them away so that they couldn't see me in the game again. But one note was a pile different. It came from the gent that had lost the bulk of the fifty thousand to me. He'd won from the others, but he'd lost pretty heavy to me. He was along about middle age, grey haired, hard as tacks, smooth as they make 'em. He sends me a fine little letter. He says in it that he's sorry that the game had to be broken up, and that he wishes that just he and I could get together and resume the game and play for some real stakes. It has been some time, says he in the note, since he'd sat down to a game with a gentleman who did not care how high the stakes ran, and therefore he really wished that he and I could sit down to a table at his home and play stud, because it was a better game than five-handed poker.

"Well, when I heard that I plumped down into a chair near the window and fanned myself for a while. When I come to and my brain began to function again, I sent him a little note telling him I'd be plumb tickled to play a game with him at his house or any other house. Then I slipped downstairs in a sort of a haze and asks the clerk about Judge Howick.

" 'Well, he's worth three or four millions any way you look at it,' says the clerk.

"I staggered away and sat down again. I seen plain that my big time had come, and that I was due for my killing, and then retire and maybe found a college or build a church or something like that, and get my picture pasted into the magazines showing me beating a golf ball to death on Saturday, or teaching Sunday-school on Sunday, or signing cheques in my palatial offices on weekdays—I say, I was seeing myself like that, sort of in moving pictures with me for the hero every time, when in comes the Judge himself. He gives me a wide smile and a strong hand, and ten minutes later we're on the way out to his ranch, with the dust chugging up from the hoofs of his span of high-steppers and my luggage slung into the rear of the rig.

"The Judge was so damn agreeable he pretty near melted in the mouth all the way out. He didn't talk at all about the game of the night before or the games to come. He was just telling me about his ranch and about how dead interested he was in raising fine cattle, and how his heart was all wrapped up in his little niece and nephew—but maybe you see how the thing works out? I hear him in a sort of a happy dream, just thanking God every time we go over a bump that I'd brought along every cent of that fifty thousand so that I'd have the stake and the backing I needed. And then we land at his place. Not all at once, you see, but gradual.

"We slide through about fifty thousand acres of hills and valleys, and farm lands in the bottoms and grazing lands on the hills, and finally we come in sight of his house.

"It stands on the top of a flat-headed hill, with a flock of palm-trees, and such-like, standing around it, and the house itself just showing through here and there—one of them pink-plaster Spanish affairs, you know, with blue window trimmings. It looked nice and quiet. It didn't make no more noise than a million dollars.

"That was until you got into the inside court, the patio. That was done up for a winner. Yes, sir, you never seen the beat of that, Charlie. It had real honest-to-God columns all around the sides—marble columns with fool carving strung all over 'em. And there were arches in between the columns. Why, Charlie, a church couldn't of been built more plumb expensive than that house is. Everywhere I turned my head I seen a dollar sign.

"The Judge eased me out of the rig, and a couple of nigger boys comes running. A couple? No, there was a whole flock of 'em. One of 'em got my duster. One grabs my hat. Another couple hooks on to my suitcase. Well, that was the way I managed to stagger to my little room, which was only about as big as this whole restaurant, throwing in the kitchen for luck. It had a bath off to one side and a little private sort of a garden over to the other side, with glass doors opening out on to it, and more colours in the flowers than you could name in ten minutes.

"But I'll cut out the trimmings and give you the facts about what happened in that there house— Casa Loma they call it. We got through a fair lot of drinks that day, and came down to the evening all ripe for a buster of a game, and a buster of a game it sure enough was.

"Stud is my particular pet. Maybe you know that. It hurts my feelings to take money away from the best of 'em, when it comes to stud. And that night I had the pasteboards talking to me like I was their daddy. There wasn't nothing that I couldn't do to them cards. And I tied the Judge into knots. He kept a-shaking his head and sighing and smiling. And then he'd order in another drink.

"Every time he ordered a drink a couple of them big coons showed up, and they sure looked like a bad time, them darkies did. I never seen so much muscle roaming around loose on a couple of gents as the two coons that handled that liquor hand. Each of 'em was as big as Joe Hoyt at his palmiest."

Here King Charlie shook his head. "I reckon that's stretching it," he said.

"It ain't, I tell you," insisted the Dean. "I tell you, the Judge must of hand-picked the most of Africa to get two as big as them and as well matched. They had to go sideways through the door, and when they took up a glass it looked like they couldn't help smashing it. And when one of them darkies leaned over I seen the outline of a big gat on his back pocket printed as clear as black and white.

"It was easy to see that they was the Judge's pet bulldogs as well as his drink-mixers. But I didn't pay no attention to them. Why? Because I was blind. I jumped mighty quick whenever the Judge give 'em a look, but that didn't register in my head as meaning anything in particular. I went right on playing and winning.

"Winning? You never seen so much money stacked on any one table. The Judge began to sign I O U's, and pretty soon I had 'em stacked up like one dollar bills, and nearly every I O U was for a thousand or more.

"About midnight the Judge allowed that it was enough for a start, and he give a sign to one of the bulldogs, and the big fellow slips an arm under the Judge's shoulders and lifts him out of his chair and takes him off to put him to bed. He was that far gone with the booze.

"I took up the winnings and mosied off to my own room, with three or four coons to open doors for me and bow me through. When I got inside my place I made a quick dive for the lamp and shoved the pocketful of I O U's on to the table.

"Seven hundred thousand dollars was what I made out there, all wrote out in the Judge's own handwriting, and all as good as gold for jury evidence if I had to go to law to collect. Well, my knees pretty near buckled under me, while I stood there looking at myself as a future regent of a University or bank president, or something foolish like that.

"When I went to bed I lay awake for a while having day-dreams, and then I went to sleep and was president of a railroad all night, and spent my time kicking hoboes off of the rods. But when I woke up in the morning the first thing I done was to reach my hand under my pillow. Sure enough, I found my wallet there. I pulled it out and decided that I'd cast an eye over my winnings and read that signature of the Judge's a few dozen times by way of starting the day off right. But when I opened the wallet there wasn't a damned thing in it. Only thing that I seen was a calling card. My fifty thousand was gone and all the I O U's were gone too.

"I hit the ceiling with a yell. Five minutes later I busted in on the Judge.

" 'I been robbed!' I shouts.

" 'Impossible,' said the Judge, as cool as ice.

" 'Every I O U is gone,' says I.

" 'What I O U's are you referring to?' says he.

" 'Them that you signed last night,' says I.

" 'My dear fellow,' says he, 'I don't recall signing any I O U's. The liquor must have had even more effect upon you than I feared. Don't you recall having lost your cash during the game?'

"I reached for my gun, but just then I felt a sort of a shadow fall over me. I turned around. One of the big black fellows was standing right behind me with his hand dropped into his coat pocket. Sure enough he had a gun turned on me ready to blow me to bits. In spite of himself, he couldn't hold back a grin that split his face right in half.

"I turned around to the Judge, and he said:

" 'Now, my friend, I hope your reason and memory have been restored.'

"I seen that it was no use. If I tried to make a kick he could have me locked up. His niggers would swear any sort of evidence against me. Besides, my record wouldn't look none too good if they started prying into my past.

" 'Judge,' says I, 'I see that it needs a training on the bench to keep a man's head clear while he's drinking.'

" 'Ah,' says he, smiling as cool as you please, 'my title is purely honorary, thank you!'

"And that morning one of the niggers drove me back to town. And that's the reason, King, that seven hundred don't mean nothing in my life. You understand? Nothing means nothing to me until I get a chance to come back at him. And that's why I've told you this story—because you got the means to help me out."

Chapter Five

Once again King Charlie looked sombrely upon his company as though suspicious of the sanity of the Dean. Then he said:

"Look here, pal, I know you got me backed into a corner and you got a right to ask anything I can do. But all that you and me and ten like us could do wouldn't budge the Judge. Howick seems to be one of them gents that can pull a crooked deal now and then, but who have the country behind 'em and—"

"Behind him? I should say not. The record of Howick is just short of good enough to land him in prison. He's worked up from nothing, and he worked up by grub-staking prospectors and then beating them out of their half of the claims when they landed something worth while. He's the best hated man in Texas, and you can lay to that! If he was to go down, the police would sure weep if they had to arrest them that stung him. Old Howick knows it, and that's why

he's got his place full of those man-killing niggers.
They'd as soon wring a gent's neck as look at him,
and that's why the Judge has them out there. He
knows that he has to fight his own battles, and he
keeps a standing army of his own to do it. But when
I got to thinking things over I seen that I knew only
two men that could help me. One was Joe Hoyt; because Joe is the only man I know strong enough to
handle one of those big black fellows. And the other,
King, is a man that nobody but you can get to go
with me, and he's the only man that I know of in the
whole world that's smart enough and dangerous
enough to tackle Judge Howick. That's Billy English."

King Charlie pushed his plate back and shook his
head.

"If you want to get even because I lifted that wallet," he said, "take me out and fill me full of lead, but
don't ask me to try to lead Billy English crooked. Besides, I couldn't do it."

"You couldn't? Ain't you his father?"

King Charlie sighed and dropped his head. How
often would that tremendous lie he had told rise
again to haunt him? With that lie he had forced an
honest youngster to go wrong. In spite of that lie,
Billy English had torn himself away from the life of
the long-riders and had chosen honest work.

"Dean," he said, "you don't understand. It's ten
years since Billy has seen me. I've seen him, but it
was only by sneaking up close and peeking in, you
might say, every couple of years. The rest of the time
I've spent back around York, where I'm to home. But
every couple of years I've sneaked out and taken a
look at Billy and the girl—"

"The girl?" echoed the Dean. "I didn't know that
he was interested in any skirt—"

"You forget. I mean the little five-year-old kid that
him and Joe Hoyt and me and you, Dean, swore that

we'd try to help after her mother died in that damned
lodging-house—"

"Louise Alison Dora Young—I remember," cried
the Dean suddenly. "Lady!"

"Lady," nodded the King gravely. "That's what we
called her. But what one of us has kept his word by
her? Only Billy. He cut out the crooked work. He
went straight for the sake of that kid. He was only
sixteen when he started slaving to make a home for
that little youngster. He's twenty-six now. He started
in with nothing. And I've seen him four times, and
every time he'd done something more. Right now he
has a nice little herd of cows started. All of the folks
in that part of the country swear by him. Lady has
growed into a fine-looking kid. I seen her two years
back. Kind of long in the legs and wobbly in the
knees, but a disposition like a day in May and a smile
like a bird singing. She—"

"Look here, Charlie," said the Dean grimly, "are
you writing a book about Lady, or are you telling me
whether or not you'll get Billy English to help me
out? I know that he's gone straight. That's just because he's a fool. Why, when he started he was only
a kid—only fifteen—but inside of a year he had the
makings of the best yegg I ever seen. He could read
the mind of the tumblers and he could make his guns
talk Latin for him. He went straight. Now I'm going
to do him a good turn and show how, by making one
more crooked turn and taking one more long ride,
he can make enough to set up a real home. Understand? Howick is so hated and he hates everybody
else so much that he won't do business with banks.
He keeps his cash in his own safe, and he has his
own safe guarded. All with his own men. Charlie,
listen!"

He laid a hand of iron upon the wrist of the older
man, and he leaned across the table.

"There's at least a cool quarter of a million in that
safe of his. Understand? A share to you and another

to Hoyt. Two shares apiece for Billy English and me. Is that square? Forty thousand for you, King?"

King Charlie leaned back in his chair, his mind distraught with anguish. In him there was an honest desire to play fair, to keep from tempting the youth who believed that he was the son of the tramp, King Charlie. But it was only a few moments before that he had had in his hands the seven hundred, and the thought of fifty times that sum dazzled him. And, like all of the criminal class, a crime proposed was to him a crime accomplished—the mention of the quarter of a million established exactly that sum as the prize, and established it so clearly that he could almost see the denominations of the bills in the drawers of the safe. So he wavered, fighting the battle back and forth until he heard the insidious whisper of the other:

"Remember, Charlie, if you can't do this for me, there's another out, and that's for you and me to meet outside and—"

King Charlie nodded.

"You've got me, Dean," he said. "I'll do what I can. But how do we get to Billy's place?"

"We start in the morning. Meet me here."

And without another word the Dean rose and left the place. After he was gone, leaving his untouched food behind him, but tossing to the King a bill which would pay for the meal and buy a bed for the night, the old tramp drank another cup of coffee and pondered. His first thought, of course, was to flee, but he knew well enough that, without money, his course along the rails would be much slower than that of the Dean. He could not hope to distance the younger and more active man, and the end of the chase was sure to be a scene of bloodshed when the Dean took vengeance for this second act of treachery.

He was being played on a long rope, but he could only use it to hang himself. So he paid the bill, left the restaurant, and found a bed. In the morning he rose early and went straight back to the restaurant, where, as he half suspected, he found the lean form of the Dean waiting for him. The latter allowed him only time to make the briefest of breakfasts, and then, when a train whistled, bound West, tore him from his chair and started him towards the track. It was a lumbering freight, heavily loaded. They took the rods side by side, and during the day the Dean impressed upon the King again and again the undying hatred which he felt for Judge Howick. It was not only that he had been basely tricked, he told his travelling mate, but it was because Howick had violated the code of honour among thieves. A crook himself, he yet sheltered himself behind the standard and the position of an honest man with the strength of Society at his call.

They stayed with that train until late afternoon, when they dropped off and took a branch line, riding the cushions into a cattle country. At the end of the line they climbed down and found themselves in a typical little cow town.

"Here's where we ought to find Joe Hoyt," said the Dean. "I've kept track of him the past ten years. He's spent seven of 'em breaking rock—so he ought to be in good trim. He's only out for the last six months, matter of fact."

"Then he'll be sore-headed and mean as a grizzly," said the King.

Very much like a grizzly was his appearance, at least, when they came upon him. They found him readily upon inquiry. His name was changed, of course, but his description was unmistakable, and they found him seated upon the veranda of the hotel gazing towards the western hills, where a long line of cattle ambled against the red of the sunset sky. He was a vast-shouldered man, without much claim to a neck, but with a huge head growing directly out of his chest. His arms were of great length, and when he stood up they arched out pronouncedly from his sides, because of the swelling muscles. His hair was a grey mane, as coarse as the mane of a horse, and quite long, so that when he removed his sombrero it was apt to fall in a ragged shower low on his forehead.

Upon the King and the Dean he turned a lacklustre eye of one who did not at all recollect them, and the Dean smiled upon his companion.

"He's still got some wits left under that thick skull of his," he said. "I'll open up the talk."

He stepped close to Joe Hoyt.

"Well, stranger," he said courteously, "appears like you was thinking pretty hard just now. Are we intruding if we ask you a few questions?"

"Talk," said Joe Hoyt, "is tolerable cheap. Talk don't bother me none. So blaze away and tell me what's what. Are you new to these parts?"

"Plumb new. What do they raise around here?"

"Hell," said Joe Hoyt without lifting voice. "Mostly they raise hell."

"Maybe you're a farmer yourself in that class," suggested the King.

"I raise greenbacks," said Joe Hoyt with perfect seriousness. "That's the crop that I hope to harvest, bo."

"Have you got it sowed?"

"I run out of seed," said Joe Hoyt.

Then he glanced over his shoulder and made out that they were in no immediate danger of interruption.

"What's the game?" he asked. "And how in hell are you?"

"Flush," said the Dean, "and a fine plant all worked up—one that we need you in on."

The big man sighed.

"I been sitting here waiting and waiting and waiting," he said, "and waiting for something to happen. And now luck has turned my way. Dean, when do we eat?"

King Charlie

"You see," said the Dean, chuckling, "he ain't lost his old tricks. He's still strong on the eats. Have you got your grip yet, Joe?"

Joe Hoyt leaned over close to the chair in which the Dean had seated himself. He slipped his hand under the seat of the chair and without rising, without showing the slightest strain, he lifted the chair and the Dean in it and brought him nearer.

"Sit nearer," said Joe Hoyt, "my hearing ain't up to what it used to be."

The Dean nodded.

"Ten years," he said, "ain't changed your muscles any, partner. Now listen to me."

Chapter Six

It was twenty-four hours later. Crouched outside the window, Joe Hoyt and the King and the tall Dean looked through upon the interior of the house. What they saw was the simplest sort of a rancher's cabin. There was only one room below. The stove for cooking and for heating the place was in one corner. The homemade table was in the centre, with the axe-marks visible on the legs which supported it. The chairs were of almost equally crude manufacture. The floor was of the rudest planks, with the skin of a puma here and the skin of a bear there to soften the boards, skins so badly mutilated that they would have brought no price as pelts in the market. A saddle hung by the stirrup in a corner. A bridle was draped on the horn. Revolver and gun belt were hooked across the top of a rifle which leaned against the wall. A ladder showed, to one side, the way to the trap above which opened the entrance to the sleeping quarters in the attic.

King Charlie

But the centre of interest on which the three observers focussed their attention was that circle of lamplight around the table where sat Billy English, tilted back in his chair and smoking a cigarette with the enjoyment which only comes at the end of a long day's work. He looked all of his twenty-six years, and more than all of them. He had taken the burden of a man's responsibilities at a period when most men are still without a serious thought. And with ten years of constant and heavy labour behind him, his lean young face was seamed and saddened by worry. Yet his blue eye was bright and intense and restless in its rovings, though it now fixed steadily upon the girl at the opposite end of the table.

Her back was towards the window. They could see chiefly the rounded nape of her neck and the heavy braid of yellow hair which slipped down past her shoulders and stirred in all its shimmering length whenever she moved her head. She moved it often, now looking up from, now down upon the book from which she was reading aloud to him. And as she read a slender, brown hand would fly out in an expressive gesture, or her head would turn a little in the excess of her emotion, and the watchers caught sight of a white, gleaming forehead where hats had sheltered her from the sun, and a pleasant profile of a fifteen-year-old girl.

Her auditor, at least, seemed to find more of interest in her face than in her words. He had not that intent look which comes to a listener to the spoken word, but he pored intently upon her face as though it carried a heart-filling message to him, the same thing over and over and never wearying.

"That's her," said King Charlie. "And that's him. Would you ever of knowed 'em?"

"Never would of knowed either of 'em," said Joe Hoyt, greatly wondering.

"Would of knowed both of 'em if you hadn't been within a thousand miles of me when I seen 'em," said

197

the Dean. "I can tell the girl by her looks. I can tell Billy English by that look in his eye, as if he had just finished fighting somebody, or else was just about to fight somebody. Never seen so much bull-terrier in any man's face as there is in his."

They knocked at the door now, and it was presently opened to them by Lady. At the first dim sight of three men in the night, she smiled instinctively. Plainly she had been taught to trust all men. It was only when she caught sight of the lowering face and the tremendous bulk of Joe Hoyt that she gave back a startled half step. As she turned, the lamplight gleamed a ruddy gold along her hair and outlined all of her features with a glow. And the three men in the outer night caught their breath of one accord. It was not her beauty of the moment so much as the promise of her beauty to come and, above all, a brave-eyed, clean-lipped girlishness which went to their hearts. She had turned a little towards Billy English as she stepped back.

The latter came out of his seat like a panther, which sleeps coiled up one instant and the next is leaping at the throat of that which awakens it. So he came towards the door, a meagre form not above average in height or bulk, and small indeed compared with the lofty Dean or burly Joe Hoyt. Yet he was large enough. He made up by the perfect balance of eye and hand, the speed of movement, the symmetrical proportions which would enable him to put forth surprising efforts, for the lack of sheer weight of bone and muscle.

The moment he peered into the night he exclaimed, and then strode out and caught King Charlie by both shoulders.

"By God!" he said, "I've been waiting—and here you are."

Then he turned on the others. His first enthusiasm suddenly waned. His greeting was icy cold.

King Charlie

"How are you, Dean? How are you, Hoyt? Come in."

They accepted the invitation: all silent, because he had not offered to shake hands with any saving the King.

"Lady," he said, turning to the girl, "I want you to know some folks I used to be acquainted with. This is Charlie—King; this is Mr.—Dean; this is Mr.—Josephs."

He hesitated each time a little as he turned their sobriquets into proper names.

"This is Louise Young," he said to the men, and she went from one to the other around the little semicircle and shook hands with them. "Run upstairs," he added to her. "I got to talk business to these old—friends of mine."

The girl paused only an instant, and in that interval she fixed upon the trio, each in turn, a glance of terror and the utmost penetration. Then she went obediently up the ladder and disappeared above them. No sooner was she gone than the attitude of Billy English changed and his smile went out.

"Now," he murmured sternly, "talk soft. She guesses that something is wrong, and she has the ear of a deer. What are you fellows up to?"

He put King Charlie out of the conversation, so to speak, by turning a shoulder upon him, and in the meantime he fixed the other two with a cold eye. "Talk out," he said. "You two never travelled together before for any good, and I'm damned surprised if you're travelling together now for the sake of your health. What is it you want?"

Joe Hoyt was beginning to bridle under this stinging stream of sarcasm, but the Dean interposed with soft words.

"First of all," he said, "I want to know why you're so hard on us, Billy? We used to be pals once. Why are you so hard on us now? We ain't going to steal the girl away from you, Billy."

"You've left her in the lurch for ten years, though," said Billy fiercely. "You left her for a kid, like I was ten years ago, to take care of. How in the name of God I was able to pull her through the first couple of winters I dunno, what with her sick most of the time and me part of the time. But if I managed, it wasn't no credit to you, none of you. You swore you'd stand by her and help her out. And here's the first time in ten years that you've showed up."

The Dean raised his hand to protest against the torrent of angry words.

"It's easy to talk without really knowing," he declared, "but just wait until you know a few of the facts, son. Here is Joe has been in the pen for six years. Here's me that have run in such rotten luck that I've hardly been able to take care of myself, let alone helping to take care of anybody else. But the minute I got a chance to help I come. It took ten years for that chance to show up. But when it came I started for you—"

"Because you need me," said Billy, "and because you hope you can work me in on one of your crooked games, but I'm through with all that. I'm clean through!"

The Dean was a little taken aback because his motives had been so readily deciphered. But he gathered himself together as well as he could and confronted Billy English again.

"You're hot under the collar now, Billy," he said. "But you'll get over that. Wait till your father has had a chance to talk to you."

Billy English turned like a flash upon King Charlie, and, with a strange mixture of pity and horror, of sadness and hatred, he stared at the old tramp, who now had mustered his bravest air as he clapped Billy upon the shoulder and said: "You mustn't go off half-cocked like this. You got to give people a chance to explain themselves. If you won't listen to the Dean, just listen to me!"

King Charlie

The other shrank from under the extended hand. The Dean called Joe Hoyt away with a gesture, and they went towards the stove to make a pretence of warming their hands while their orator strove to convince Billy.

The argument which he advanced was short and vigorous.

"How long you been living here, Billy?"

"You know as well as I do—ten years."

"How many days' work have you missed in that time?"

"I dunno. Maybe three or four weeks when I was sick."

"You been riding the range hot and cold, wet and dry. You been out in all sorts of weather—I can see it in your face, Billy. You look all wore out."

"What of it?"

"What of it? Why, just this: What have you got out of it? Where are you now ahead of where you were ten years ago?"

"Ten years ago Lady was a baby five years old. I've give her ten years of an honest life. She's got her schooling in them ten years, and she's lived clean and happy."

"That's what you've got ahead?" said the King. It was more than he had expected, and he was fighting for a moment of time. "Is that all?"

"It's enough," said Billy. "I can get along without being rich. Besides, I got some cows. Every year the herd grows. I like the business. And I get along fine with the folks in these parts. I ain't got much in the way of dollars to show for my work. But I got some results, and maybe before I die I'll have the dollars too. I'm not worrying about that. The main thing is that Lady has had a chance—"

"To live like a lady?" asked the King sharply.

"A lady? What d'you mean? If being honest and around honest folks and growing up polite and kind-hearted—if that makes a lady, then she is one."

"But you and me both know that that ain't the only thing. Remember the way her mother talked. Remember the way her mother had her dressed. Billy, she was meant to be raised like a lady of leisure, and you know it. And out here, what are you raising her up to be? The drudge on some ranch—that's all! What sort of advantages have you got to show her?"

Billy English dropped his head.

"What school is she going to *now?* She's gone through grammar school. Where's the high school to send her to? But better still, she'd ought to go to a finishing school, where she could learn swell manners and get the ways of a lady as well as the name of one."

"I never thought about them things—not in that way," muttered the younger man. "Maybe you're right. But how 'm I to do all that?"

"That," said King Charlie, breathing a sigh of relief as he neared victory, "is what I've come to tell you about. I ain't suggesting that you do anything for your own sake, but just for the sake of the girl."

Billy English started to speak, then changed his mind and dropped into a chair. From the corner by the stove the Dean waved his arms in sign of victory and urged King Charlie on.

Chapter Seven

Judge Howick rose from his chair and made a signal. Instantly a giant negro stepped from the shadow of the patio arcade and drew back the chair so that when he resumed his seat in it he was turned half towards the sun and half away from it. For the sunlight was not a brilliant red gold, having reached that low point in the west when the white heat which it carried all day began to be lost and filtered away through the screen of atmosphere before it reached the earth. The Judge stretched himself into a new position of comfort and regarded the angle which the shadow of the opposite roof made on the side of the arcade. It had been rapidly sloping athwart the floor of the patio, and now it was climbing the columns inch by inch.

"It's time for them to be here," he said aloud. "I've told that fool Murphy to make faster time between the house and the station. Eh, Jules?"

The big negro who had just moved the chair, and

who now attended the master silently and with folded arms, stepped forward again to answer.

"He says it kills the horses when they make the drive in an hour, sir," he said. "He aims to make it a little less because—"

"Damn his reasons and damn him!" exploded Howick. "I told him to make the trip in exactly one hour. If he uses up a few horses that makes no difference. What in hell is a horse or two here or there? If I can afford to spend horses in order to make fast time, who's to say no to me, eh? Who's to stop me, Jules?"

This last was delivered in a roar of a voice, and big Jules spread out his hands in a gesture of resignation. The Judge now jerked out his watch and stared at it.

"He's got three minutes left," he said, "and—"

The savage look turned to one of gloomy disappointment as he heard the crunching of the hoofs of horses far off on the road. It seemed that he would have treasured the opportunity to fall upon poor Murphy. But now the buckboard came to a halt in front of the patio, and there appeared two downheaded greys who stood dripping sweat from their bellies, flecked with the white foam of their labours here and there.

Murphy himself, an active little man with an expression of black rage now on his face, appeared, conducting another and taller fellow. As they came up, Howick waved the one to a chair and turned inquiringly upon Murphy.

"Look!" cried the latter in a choked voice, "look at them hosses! The near mare is half killed and the off ain't much better. Neither of 'em 'll be good for a damn lick of work for a week!"

"Then don't work them for a week—or work them to death, damn them, and buy some horses that *can* stand the trip!"

"The hosses ain't born that can stand that trip regular. If they can make the trip in, they can't stand the trip back on the same day. It'd kill the best that ever walked. Maud S. couldn't make that double trip and stand up under it."

"Let the worries of the stable stay in the stable," said Howick sternly, "and this is the patio of my house."

Murphy exploded with a shout of horror and rage.

"Because you pay money for your hosses, d'you think you got a right to *murder* 'em?"

Howick raised his hand and pointed.

"Get out," he said, "and don't come back until you're ready with an apology."

Murphy hesitated, trembling with fury, and then turned and fairly ran from the patio. The man whom he had brought into the enclosure now gingerly took his chair, still with his head turned to watch the place where Murphy had disappeared.

"That fellow will do you harm one of these days," he said. "He means no good to you, Mr. Howick."

"None of 'em do," replied the latter quietly. "There's hardly a man on my place that wouldn't knife me if I turned my back on him. That's a fact, Johnson."

Young Johnson regarded his host with more critical interest than surprise.

"I'd rather tame lions," he said. "I'd rather lie down among man-eaters than stay around men I know hate me. That fellow Murphy, now—his face sticks in my memory. I seemed to remember having seen him somewhere and—"

"Stop worrying about that. Of course you've seen him. He's Jack Murphy, and you've seen his picture in the rogue's gallery. He has two killings to his credit, but they were never able to hang much on him—never enough to send him up for it. I got hold of him. He has one weakness—he loves horses. So I find him useful. Also, he amuses me!"

"Because it drives him nearly crazy to have to drive

his horses at the rate you demand?" asked Johnson with a slight sneer.

"You ask too many questions!" snapped Howick. "Suppose I were to send someone to ask as many questions of you?"

Johnson changed colour.

"To get down to the business of my report," he said in a brusque and matter-of-fact manner.

"Go ahead with it, then. Have you been watching him as far as this? How far East did he go?"

"East? He didn't go East."

"Not East? You don't mean to say that a gambler of his talent is wasting his time in the West?"

"That's just what I mean. He's gone West with his grievance."

"Grievance?"

"I mean, what he calls a grievance. He persists in saying that he was robbed of fifty thousand dollars in your house, together with an enormous number of I O U's which you had signed."

"A peculiar illusion," said Howick, and smiled mirthlessly. "But go on with your story. Instead of going East, he went West to play in some of the small towns until he had secured a stake again?"

"He hasn't been gambling lately," said Johnson.

"No?"

"No, he has been gathering men instead of dollars. Three men, Mr. Howick."

"What the devil does he mean by that?"

"He means trouble for you, sir."

"Trouble for me?" Judge Howick broke into uproarious laughter. Then he rose, paced up and down a few times in the keenness of his delight at the thought, and then planted himself in his chair again. "This promises to be a good game," he went on. "He's got together three men, and the four of them are going to give me trouble, eh?"

"I wouldn't smile," said Johnson. "I take it a little seriously."

King Charlie

"Perhaps you would. That's because you haven't been through what I've been through. I know these things, Johnson. I love peril. A touch of danger is the sauce that makes existence worth while. But why in the name of heaven do you think that I, surrounded by men who would die for me simply because they know that they would damned soon die without me—guarded by such men as these, why under heaven, Johnson, should I fear four lone men? Who are they?"

"One is an old tramp, well over sixty, and afflicted with the prison trembles, or shakes, as they call it. That's a sort of nervous ague, you know."

"A formidable start," observed Howick with a grin. "Who are the others?"

"A gigantic fellow named Hoyt, just out of prison after serving a six-year term, and ready for any sort of deviltry. He has a long record behind him."

"If the law has been clever enough to catch him so many times, do you think that *I* shall have any trouble with him? This Dean, man, isn't as clever as I thought. Has he lost his mind that he thinks of tackling me with such a picked-up aggregation of loafers and ex-convicts? Who's the third man?"

"A youngster twenty-six years old."

"I fear no man under thirty," said Howick instantly. "They may possess both skill and courage, but without mellowing experience they are not dangerous. But what's his record?"

"For ten years he has ridden range."

"Dean *is* mad!"

"I think not. I have made inquiries about the gang of them. Nothing was very definitely known. But there is a pretty generally believed rumour, according to a man I met from Colorado, that Billy English once operated with Hoyt and the Dean, and they made a terrible trio. Dean was the schemer, Hoyt was the bulldog and the muscle of the party, and Billy English—he was only a kid of fifteen or sixteen then—was the fighting edge of the instrument. It was a good enough tool to cut through pretty strong safes, Mr. Howick."

"Ah, you think they contemplate burglary? Burglary of *my* safe?"

"I make a reasonable surmise that they do," said Johnson coldly.

"Where are they now?"

"Here."

"What?"

"I mean it. They must be somewhere among the hills near the house. I suppose right now they're boiling down the powder to make the soup."

The nearness of the danger sobered even the confident rancher. But then he shrugged his shoulders.

"The point is," he said, "that they don't understand my system of guarding the safe. Do you understand it, Johnson?"

"No."

"Then suppose you take a turn down in the cellar with me. You'll be amused."

They passed down a wide and easy flight of stairs which opened on to the patio arcade and passed from this into the series of capacious rooms which formed the cellars of La Casa Loma. For, since the weather during most of the year was bitingly hot, far more of La Casa was an excavation in the living rock than showed above the ground. There were two and even three levels of lofty rooms.

"It's been a fancy and a hobby with me," the owner explained. "Digging these rooms has made me feel like the proprietor of a *bona fide* donjon."

They spent a full half-hour wandering through the lower regions of the house and examining the workings of the defences of the safe. When they came up again Johnson was white and sick of face.

"Well," said Howick cheerfully, "confess that you have never seen defences like that around a safe."

"I confess," said Johnson, "that I have never seen a safe surrounded with such traps. The safe, it seems, is only the bait."

Chapter Eight

The resolution of Howick was that he would remain on the alert during every instant of the evening. But there is nothing so fatiguing as the constant expectation of danger which is delayed over even the shortest interval. Before ten in the evening, the Judge as he was called for no known reason, began to yawn and stretch his thick, strong arms, and finally he turned and asked Johnson with a curse how he could manage to keep awake so long and so easily.

"It's because you don't give a damn what happens to me," he complained. "There's no strain on you, Johnson."

"None at all," said Johnson. "If you think a moment, you'll see that it's better this way. You've hired me as a combination bloodhound and bulldog; you'd better keep me in that capacity. If I begin to worry I'll be less efficient."

The rancher glowered at his private detective. Like all of the other men in his employ, he knew that he could trust Johnson simply because he had enough "on" the detective to send him to prison. But though he ruled all of his people by fear and money, there were times when he realized that there is something more important than that which can be bought for cash.

"Your heart isn't in your work, Johnson," he said. "I know that."

"Of course not," admitted Johnson frankly. "That isn't the point, is it?"

Howick favoured him with another vicious look, and then yawned again.

"I'm going to bed," he announced at last. "How are the men posted?"

"Just as you ordered them to be posted," said Johnson. "I had them all in their places before dark."

He looked up, instinctively, as he spoke. The patio was a pool of black shot across, here and there, with an uncertain glow from hanging lamps under the arcade. It required some concentration to make out, far above, the dim twinkling of the stars. In the centre of the patio, since the night was coming on unexpectedly hot for this season of the year, the fountain had been set to playing, and its crisp whispering ran up and down a soft scale as the wind dipped into the enclosure and shook the head of the column of spray.

"Well," said Howick with another frown, "it's a foolish thing to be besieged like this—a whole fortress by four rats!"

"A rat," said Johnson coldly, "can sink the biggest ship in the world, if the ship is made of wood. And four such rats as these could gnaw even through the walls of a fortress, I should think."

"Do you mean that?" cried Howick in alarm.

"Nonsense!" said Johnson. "What can they do? We have about twenty trained fighters, haven't we? I've scattered half a dozen around on the high points near the house. It will take careful work to get through that line of outposts. But if they do come closer, they will be met by a dozen expert riflemen scattered around the house and instructed to shoot to kill. But even supposing that they were to penetrate through these and come to the core of affairs—the safe itself—why, Mr. Howick, don't you think that that trap would be strong enough to take them all and keep them for you?"

He blinked and shivered a little as he made this suggestion.

"Yes," nodded Howick, "I have a good deal of faith in that trap. The point is, Johnson, that I have no reason to fear anything, and yet when I recall the evil face of that gambler when I last saw him I'm ready to expect wellnigh anything from him. Still, they can't work by mystery and—"

Here both he and Johnson were brought out of their chairs with a bound by a shout which was almost a shriek not twenty paces from the gate of the patio, and at the same time their ears were struck by the sharp and ringing report of a rifle.

From the shadowy arcade, the two monster negro guards, Jules and his brother, sprang to the centre of the patio. They had taken off their coats and their shoes and socks. They were dressed in skin-tight, sleeveless shirts. Their huge bare feet gripped the stones of the patio pavement. The muscles of their great arms bulged and slipped at each movement. For all their bulk they were agile as two huge cats. One carried a crooked knife with a point so keen that the blade seemed to taper off to a ray of light. The other bore a long revolver. His knife remained in his belt.

That first leap forward had been a blind one, the result of long training that, no matter what happened, they must first protect the life of the master. Afterwards they sprang to the side again and towards the gate of the patio, and crouched there in tigerish silence, ready to spring upon and rend the first assailant to enter.

Howick, white with excitement, looked with a flash of profound pleasure upon these trained man-killers. Then, his gun in his hand, he waited developments.

They were not long in coming. There was a stir of voices, and then two of Howick's men came through the entrance half carrying and half shoving before them as a prisoner a tall, rosy faced old fellow, whose hat had fallen off, exposing a grey head.

"It's King Charlie," said the private detective. "It's the old tramp himself. Has the old fool gone mad and made a forlorn attack on us?"

The prisoner was brought to a halt before the little table at which the rancher and the detective were standing. They now sat down again.

"Jules!" called Howick.

The huge negro was instantly before them, moving as silently as a cloud shadow that slips across the hills.

"You boys can go back," said the rancher. "First tell me how you got him."

A scar-faced fellow stepped half a stride forward as though taking upon himself the duties of a spokesman.

"I was lying out on the hill," he said, "when I thought that I seen something moving down in the hollow. I give Dick, here, a rap in the ribs and whispered to him to look. He seen it too. We thought that the four was about to try a rush from that direction, but we thought that we'd wait and see a bit more before we turned in an' reported. And pretty soon Dick, who's got uncommon good night-eyes, made out that there was only one. We waited till he got close, then I shoved a slug right over his head. He jumped up and held up his hands. 'I surrender, boys,' says he, and here he is, sir."

"Very neat work," said Howick. "I'll remember you

for it. Now get back to your post. There are three more, and when they show up they may not be as easy as this one."

As they turned away big Jules sidled forward until King Charlie was forced to look into his grinning, wicked face. Then he returned to his post behind the prisoner.

"And now," said Howick, "what are *you* doing around here at this hour of the night?"

"Me?" said King Charlie. "Why, I was just taking a stroll and waiting for the moon to come up. When I seen your house, I thought it looked big enough to give me a handout, so I started for it. On the way a gun goes off in front of me. I jumped up—"

"You jumped up? You were crawling up the hill then?"

King Charlie became suddenly silent.

"I ain't much of a talker," he declared. "I've said my piece. That's all you get out of me."

Howick glanced aside at the detective.

"I think what he knows might be worth extracting, don't you, Johnson?"

Johnson frowned, and then, as understanding came to him, he changed colour.

"That's up to you to decide. For my part nobody knows *anything* that's worth a price as big as that. But you're the doctor."

"You're too squeamish, Johnson," said the rancher "That's what keeps you back in the world. You have too many nerves. You let them get in your way. Much better to take my attitude. Keep your nerves in their right place—out of sight. Jules, bring Charlie along after us—to my room."

He led the way with Johnson at his side into the house, and to a big room in the end of one of the wings. Here the owner of La Casa Loma had outdone himself. The click of their heels was lost in a soft, thick carpeting. Old Italian furniture glimmered in dull polish under the lamplight.

Here Howick threw himself into the depths of a big chair, pointed Johnson to another, and then ordered Jules to strip the shirt from the back of his prisoner, first tying both his hands and feet. Jules replied with a grin which showed the glint of white teeth, and laid hand on King Charlie; but the latter had fallen into a violent trembling. At sight of this Johnson leaned forward with a curious look.

"That's the penitentiary shake," he said. "The King must be an old timer. Mr. Howick, I think he'll talk now, if he can in spite of his chattering teeth."

"Will you tell us what you know?" asked Howick. "Or do you want a taste of a persuader?"

King Charlie rested a shoulder against the wall and slumped close to it. He seemed on the verge of a collapse.

"I'll talk," he said. "God knows I want to stay straight with the boys, but—I couldn't stand it."

"You show good sense," said Howick, though there was a shade of disappointment in his eye. "Now, King Charlie, if that's what you're called, tell us what your companions are up to?"

"I was to make the feint from this side," said King Charlie. "I was to come right up towards the patio and get myself caught. But the other three, after the noise on this side, were to tackle the house from the far side."

There was an exclamation from the rancher.

"My God, that's nerve for you, Johnson! He throws himself into the fire. Do you know that this means a fat prison term?"

"I'm used to that," answered the King heavily. "That wouldn't stop me. Besides, we expected to make enough to make it worth while. But—we didn't look for you to try torture. We knew you were hard, but not this hard."

"Ah," murmured Howick. "You see that I fool them, Johnson, in exactly the same manner that I fool you. Jules, tell your brother what I've heard. Let him go to the boys and tell them to gather and watch the far side of the house. They needn't mind about this. Then, come back and stand at the door. Hurry!"

Jules was gone at once, and Howick settled back again.

"Go through the King, Johnson, will you?" he asked. "See what weapons he carries."

"He's been searched already," said Johnson, "and they've done a good job."

"Then untie the ropes and let him sit down. You can put that pair of handcuffs on him, if you will. Ah, now we're fixed for a comfortable little chat."

He lighted a cigarette, and regarded the shivering and down-headed victim with mingled scorn and cruel pleasure.

"How much," he said, "did the four of you expect to take out of the safe?"

"Fifty thousand," said the King heavily.

"Only that much? Ah, I see why you have failed. Lack of imagination, inability to see the truth simply because the truth is bigger than you are." Here he turned to Johnson. "My friend, if I were to go in for this work, I think I could make a success of it."

"No doubt about it," said Johnson. "You have the nerve for it and the mind for it."

Howick regarded him closely, to make out the truth about this rather dubious compliment, and in the meantime there was a whisper of naked feet along the flagged passage outside the door. Jules, having accomplished his mission, had returned.

A moment later there was a shot and then a volley on the far side of the house.

"They're at it!" cried Howick. "The fools have run right into my trap. Johnson, I'm more and more pleased with myself. I begin to think that most of my talents are wasted in this peaceful life."

Here King Charlie, looking towards the door, and fascinated by the glowing eyes and gleaming teeth of

Max Brand

Jules in the semi-dark outside, saw that worthy's head suddenly jerked back, and the next instant his whole body was jerked out of sight and fell with a heavy thud.

Chapter Nine

"What the devil is that?" asked Howick.

The explosion of rifles had not been repeated. Now there was complete silence over the house.

"What happened to Jules at the door? Jules!" called the rancher.

"He stumbled and then he went down the hall," said King Charlie.

"Stumbled—went down the hall? What in hell does he mean by leaving the door when I've told him to stay there? I'll have every inch of his black hide torn from his body if he—"

He converted his fury from words into action, springing from his chair and hurrying to the door.

"Jules!" he called loudly, and then stepped out of sight into the hall.

Silence resulted.

King Charlie leaned back in his chair and yawned. But Johnson, the private detective, leaned forward and watched the old tramp with keen eyes.

Max Brand

"You old devil," he said suddenly, "you've been covering something up. That yawn is too elaborate to suit me. You ought to be thinking of a ten-year stretch instead of sleep. What's the truth about—Howick!"

He broke off his questioning to call cautiously after the rancher, but there was no response, and then he stepped out towards the door.

"Howick!" he called a little louder, and drew his revolver.

It was still not levelled, however, when a masked man stepped swiftly and noiselessly into the doorway and covered him with a weapon held as steady as a rock.

"Now watch that gun-hand of yours, stranger," said the newcomer in a soft, almost a purring voice. "Be careful that you move slow when you put that gun on the table over yonder. If you make any sudden starts, I'm going to drill you. Move lively, but let your hand work slow."

There was something so businesslike in this command that Johnson, without an attempt at resistance, backed to the table under the window, deposited his gun on it, and then shoved his hands above his head. The masked man, in spite of his haste, had time to remark scornfully:

"Look at that! They were too much rushed to take the key out—the blockheads!"

He twisted the key of the handcuffs, and King Charlie rose from the chair, a free man, and slipped them over the wrists of Johnson.

"I sure hate to see this happen," he assured Johnson with a grin. "But you were starting in to ask me embarrassing questions, stranger. If you keep your mouth shut no harm'll come to you. I remember that you weren't for putting the screws to me to make me talk. I'll keep that in your favour, Johnson."

Johnson, securely handcuffed, was pushed back

218

into a chair. The King then hurried to the door with his rescuer.

"You never worked better in your life, Billy," he said to his companion as they entered the hall. "You never done a neater or a smoother job. Never! Don't seem like you *could* have been away from the game for ten years."

"Shut up," said Billy English sternly. "We got no time for chatter. Help me get these back into the room."

There on the floor of the flagged hall King Charlie saw the cause for the disappearance of both the huge negro and the rancher. The negro lay on the floor with his mighty arms cast out. The rancher was huddled in a heap.

"Are they dead? Did you kill 'em *both?*" gasped King Charlie.

"You blockhead—I never kill. There ain't a game in the world that's worth that price. Chloroform over the face and a knee in the small of the back fixed the nigger. Don't you smell it still? He won't be kicking for half an hour, and we'll be out of here by that time, God willing—out of here or dead, one of the two. Give me a hand."

Their united efforts enabled them to drag the great negro into the master's room, and there they slumped him to the floor, a loose-mouthed hideous mask of a man, more terrible than death in his enforced trance. Then they returned and brought in the rancher.

He had been struck sharply across the side of the head with a blackjack. The skin had been broken by the force of the blow, and a small trickle of blood was running down his face. But otherwise he was uninjured, as Billy assured King Charlie.

"I tapped him careful—so careful it wouldn't have cracked the skull of a kid. But he sure has a paper head. He went down without so much as a gurgle.

Here—he's coming to. Get a rope on his hands, will
you?"

King Charlie, working with great deftness, threw
a double loop over the wrists of the prisoner, and he
opened his eyes to find himself helpless, with a revolver shoved under his chin by way of a stimulus to
a quicker recovery.

"I'm dead—they've killed me—help, Johnson!"
gasped Howick, as he sat up.

Then, his senses clearing, he was suddenly aware
of the gun and the masked man above him.

"Oh, God!" he said. "I'm done for."

"You are," answered Billy English, "if you peep. Sit
still, Howick. You're an old hand at cards, they say.
Then you ought to know that this trick is ours, and
it's against the rules for you to make a fuss when you
haven't a chance. But I'll go a bit further, and read
out of the book of you. You damned blackhearted
rat, I've heard about the way you work, and you keep
in mind that the only reason I don't cut your throat
is because I hate to get my hands dirty. If you let out
one yell, or if you try to bring attention of any kind
here, I'll finish you, Howick, before I take another
step. It'd be a pleasure at that."

Howick was silent, blinking into the face of the
masked man, and moistening his lips in a desperate
effort to answer. Finally he forced the words out.

"I'll keep quiet, boys," he whispered. "You don't
have to be afraid of me. I'll play the game now that
I see I've lost."

Billy English turned his back on the prisoner, and
kneeled beside the prostrate negro. He pushed up the
eyelid of Jules and regarded the eye. Bowing his
head, he listened to the heartbeat and the breathing
of the senseless man.

"Nothing could be better," murmured Billy. "He's
doing fine. Won't wake up for an hour, maybe, and
in the meantime he's having a fine sleep. No danger
to him at all. But I thought it would be a thousand

years before that big ox stopped wriggling, when I was holding the rag over his face. Where are the rest of the boys, Charlie?"

"They'll be here in a minute. They have to run around to this side of the house after they made the bluff to tackle them on that side, and they'll come slow on the way into the patio. And—"

Here he stopped short, for a voice called from the patio, and then a footfall sounded in the hall.

"We've drove 'em off, Mr. Howick, shall—"

Billy jammed his gun into the ribs of the rancher.

"Stop that man!" he commanded.

"Who's there?" called Howick.

The footfalls stopped suddenly.

"Jordan."

"Jordan, go back to your place. Who told you to come in?"

"Horn."

"Tell Horn to stay there."

"You don't want us to swing some men back to this side of the house?"

"No—I don't need advice. Get out!"

The footfalls retreated hastily. The rancher looked up with despair towards his captors, and a moment later a huge, squat form filled the doorway, and Joe Hoyt was before them with the lofty form of the Dean immediately behind him.

The latter stalked at once towards the rancher, and then removed his mask.

"I been wearing this for the sake of some of the others, Howick," he said; "but when it comes to you, it sure goes to my heart to think of calling on you and going away without you having a chance to see my face. Here I am, Howick. I told you that I'd come back, and here I am to cheer you up and sit in at another little game with you."

The rancher scowled fiercely up to him, but he returned no answer.

"Get up," said the Dean, and kicked Howick

sharply. The latter started to his feet, his face convulsed with passion.

Here Billy English pressed close to the Dean and laid a hand on his arm.

"No more of that!" he commanded.

"The dog!" answered the Dean. "If I busted every bone in his body it would be less than what's coming to him."

"Don't touch him," said Billy English ominously. "No matter what he is, he ain't to be touched while he's helpless. That's doing as bad as he done to you. Tell him what he's got to do, though."

"You're going down with us," said the Dean. "You're going to take us on a personally conducted tour into the cellar of La Casa Loma, son, and down there you're going to lead us into the room where you got the safe, and there you're going to work the combination for us and show us the way to the inside of your cash on hand. You understand?"

There was a faint, choked wail from the rancher; but the protest died away when he had glanced at the savage face of the Dean.

"Fix that one, will you?" asked Billy of Joe Hoyt.

The big man stepped to the second captive. His ministrations were swift and effective. When he stepped back the private detective was bound hand and foot and gagged. He could neither rise from the chair nor cry out.

"Douse the lights," said Billy, putting out the one nearest to him, and in an instant the room was blanketed in the thickest darkness. The victors filed off through the doorway with their captive.

Chapter Ten

Left alone in the black room, poor Johnson meditated upon the fate which lay in store for him.

Five years before, for the commission of a petty act of theft, he had fallen under the shadow of the law and faced a prison sentence and a ruined reputation if his employer chose to prosecute the case. But here the rich rancher, Howick, had stepped in and saved him.

At first he had blessed the rancher, but he had been shown before long that Judge Howick never performed an act of charity. All that he did was done with a purpose, and the purpose now was to secure a private sleuth for his own uses. So Johnson had become the slave of the rancher.

His bonds were not heavy and they rarely chafed, but always he was conscious that when the hour came he would be at the complete disposal of Howick. Even now he was liable to ruin, for if this adventure turned out as it now threatened to turn out, there was no question but that Howick would turn upon and tear all of those who were near him. He would first of all hate the man who had been the witness of his cringing and his humiliation. Yes, upon Johnson he would loose the full malignancy of his nature, and that, for the detective, meant destruction.

So that he had not even the privilege of rejoicing whole-heartedly in the downfall of his master. The only manner in which the Dean and his compeers could free him from dread would be by ending the existence of Howick. And he had heard too much from the lips of the controlling member of the quartet, Billy English, to hope that the latter would allow a murder.

But if Howick could not be destroyed, he must be saved. There was no alternative, if Johnson hoped to save his own hide. So he turned over in his mind the possibilities.

He was locked into a strong room, tied hand and foot, and secured to a heavy chair. He was gagged so that his mouth and jaws ached, so severely had Hoyt pried them apart, and he could barely breath.

But in the room there was an agency which, if he could employ it, would at once set him free. That agency was big Jules. But Jules was tied in a manner no less effective than his.

Yet he started hitching the chair across the floor. It was slow and heavy labour, and when he worked he began to breath harder, and when he breathed harder the gag wellnigh choked him.

Half-throttled, his face swelling with the blood that rushed up towards his head, he nevertheless kept on, moving the chair an inch at a time, until his feet struck a soft mass. That must be Jules.

Yes, as he sat still and strove to regain his own breath, he could hear the faintly stertorous breathing of the senseless negro.

Then he raised his feet as well as he could, worked

them down the leg of the negro, and securing a bit of the flesh against the stone, he ground down mercilessly.

It must have almost torn out the flesh like pinchers acting upon him; but still that agony did not rouse the negro. Johnson strove again. This time he succeeded in fetching a low groan from Jules.

It was like the growl of a fierce dog, and now he desisted for a moment. What if the negro did return partially to his senses? Would he not at once attack the creature that tortured him? Maddened by the pain, would he not fly at the throat of Johnson in the darkness?

For with no voice could Johnson reach the other. He could only wait and pray that the negro, if his brain cleared from the effects of the drug, would fumble about until he recognized the plight of the other man in the room and strive to liberate him, particularly since he might feel that it was the master who was in this condition.

An interval passed, and then Johnson ground his heel again into the flesh of Jules. There was a louder response this time, but still the body of the tortured man did not stir. Johnson sat back in his chair, almost fainting with the suspense and the excitement. It was like prodding a wild tiger and hoping that he would spring the other way.

Finally—it might have been ten minutes or an hour, for all Johnson knew—the slumberer roused and sat up with a gasping oath. Johnson strove with all his might to speak, but he could not make a sound.

Then it seemed that the torment of the bruised places which Johnson's heels had reduced to a pulp fully brought back consciousness to Jules. He sprang to his feet. In the dark his sweeping hands struck the form of the bound man. He caught up Johnson, chair and all, and crashed him down to the floor, splintering the wood of the chair-legs into a thousand shards.

That crashing noise seemed to bring back some of his senses to poor Jules. He fell upon his knees, moaning from the anguish of his tormented body. Then, fumbling with his great thick hands at the form of the silent man, he reached the cords—he felt his way to the gagged mouth—he tore the gag out.

"Jules—thank God!" gasped the prisoner. "They've taken the master—they've taken Howick. He's down in the safe-room in the cellar with the four of them. Get the rest of the boys! Quick!"

Chapter Eleven

The four and their prisoner, in the meantime had gone down the hallway to the patio, stolen along this under the shadows of the arcade to the stairway leading to the lower parts of the house, and then, guided by the reluctant rancher, they went down into the musty darkness.

Here, lighting a lantern which he found hanging from the wall at one side, Howick seemed to regain some of his poise and his courage. As a matter of fact, he was telling himself that if he could take the most roundabout way of reaching the safe-room, he would probably have taken so much time that some of his men might have a good chance of returning to his room, where they would find out what had happened.

It seemed impossible that he could be actually in the hands of four weak men while a score of his own stanch fellows were within easy hailing distance. He could hardly believe the senses which told him that he was deliberately showing the way to the plunderers of his fortune. In the meantime, he wound off to the side, taking the four through a long succession of storerooms and vacant chambers until finally the hand of the Dean fell sharply upon his shoulders.

"If you're killing time on us—" said the tall man.

That was all, but the rancher knew that he could gain no more in that manner. He conducted them, accordingly, straight to the door of the safe-room. From the outside there was hardly a sign of a door, only an infinitesimal crack in the surface of the rock, for the door was simply a huge slab chiselled out of the side of the wall. The lock itself was set into the main body of stone, and not into the door. Into it Howick fitted his key, and presently the stone panel sagged in, and a moist breath of cold air flowed slowly out around the four.

Stepping inside, they found themselves before a huge safe.

"Watch for the boards on each side of those two main doors that lead up to the front of the safe," cautioned the rancher. "They connect with levers that start water running into the cellar. In three minutes after the flow of water starts the whole cellar is full to the top, and the gentlemen who call to see my safe are washed out. You understand?"

"Neat idea," said the Dean, "and, as a matter of fact, it sounds like exactly the sort of a plan that you'd form, Howick. Now, the point is that the door is open and that the water would run out of the cellar as fast as it would run in. But the next thing for you to do is to open the door. Don't try to tell us that you've forgot the combination."

But the attitude of the rancher had undergone a strange alteration. He no longer either cringed or snarled at them, but with perfect politeness he now said:

"My friends, I have always fought hard, and I hate to lose, but when I see that I am hopelessly beaten,

I trust that you will find me a good loser."

So saying, he fell upon his knees before the lock and worked at it busily for a moment, then the tumblers clicked and the heavy door swung slowly open.

Inside they found themselves confronted with another and a smaller door.

"You see," said Howick politely, "that one blast would not have turned the trick with this safe of mine, and before a second blast could be set, I trust that the noise of the first one would have roused my men. But now that you have me with you, you don't need nitro-glycerine."

Still smiling, he worked at the combination on the smaller door, and when this also opened, he drew out a small, steel-jacketed drawer in either hand and extended them towards the four.

"There you are," he said. "There are the cash savings of my lifetime. Help yourselves, boys. Then run through the rest of the safe and you may find some other things of interest."

They gave him side glances, and then, led by their greed, they snatched the drawers from him. As he had said, they were both jammed with greenbacks. It was impossible to even approximately estimate so huge a sum of money, and as they raised the lamp over it the faces of the four showed curious differences in expression. That of the Dean, for instance, showed the most fiery pleasure and gratification, as of one who deserves what he gets. King Charlie was frankly awed; Joe Hoyt was dazed; and only Billy English was for the moment saddened, and seemed to be thinking of the possible consequences of this act.

It was he, too, who suddenly turned and cried: "Howick!"

And his gun leaped into his hand.

For Howick had slipped back towards the door as the four leaned over the money. Now he checked himself on the very verge of leaping out and came back to them, giving the heavy door, as he did so, a passing twitch with his fingers of sufficient strength to start it swinging shut.

"Get the door!" cried Billy English to Hoyt, who was nearest to it, but as the slow-thinking giant did not instantly comprehend, he himself leaped like a flash for it.

He reached it just too late, for the heavy mass of rock shut as his fingers reached for the edge. He seized the knob of the door and wrenched at it, but the lock closed with a spring. Then he whirled upon the rancher.

"Let's have your key!" he demanded.

And then he saw that Howick, white of face with excitement and malevolent pleasure, was standing with his arms akimbo and smiling upon them.

"Friends," said Howick, "I'm sorry to say that the key is on the far side of the wall. If you want it, dig through the wall with your finger nails and get it!"

There was a stifled howl of rage and terror from Joe Hoyt, but as he turned to throw himself at the rancher, Billy English, always a master of the other three in the most rash moments of excitement, now interposed.

"Don't be a fool, Joe," he said, "Howick is only joking. He knows that we'd tear him to pieces if he didn't have some means of getting us out of here, and we'll put the screws to him until he tells us how."

"Fool?" repeated Howick hoarsely, and he shook his triumphant fist in the face of the others. "I'll teach you how much of a fool I am. There's no other way to get out of this than to put a key into the lock. And I have no key. You can search me to the skin. There's no other way. Don't I know that if there were another way you'd tear it out of me? But no, my friends, the only way you leave this room is when the door is opened from the outside, and when that happens you can imagine who will be waiting for you on the opposite side of the wall. But if you try to even things up at my expense in the meantime—why, gentlemen,

King Charlie

I need hardly tell you the difference between being sent to prison for robbery and being hung for murder."

All that he said was too entirely convincing. The money which they had stuffed into their pockets now became worse than useless. They flew at the door and wrenched at the knob, but the door merely quivered, and Joe Hoyt, recoiling as his hand slipped off the knob, stepped back off the straight boards which led to the front of the safe. The boards upon which he staggered gave with a slight, metallic sound; there was a faint whirring of a powerful pump, and then a great stream of water began to crash upon the floor of the vault-room.

There was a scream from Howick, all of whose assurance was stripped from him in a trice.

"You fool—you devil—we'll all drown like rats!"

Chapter Twelve

Where, then, was the courage of the stoutest of them? Howick was a raving, screaming coward, tearing at the wall with his bleeding finger-tips. The tall Dean leaned against the safe with his face in his hands, and King Charlie stood gripping the hands of the dazed Billy English as though the youngster who had saved them so often in crises could save them again now.

Only Joe Hoyt showed the courage which makes men act. The water was rushing across the floor. In a trice it was ankle deep. Then the lantern slipped from the hand of the Dean and was instantly extinguished in the water.

A yell rose from the prisoners. With that tide of rapidly rising, icy water, the rushing noise, and the choking darkness, it seemed that the bitterness of death was already theirs.

But big Joe Hoyt, too stupid and unimaginative to be crushed by his anticipations, waded forward through the deluge crying: "If we're going to get out, we got to get out by springing that lock, and if we spring that lock I'm the man to do it. Lemme get at it."

Fumbling forward, he encountered the body of Howick. He hurled the rancher to the side with an oath, and the next instant his big hands were fixed upon the knob of the door.

But the others, having heard his words, now gathered close behind him. To none of them would it have occurred to attempt to break the spring of that lock by sheer pressure. Even with a jemmy they would have doubted their ability. But they had seen him do tremendous feats of strength before, and now they rallied close around him with the water swirling at their hips and staggering them with the force of its current. Even the rancher, scrambling back to them, was pinning his hopes on the strong man.

"The door's strong enough," he said, "but maybe the lock ain't so strong."

"Try it!" called the others.

And Billy English, putting his hand upon the shoulders of the strong man, felt the shoulders turn to iron as the muscles tightened with the effort. His whole great body quivered; there was a loud creaking noise, and then Joe Hoyt staggered back with a gasp. Water had risen to the height of the knob and his grip had loosened and slipped off.

Water, indeed, was now swirling up to his shoulders, up to his chin. The scream of the rancher, as he made out that Joe had failed, was a death-cry.

But dauntless Joe Hoyt had still the courage for another effort. This time, stooping, the water covered the top of his head while he fixed his mighty grip upon the knob of the door. And all immersed in the deluge, with his lungs heaving and burning under the suffocating strain, he heaved up again.

There was a wrench, a thin ray of light plunged through the darkness, and then the door was tugged in and the water roared out into the hall beyond. They were free!

Another peril was on them, however, the moment the blessed light struck them; for the keen voice of the rancher was shrieking to his men, bidding them come to his aid, and trusting to the darkness to protect him from the wrath of the four.

It was the voice of Billy English which again saved him from destruction, as the Dean rose to shatter his skull and silence him with the blow of a revolver butt—the voice of Billy English commanding them all to rush on and hang together.

And so, staggering in the leaping current of the escaping water, they floundered to the first stairs and up these. But as they did so, a door was wrenched open above them and in the lighted square, behold huge Jules, with Johnson beside him. They showed for an instant, amazed at the sight of the four hurrying up from below, all four dripping like half drowned rats. Then they whipped up their guns.

But Billy English had drawn his weapon at the first showing of light, and while his three companions rushed blindly and frantically into the teeth of destruction, as though they hoped to smash their way to liberty by the sheer weight of numbers, he himself had swerved to one side, and taking deliberate aim, he now fired twice in quick succession.

The first bullet, nicely aimed, snapped the upper arm of Johnson. The second bullet, with hardly less accuracy, ploughed through the thigh of the big negro. He went down with a crash, the gun exploding from his hand. He slid halfway to the bottom of the stairs with a yell of pain and rage, and past him dashed the four and found the blessed air of the open night in the patio above them.

Half a minute too late Johnson had roused the negro from torpor.

But all of the circle around the house was now alive with the voices of shouting, cursing men who were beginning to realize that something was wrong, and who now came rushing back as they heard the sudden crashing of firearms. Half a dozen of them swirled into the entrance to the patio, and Billy English pumped three shots in quick succession into the masonry beside them.

At the same time he shouted: "Hold the patio against them, boys. That's our chance!"

But as the men of the rancher tumbled back in alarm from the gateway, Billy turned to his companions.

"Start back through the rear of the house," he commanded.

"Back there? That's where they're all stationed now!" cried King Charlie.

"That's where they were a minute ago, you mean," answered Billy. "They'll be gone now. We'll slide through the gap. We can't make our own horses. Probably they got some of their own saddled. We got to pray for that. Dean and Hoyt, you run first, and I'll stay behind with King Charlie."

The other two, with grunted acknowledgment that this was sound advice, plunged away for the rear of the patio and then through a room, diving out of a window at the rear of La Casa Loma. King Charlie and Billy English followed them as fast as the older limbs of the tramp would permit. But once outside the walls of the house they found themselves in a comparative silence. There were shouts and guns exploding from the front, where it seemed that the men of the rancher were blocking the entrance to the patio and firing at random into its darkness. But they had not yet carefully spread the cordon around the whole building, and through the gap in the rear the fugitives ran in perfect safety until they reached the secondary shelter of the barns. There they found that there were no saddled horses, and at the same time two or three men from the house discovered them and started a heavy rifle fire.

King Charlie was detailed to hold the rear of the barn, confident that the rancher's men would never dare to rush across the open, starlit space to get to close quarters with them. He kept up a steady fire, aiming at nothing, while the other three quickly selected three of the best horses, saddled them, and in another minute they were under way.

And as they went down the slope they heard the screaming voice of Howick behind them offering ten thousand dollars a head for each of the four robbers. But they were off to a flying start, well mounted, in country adapted for a get-away. By the time the first grey of the dawn began to roll over the hills, they had dropped all signs of the pursuit far behind them.

"But where," said Louise Alison Dora Young, "where does all this money come from that will send me to school?"

"Why," said Billy English, "I'll tell you about that: When your mother died, Lady, she left me quite a bunch of stuff—jewels and suchlike. I turned all of that into money and I soaked it away in mining stock. That sounds like a fool thing to do, eh? Well, the money was buried all these years, but just the other day it turned up that the mine had just struck pay dirt again and now its paying big—"

"But then you'll go back East with me, Uncle Billy?"

"How?"

"If there's as much money as that, we can surely go together."

"Go on that money?"

He shook his head with a profound conviction.

"The only thing that'll make that money good," he said, "is to spend it on you, honey. Besides, my place is out here riding herd!"

"Oh, well," she said, "my place is here, too, then. I'd be too lonely without you, Uncle Billy."

"That's fool talk—plumb fool talk!" he declared.

King Charlie

"I've made up my mind about it—that's all, Lady. You're going East to school."

She was silent. A thin voice coyote began a sobbing wail in the distance.

PART IV

PART IV

Chapter One

The sway of the stage, as it sagged heavily over the brow of the hill, threw her head back, and there she let it stay with her glance wandering, for a moment, among the blue deeps of the sky. Far above a hawk floated, and far above the hawk there was another, smaller speck. That, perhaps, was an eagle watching the hawk's hunting with a jealous eye.

Louise Alison Dora Young observed these things with an eye which sensed the picture rather than noted the fact, if one may catch the fine distinction. She smiled into the blue of that sky with the perfect knowledge that her smile was visible in spite of the wide shading brim of her hat, and when she uttered a little exclamation of artless delight and caught her breath audibly, musically, let no one for a moment dream that she was not well aware of the artlessness and the music. Neither did she fail to comprehend that the hand which she raised to the edge of her hat showed a more delicate and more spirit-thin whiteness against the impalpable background of a Western sky. Indeed, she approved of her attitude so strongly that she would have held it for a considerable period had it not occurred to her that the contrast between the blue of her eyes and the blue of the strange sky might be interesting to her companion.

Of course, her companion on that seat of the stage was a man.

That baby-eyed, soft-mouthed, blank-faced expression which stupid man calls thoughtless innocence is, of course, the effect of consummate craft. All of those who can will use it. Because it has an effect of mortal suddenness upon the most sedate of men. The wiser men are, the more easily they fall into the snare of wide eyes. We may be sure that poor Solomon's thousand were a thousand doll-faces. To do their thinking for them—that was a very easy thing, he imagined. And the beauty of it all probably was that to the end they fooled him, just as beautiful Louise Alison Dora Young was fooling poor Jack Granville on this day of days.

Not that Jack was a Solomon. He was quite a distance from even aspiring to entry in that class. He was, instead, a wide-shouldered, grey-eyed, erect youth, who knew how to curve a baseball across the corners and how to boot a football between the posts from the thirty-five yard line. Of course, these were acquirements which had made him famous and had earned him more inches of headlines than the President and any three Senators of the year. His college, a scant month before, had just finished voting him the "most popular," "best dressed," "versatile" man in the senior class which was now graduating, to the sorrow of Alma Mater; above all, it was said that he had done more for his college than any other member of his class. No doubt he had. If the advertising he had given that college were to be paid for by the inch in the great New York dailies, the combined salaries of the Greek and Philosophy Departments would have been found inadequate to meet the bill.

Such was the greatness of handsome Jack Granville, honest Jack Granville, mighty Jack Granville. And when he found himself stepping through the gates of his college and into the "world," he had to stop and rub his square chin and shift feet more than once before he could make up his mind as to what was next in order to be done.

Making money was not of interest. In fact, it was about as silly as pouring water into the ocean to fill up the sea. His great-grandfather had first raised the always solid fortunes of his family to the level of wealth. His grandfather had multiplied the sum total by ten, and his father had taken control of the immense estate and swelled it by four times the original size. That father was still, in the sprightly prime of his later forties, quite ready and able to sit at the helm in Wall Street and steer smoothly on past winning posts.

Therefore, why should Jack Granville wish to make money? It would be ridiculous.

But then, what the devil *should* he do?

It was suggested to him by an aesthetic aunt that he should go to Europe and study art and stand by ready to convert nine-tenths of his father's millions into oil paintings as soon as that worthy gentleman died; but Jack pointed out that his paternal relative was quite likely to live to ninety—indeed, that he gave actual promise of doing it, and that if he suspected anyone were waiting for his death he might double even that venerable age. Besides, there was another objection—the steady grey eyes which could so accurately judge distance when the gloves were on his hands and there was an opponent's chin within striking distance, were absolutely unable to focus upon the smile of Madonna; and he had been known to make a horrible comparison between the colour of a raw beefsteak and the famous Rubens red.

Not money? Not art?

"But consider," said the family in conclave, "that he has to do something! What on earth shall it be?"

"Polo," said big Jack Granville, and went to England, and rode and smashed his way to fame on a bright summer's day.

When he came back the family took up the question again and presented it duly: What can Jack do?

Once more Jack took the answer, at least, temporarily, into his own hands, for he went on a weekend party, and there encountered among the guests a star-eyed beauty who, as he himself put it in his vulgar way, "was knocking them stiff by the score."

Among the casualties was Jack Granville. He differed from the rest, however, in an important particular. While the others, having seen her, merely flocked about and gaped and grinned about her in the calf-fashion of young men in the presence of Beauty, Jack Granville thrust out that square jaw of his, the mere sight of which had been sufficient to dissolve a sturdy football line, and determined to fight for her to the bitter end.

So he started at once and, on that first evening, danced no less than eight times with her, made himself horribly talked about, and concluded a giddy and joyous evening with his hopes in the seventh heaven and his fighting heart fully consigned to the battle.

He told himself when he went to sleep that night that he would not propose, as a matter of decency, until the third day, and he stayed by his promise to himself, and proposed on the third day.

Afterwards, dizzy and reeling in spirit, though he kept smiling through it all, he confided in Aunt Eleanor exactly what had happened.

"You were too sudden, Jack," said Aunt Eleanor. "Good heavens, boy, she thought you were making game of her!"

She herself was breathless. There was no princess in the world really worthy to share the hand and the fortune of Jack Granville. As for this Western, nameless snip—However, a pretty face had been known to topple the greatest. Thank God it was not a chorus girl.

In a breathless and broken fashion something like this Aunt Eleanor reasoned the matter out, and then asked: "Just what did you say to her?"

"I told her that I liked her a lot and that I thought we would hit it off in great shape if she could see her way clear to marrying me. She didn't smile and she didn't blush. She just looked me in the eye and made me feel like a vendor of old clothes walking down the aisle in Trinity Church on Easter Sunday."

"She wanted poetry—eloquence," said Aunt Eleanor. "She's an old-fashioned girl."

"Old-fashioned foot," said Jack. "You don't know her. She's a brick. What she said was that she liked me better than any young man she'd ever met, but that she didn't love me a bit. I asked her if I might stay around and bother her, and she said that she'd like that fine."

"Does she use such slang?" asked Aunt Eleanor, with her most Labradorian chill and lift of the brows.

"Slang?" said Jack fondly. "Nothing but the purest Shakespeare undefiled for hers. But after all, even if I get to the post with my weight assigned, I still have to parade past her guardian before she'll as much as seriously consider my proposal."

Here Aunt Eleanor started up from her chair.

"Stuff and nonsense!" she cried. "Stuff and nonsense, Jack! Does any American have to ask who Jack Granville is? Please God, no!"

"But please Louise, yes. If Lady—"

"Where did that nickname originate?"

"Her initials spell it."

"Bah!" snapped Aunt Eleanor, who would have made an excellent man had there been need. "This whole affair is ridiculous. Carry you three thousand miles into the West to get the approval of her guardian—*her* guardian! Never mention this to me again, Jack."

And he obeyed her. But, nevertheless, here he was, not three thousand miles, but a good two-thirds of that distance into the West, having finally been told that Louise Young had decided she liked him so well that, should her guardian approve, she would consider herself engaged to him. And now, in this old-fashioned stage-coach, they were labouring and creaking and sweating and rolling through the mountains towards the ranch-house of the man.

He had looked up towards the dizzy height of the heavens. He had seen that slim-fingered hand wavering against the blue, and now he received the double shock of blue, blue eyes that turned the sky pale, and red, smiling lips. He caught his breath. His own eyes grew dim.

'Louise," he said, forcing himself to speak commonplace words, but worshipping her with all his heart, "Louise, you've never told me about your guardian."

"Haven't I?"

"Never. You've told me the rest—that you never knew your father or your mother."

"And that really makes no difference to you?"

"My dear," said Jack Granville, and then fell acoughing as though choked by the stinging alkali dust. He continued at last: "Not the slightest difference. I would take you if you had no name at all." He went on: "With such a free spirit as you, Louise, I've always wondered why you should be so subservient to the wishes of a guardian."

"I'll tell you all about it. When I was five my mother died, and she was all the family I had. I was left with a nameless-name, you might say, and nothing else. But Uncle Billy saw me, and—"

"I thought you said you had no family?"

"I meant it. He is not relative. He saw me. He was just a young cowpuncher with a heart of gold, Jack, you see. He took me, gave me a home, treated me like a daughter, sent me to school.

"I couldn't see it then. Children are blind to the sacrifices which are made for them, it seems. But I see now that he has practically given up his life to me. He started very humbly as a small cattle owner. But no matter how humbly he lived there was always plenty for me, and when I went away to school, the schools were the best. He has educated me like the daughter of a millionaire. He has dressed me like the daughter of a millionaire."

She raised her hand, her sleeve slipped back, there was exposed a bracelet of thin, woven gold with a clasp worked in great emeralds.

"He's never spared money on me, but he himself couldn't be told among a hundred dusty cowpunchers. Oh, Jack, he's the dearest, quietest, kindest man in the world!"

Jack Granville struck his big fist heavily against his knee.

"By the Lord," he exclaimed, "a yarn like that warms a man's heart! It's a fairy tale. It's too good to be true. I'll be glad to shake hands with him, I'll tell you. Why, Louise, no matter what demands he makes on you, you'd be damned black if you didn't do exactly what he asked. Wants to see the man you're to marry? Of course he does, and of course he has a right to. How old a man is he, Lady?"

"Oh, middle-aged."

"What does that mean—forty-five?"

"Oh no!"

"No? Forty?"

"Not forty."

Big Jack Granville sat up.

"Not forty? H-m-m! Let me see—you're twenty-one, Lady?"

"Yes. What has that to do with Uncle Billy's age?"

"Nothing, I guess," said Jack. "Nothing, I hope. You say he isn't forty?"

"You're acting very queerly, Jack."

"Am I? I'm sorry. I always act queerly when I'm thinking hard. I'm not used to hard thinking, you know. I'm really curious about your guardian's age—this man who doesn't want you to marry until he's had a chance to look over the man."

"Oh, he's away, 'way past thirty, Jack."

"Ah! We're getting still further down, eh? Thirty-five, eh?"

"No, but past thirty. Thirty-two, to be exact."

There was a deep exclamation from Jack Granville.

"Thirty-two—you're twenty-one. I begin to see why he has to take a look at the man you're to marry. Eleven years older. Why, my grandfather was twenty years older than my grandmother when they were married!"

This time it was the turn of Lady to sit up stiff in her seat.

"Jack Granville!" she cried. "What do you mean? What *do* you mean?"

"Figure it out for yourself," said Jack.

She had turned a violent crimson. She was trembling from head to foot.

"Don't you see," she stammered, "that—that Billy—why, of course he never—why, Jack Granville, what a perfectly crazy idea!"

But Jack Granville, biting savagely at the end of a fresh cigar, watched the hanging hawk swoop suddenly down and shoot out of view, striking at some unseen victim. He did not answer Louise.

Chapter Two

It was five long years since Lady had seen the old house in which she had spent the latter portion of her childhood, and now, with shining eyes, she urged the horse which they had hired in town after leaving the stage to a sharper trot that whirled them over a low hill. Before them was a shallow valley with a great mountain lifting up behind, and just between the valley and the mountain there was a small shack. A crooked stove-pipe leaned above it. A shamble of old barbedwire fences stretched around it. Miserable sheds and broken-backed barns were scattered here and there.

Lady uttered a glad little cry. "Faster!" she called to the horse. "That's the place, Jack!"

Jack Granville glanced at the dreary prospect. Then he turned to the radiant young beauty beside him.

"That's it!" She was jumping up and down on the seat. "That's home!"

"If one man can make *that* place home," said young Jack Granville, half to himself and half to the girl, "he must be quite some man—quite some man, I should say."

"He won't expect us—dear old Uncle Billy! He'll never dream that I'm within two thousand miles of this place. Oh!"

The last was a shrill little cry, as she put the horse into a pounding gallop that set the rig jouncing and bouncing over the rocky road.

Presently they were out of the buggy before the house, and her young voice was ringing up the hillside: "Billy! Oh, Uncle Billy!"

Jack Granville set his teeth and waited, but as the girl ran up the path there appeared in the door of the shack a thin old man, with white, white hair, and leathery red cheeks, and gleaming eyes, and a carriage as erect as a youth of twenty. That was more the sort of an Uncle Billy that Jack Granville would have been glad to see. The ancient man came swiftly through the door, tossing a cigarette far to one side. He was dressed in a red flannel shirt open at the withered, wrinkled throat. One suspender stretched across his lean shoulder, drawing up his trousers almost to his chest. The result was that they showed a considerable bit of narrow shank below their bottom edge, and that leg was clad in a tumble of socks as red as the shirt. Yet this dusty veteran came down the path, met the girl, and caught dainty Louise Young in his arms and then lifted her clear of the path.

"Oh, King Charlie, King Charlie, King Charlie!" cried Lady. "It's five long years!"

King Charlie's eyes were wet, and not with the rheum of age.

"I know," he said. "Five years, and every minute I've been thinking about you, honey. Every minute I've been missing you. Billy and the rest, they're young. They can get along without you. They have other things to do. But me—I'm old. I'm set in my ways. New things don't find no way into my heart. That's why I've been longing for you, Lady. Just sitting here longing for you."

"You're joking now," insisted Lady. "I know that you've been running around the country from Montreal to New Orleans and from 'Frisco to New York, and going blind baggage every step."

"Blind baggage—at my age? No, no, honey—the slow freights are fast enough for me."

She shook her head.

"They'll never be!" she cried. "I don't care how old you say you are—your heart is younger than mine this very minute, King Charlie."

She broke off to greet a newcomer, one of the most villainous fellows that Jack Granville had ever seen. He was perhaps fifty, a little more or a little less. His hair was grey and hung in stiff, uncombable shocks over his forehead. His dress was not much more presentable than that of the strange being called King Charlie. His frame was literally gigantic in width and in depth, and though he was of less than average height, and though advancing years must have somewhat stiffened his muscles, yet it seemed to Jack Granville that he was seeing the first man whose sheer power of muscle he would dread contending against. The grip of that brown, broad hand, for instance, seemed great enough to rip the muscle out of his arm.

This huge grotesque ambled down the path, and dainty Louise Young fled to him just as she had done to the first man.

"Uncle Joe Hoyt!" she cried. "Oh, Uncle Joe!"

He did not lift her in his prodigious arms as King Charlie had done, but he caught both her hands and held her off at a distance and looked her over with a strangely proprietary eye.

"You ain't spoiled," he said. "You're just the same. I knew that they couldn't spoil you. Charlie, here's, been saying that you'd never come near us again—and here you are. I always knowed that you'd come back to us just the same as when you left. When a girl is a lady, it don't make no difference what happens, she's always the same to them she loves and them that loves her."

Jack Granville had remained down the path, rooted to the ground. Now, as she turned back to him, he managed to advance.

"Uncle Joe—King Charlie," she said, "I want you to meet a new friend of mine, Mr. Jack Granville."

And they shook hands, and Jack Granville felt that never had he been so searched with glances as he was searched on this day. For the two men measured him up and then down again. What they saw, however, they seemed to fairly approve of, for they shook hands strongly. Strongly? Yes, in the immense grip of Joe Hoyt, Jack Granville felt his own hand fairly disappear. Every bone could have been smashed, so it seemed, had the big man desired.

"And where's Billy?" asked the girl.

"He's over the hill."

"Oh, I'm wild to see him. How does he look?"

It seemed to Jack Granville that a slight shadow had fallen upon the faces of the other two. They looked to one another before they looked back at the girl.

"He's fair to middling," said King Charlie. "He'll be coming down pretty soon, I guess, and then you can see for yourself—but five years is a long time to go without seeing a man. Don't you figure that way, Lady?"

"He never would let me come," she answered, defending herself. "I tried to come. I wrote to him every year—at Christmas vacation, and every summer; but he always told me to stay away. He said that he wanted me to keep out of the West for a while. He told me he wanted me to live a different kind of life, breathe a different kind of air, and I stayed away to please him. If I had dreamed, in the beginning, that it was to be five full years, I should never have stayed. But one year slipped into another, and still whenever I mentioned it he told me to stay where I was. Until, finally, you see that I took matters into my own hands, and here I am."

They chuckled in a deep bass chorus.

"That's like you, honey," they said. "You always had your way when you put your foot down. I guess Billy will be plumb wild when he sees you."

They went inside the house. It was the drabbest, plainest interior that Jack Granville had ever seen; and by contrast Louise Young was like a jewel in a setting of brass. Life was reduced here to the main essentials. In the meantime, Lady was staring around.

"But what I can't understand," she said at last, "is why Billy will insist on keeping up this sort of a life when he has so much money? Why does he do it? Why, he must own thousands of acres by this time, and he must have more cows than a person could count in a whole day. Why doesn't he build himself a good, big house in town, and make himself and the rest of you comfortable?"

Joe Hoyt, who bore the direct brunt of this volley of questions, opened his mouth to speak, produced no sound, and turned in a foolishly helpless fashion to King Charlie.

"It's this way," said the latter quietly. "Living the way that Billy does, he just forgets what sort of a house he lives in. Yes, he could have a lot better place than this, but this is good enough to do for him. He likes it, sort of, the way it is. D'you know why?"

"Well?"

"Well, the main thing is because it's just the way it was when you left. There's your same books on your same shelf over there. There's your pictures in the corner, and he's left your room upstairs just the same. Not a thing is different."

She went to the corner of the room, she touched the books; all at once she broke into tears and turned to them with the moisture on her face and shining in her eyes.

"Was there ever a man as good as he, Jack Granville? Was there ever such a man?"

But, strange to say, Jack Granville nodded without a spark of enthusiasm. He was more intent upon gazing out of the open doorway at the pale blue Western sky and the raw edges of the mountains lifting away in ridge on ridge, like rows of vast, storm-tossed waves frozen to stone. He could feel that somewhere in them, beyond them, was the charm which made Lady love this land and call it her country. Many a time he had heard her in raptures over it, and now he vaguely understood.

In the meantime, all was jollity in the cabin. Lady had slipped upstairs and returned in a few moments completely changed. She was wearing a faded blue gingham. Her hair was done into a braid and twisted upon the back of her head. Her feet were clad in shapeless rough shoes worthy of a man, and she stood at the foot of the ladder from which she had descended and burst into hearty laughter at all three of them as they gaped at her. Then she stirred them into action.

"Jack is a guest for the first night," she said; "but the rest of you—humph! King Charlie, I want wood; Joe, water from the well! Quick! There has to be a meal ready for Billy when he comes. Oh, Billy! Oh, Billy! The first meal in five years that I've cooked for you."

After that, all was a clamour of singing and of laughter in the cabin. Jack, wandering helplessly around, was simply in the way until he was ordered into a corner by the girl. She, in the meantime, flew here and there, accomplishing something at every turn, and as she worked she sang.

He saw her hands mixing yellow flour and white

one moment, the next she was stoking the fire until the little, crazy stove smoked and roared; again, she was slicing bacon with a murderous great knife.

"There'll be eats to-night such as you never set a tooth in, Jack Granville!" she cried.

Was that the talk to come from the lips of beautiful Louise, soft-lipped Louise, blue-eyed Louise?

And yet he liked it. He liked it far better than anything he had ever heard her say in the East. He liked these swift and efficient gestures better than any of the graceful and carefully careless postures of which she was the past mistress. All that battery was abandoned. She had worn ship and presented a new and totally unsuspected battery. It was like seeing two characters in one.

And he suddenly found that if he had adored her before he had now made the discovery that she was absolutely necessary to his existence. She was his rightful mate. She had the virility, the joyous love of life. Without her he would be only half a man.

These thoughts were growing stronger and stronger in him. He stepped out from the low doorway into the sunset-time which was spreading colour and quiet through the sky. And it was then that he saw Uncle Billy English come riding over the top of the hill.

Yes, he knew at a glance that this was the man. He rode a slender-limbed black horse which picked its way daintily among the boulders of the hillside. And there was something masterful, something free, in his air which matched with Jack Granville's conception of what he must be.

He came closer. Jack made out a stalwart pair of shoulders, a head carried high, then a strongly featured face, big of jaw and wide of cheekbones. He was sufficient horseman himself to understand that the stranger was gliding his horse with a dexterous touch. Then the horseman sloped down to the narrow stretch of level ground and came up at a canter.

He halted his horse. He raised his hand in a graceful salute to Jack.

"How are you, stranger?"

Before Jack could reply Lady was in the doorway, and with a shrill shout came running to meet the other, calling: "Billy! Uncle Billy!"

Billy English slipped out of the saddle. He was revealed, when he stood on the ground, as a man of hardly more than the middle height, of a stoutly athletic build, but with not half of the generous power that lay in the limbs of such a man as Jack Granville. In appearance he looked the full of his thirty-two years, but not more. His glance was bright and quick moving. His step was more elastic and firm than is usual with cowpunchers who are only at home in the saddle.

He took off his hat; he shied it through the open door far behind the girl; he held out his arms to her with a shout and a laugh. And then Jack watched a queer thing. The laughter died away on their lips at the same time. The run with which they approached each other was checked to a halting walk. Surprise, uncertainty, was written in their faces. They flushed. They had started as though to fall into one another's arms. They ended by merely clasping hands.

And, "Lady—you've grown up—you're a woman," said Billy English.

And, "Billy—oh, Billy—aren't you a bit glad to see me?"

"A bit," said Billy, and Jack Granville could see the other rally himself with a great effort. "I'm the gladdest and the proudest man in the mountains—ain't I, Joe?"

"You're a damn fool otherwise," responded Joe calmly.

"And here's Jack Granville, a very, very good friend of mine," said the girl. "This is Uncle Billy English, Jack."

It seemed to Jack that one of those "verys" could

very well have been left out of that introductory speech. It brought Billy English whirling around upon him with a broad smile of hospitable cordiality. But it seemed to Jack that there was no real warmth to the smile. Billy English stepped closer to him and took his hand, and so doing it seemed, again, that he had swelled and increased strangely in size.

"I'm glad to know you, Mr. Granville," said Billy.

"I'm glad to know you," said Jack.

And in his heart of hearts he was groaning. For he knew that the worst had happened. They were meeting as rivals, not as guardian and suitor.

Chapter Three

Before supper was over she had entirely dropped the "uncle." It was plain Billy, delivered in a strangely constrained voice. Indeed, she rarely addressed Billy English at all. And neither did she talk much to Jack.

But now and then she raised her eyes and shot a frightened glance towards one of them or the other. It was plain that she realized all was not well. Just what was wrong she could not make out, however. She was waiting anxiously for developments, not knowing what to expect.

Only Joe Hoyt and King Charlie did not seem to feel that there was lightning gathering in the air. They carried on the burden of a conversation which would otherwise have been flat and dull most of the time. Towards the end of the meal, indeed, there was a brief exchange of interesting comment.

"You've never talked business in your letters," said Lady to Billy English, "but from the way you've supported me in the school I've felt that you must be growing rich, Billy. And yet—you haven't changed your way of living very much, so far as I can see. Tell me how you've prospered, and how the herd's grown? I think that stories of success are fascinating, don't you, Jack?"

"Yes," agreed Jack. "Mighty interesting."

Billy English, before he answered, looked steadily at one and then at the other with a joyless eye.

"Yes," he said finally, "the story of my success would be pretty interesting, I guess. But I don't tell stories well. Cows? Well, I haven't made my money out of cows."

"You haven't? I have been picturing your cattle mustering by thousands and thousands."

"H-m-m!" he answered. "I suppose you have."

"But how have you made so much?"

"By luck," said Billy.

"Oh, mining you mean?"

"A little."

"Well," she began, and stopped suddenly over an unspoken sentence as though she were afraid to continue.

Billy English had, in fact, fallen into a black reverie from which he did not rouse himself until the meal was ended. He left the girl and Joe Hoyt doing dishes and King Charlie playing solitaire gravely in the corner of the room. Then Billy English and Jack Granville went out into the night.

They sauntered to a little distance from the house and halted, as by mutual agreement beforehand, just at the point where the voices in the house dwindled to indistinguishable murmurs. There they paused and lighted cigarettes. The glow of these vaguely illumined their faces from time to time, he who spoke being always able to catch a fleeting glimpse of the listener.

"To bust right through the crust and get at the main facts," said Billy English, "I suppose that I can take it for granted that you've come out here with Lady to—er—to—"

The sentence which he had started so bravely dwindled to nothing.

"As a matter of fact," said Jack Granville, clearing his throat, "what I did come out here to do, Mr. English, was to ask you in so many words—er—for— that is to say—"

He was wrecked upon the same rocks which had received Billy English a moment before.

"You want to marry Lady, I guess," said Billy softly.

"I do."

"I could see that right off."

"Well, what's your answer?"

"My answer?"

"Yes, it seems that she won't take a step that you don't approve of."

But here Billy laughed without mirth in his voice.

"You see," he apologized, "when I sent her away to the East to school she was just a little youngster. And I'd read about skunks that would get hold of a girl like her and marry her—talk her into marrying them with smooth talk. Her pretty face—that was what I was afraid would get her into trouble. So I made her promise five years ago. I'd forgot about it until I seen you with her. Then I remembered. But that's like Lady. She'd never forget. She'd never go back on her word. She's a lady!"

He spoke more to himself than to the other.

"She is," said Jack Granville solemnly. "She's a lady. I see that you wouldn't forbid our marriage, then?"

English started.

"Forbid it? Lord God, no! I won't forbid it. Go ahead. I wish you luck—a pile of it!"

He reached out his hand, but Jack made no move to meet the extended shadow.

"You're a fine fellow, English," he said. "The yarn

King Charlie

that Louise tells me about you and what you've done for her is about the cleanest and the finest thing that I've ever heard of. And now here's my side of it. I love her. I love her more than I ever dreamed I could love a woman. I never knew how much until I see her out here where she was raised. That, somehow, finishes the picture of her. But I think enough of her to want her to do the right thing. And it pops into my head that you've spent all these years working to make a lady out of her—and that you've done it always thinking of her as a little girl. Suddenly she comes back to you—grown up—a young woman. English, I saw your face when you met her to-day. I don't blame you. All men are the same when they meet her. There's something about her that gets at a man's heart and opens it. And it was plain as day that she staggered you. You left her a girl and she came back a woman. All the difference that there is between a bud and a blossom—if you follow my meaning. Which all boils down to this: you may have changed a good deal. Well, English, I think that her duty is first of all to you. If it would make your life happier to have her—why—I'll never step between you. I'll fade out of the picture and give you no trouble at all."

He waited. There was no answer.

"Just think that over," said Jack. "And if you care to talk about it later, say the word. Otherwise I'll take silence to mean that you think I'd better start back towards the point from which I came."

He turned away, but a hand caught at his shoulder and turned him around.

"That's white man's talk," said Billy English. "I never heard a man come cleaner. It makes it easier for me to tell you that I would rather shoot my head off than come between you. I know that I'm not worthy of her."

"Not worthy of her—after spending sixteen years on her? Well, but that's aside from the point. No man's worthy of her when it comes down to that, I suppose. Still, English, I've got to tell you the whole truth. Louise won't, I know. There's too much distance between you two. She came back thinking that she could talk to you as though you were her father. She found out that it would be talking about an affair of the heart to a young stranger—that's the whole of it! Anyway, she won't talk straight to you. She'll say nothing. You'll give your consent, and then, perhaps, she'll marry me. Simply because she'll feel that she's given me her promise by innuendo, so to speak.

"But the point is, English, that I don't want to marry a girl unless she really loves me. And I welcome you in the lists to fight this thing out and make sure, one way or the other. It'd poison the rest of my life if I found out, after marrying her, that she had a secret fondness for you."

The voice of Billy English changed.

"Don't talk nonsense," he said.

"I'm not. I'm talking dusty, bitter facts. I wish to God they didn't exist!"

"You think, after all, that she—she might—"

"Good God, no! I'm not putting any words into her mouth or any thoughts into her head. You may be nothing to her at all in that way. But, there's always that damned 'but' to bother us. English, do you understand? This stuff about you not being worthy of her—"

"Don't talk about it," said Billy, "you know nothing about it and what I've done. But, Granville, you're young, you're fine looking, you're rich, but if I go out to fight this thing through, you'll wish me in hell before I'm through. You understand?"

"I'll take my chances. I understand."

"It's a fight to a finish, Granville?"

"To a finish."

"Partner, shake hands. When I seen her to-day, it tore me in two and let daylight into the inside of me. Here's a hard fight, a finish fight!"

Their hands closed.

Chapter Four

King Charlie absented himself from the house a little after supper and disappeared into the darkness whistling softly. The whistling died away.

Inside the shack Joe Hoyt was rudely monopolizing the company of the girl and thinking nothing of it. Her presence was sunshine. What wrong was there in sitting in the sun? So he continued to sit there and talk at a great rate, pouring upon her questions as to her life during all those years she had spent away from the mountains.

"But you ain't changed none; you're still a mountain girl," he would end every outburst of questioning, and she would answer meekly: "I'm still a mountain girl, Joe."

"Why, sure you are," Joe would say. "When folks once get this in their blood, they never really get it out, eh?"

"No, it's a fever—only it's a good fever. It keeps you on fire, but you never burn up!"

This comparison pleased Joe immensely.

"Look what she's gone and learned, Billy!" he shouted. "Did you hear that one? Why, she's as plumb full of ideas as tickle grass is plumb full of stickers."

In the meantime, Billy English and Jack Granville sat in the background and maintained a polite but halting conversation. Their eyes were far busier than their tongues. For they were drawing up a sort of silent schedule of comparisons.

As for Jack Granville, when he made the proposal for an open contest for the favour of the girl, he had felt, in the bottom of his heart, that this was a fine act of generosity which sounded like a great deal but which really meant nothing at all; for after a certain amount of success which he could not have avoided with girls if he had tried, there had been born in him a degree of confidence. At least, he could not but feel that he would not be overtaxed to outdistance this dusty, brown-faced, illiterate fellow of the mountain desert.

But since they had come back into the light of the lamp in the shack, his opinion began to change.

Billy English sat in the corner crossed legged upon the floor because there were not enough chairs to go around, and because he insisted that chairs meant nothing in his life. Indeed, he seemed perfectly comfortable and did not shift once. He was at work patching a bridle, working over it with an awl and waxed thread with the most painstaking care, for he was cutting a worn place out of one strap and sewing in a strong piece to replace it.

"I could buy a new bridle for half the cost of the time that I've put in on this one," he confessed, "but then a bridle is a good deal like a gun—one you know and one your hoss knows is worth a dozen strange ones."

Jack Granville remained fascinated by the play of the long, active fingers. All the rest of the man seemed rather heavily built, considering his inches; but his hands were finely finished in every detail, and they moved with such a light deftness that Jack began to look at his companion more carefully, searching his face as, in the old days, he had searched the face of the star in the opposing football line through which he intended to crash his way to many a substantial gain, and he felt that if this man were in football togs on a football field he would stand out among the rest—would be the dangerous enemy to be watched. His respect for Billy English increased with every instant. Then, now and again, at long intervals, the head of the cow-puncher raised a little, and he would flash one piercing glance at the girl on the other side of the room. Even seen in profile, those glances carried a world of meaning, which was by no means lost to Jack Granville.

He was about to open a close conversation with his rival when there sounded from the distance of the night a sharp, small whistle, twice repeated. The sound brought Joe Hoyt and the girl to their feet, and Billy English moved also, but with a difference. Without fully straightening, he lunged to his feet, scooped cartridge belt and holster, saddle, and bridle from the floor and, still without rising to his full height, he lunged for the door.

He whisked out of sight, leaving Jack Granville amazed. There had been something catlike in all the motions of Billy English. They had been both soundless and swift to an incredible degree. Once, in his Freshman year, he had seen a lithe half-back of the Crimson team who swooped upon the line in even such a manner—like a swift, silent-winged hawk, ready to clip past, tackle, or swerve around the end, elusive as a shadow to tackle, solid as steel when finally shocked against.

"What—" began Jack Granville. "What's up? What's happening, friends?"

"Not a thing that you can help," said Joe Hoyt.

"You stop worrying—stop talking. Keep your mouth shut and know nothing. That's the way you can help. Now, mind you, I want you to do what I say."

He had slumped to the centre of the floor. He, also, had oddly changed from the sluggish, dull-eyed fellow of a moment before. His eyes were on fire. His great body was tensed. He held their attention with every movement of his head or hand. Granville himself felt that he was caught and held in a vice.

"When they come in," said Hoyt, "you ain't seen Billy. He ain't been here. You don't know where he is. You don't know when to expect him back. Is that all clear?"

"But why—" began Granville.

The other turned upon him with a snarl.

"Look here, tenderfoot," he said, "if I got to waste time giving you reasons, I'll just bust you in two so you can't talk and put you away quiet till you're needed again. Don't forget that. The thing for you to do is what you're told."

Never in his life had big Jack Granville been talked to in this manner, and he could never have dreamed that, being so talked to, he would submit. But now he said not a word in protest. He sensed a grim justice in the attitude of the giant, and, also, he suddenly knew that the huge-handed fellow could do exactly as he threatened—break him in two!

He looked to the girl to see what her attitude would be. He was surprised to see that she was not white and shaking. Her silence rather proceeded from an alert readiness to do as she was told to do—a readiness to help when the moment for help arose. All at once she had fitted into her old gingham outfit—she had stepped away from the girl of silks and soft manners and smiling lips. She had become capable of, he knew not what; but he knew that she was significant, that she cut into his heart with new meanings.

"Listen!" said big Joe Hoyt.

He held up his hands. As though in answer to that

signal—a stagey thing to hear—hoofs began drumming in the distance, rushing suddenly closer until, with a storm of noise and quick shouts, what seemed a score of horsemen darted past the building.

"There he goes," shouted one of the stentorian lungs. "Sam—Pete—Lefty—drop back to the house and—"

The roar of hoofs and the speed with which they whipped into the distance cut off the rest of the speech; but enough had been said to tell Jack Granville that some body of men, most likely a posse acting in the name of the law, had come out to find no less a person than Billy English. And that warning whistle which had informed Billy of the impending danger had come from wise old King Charlie, who had walked away into the darkness after dinner.

No sooner had he come to these conclusions than horses returned to the door of the house, and then three men crammed through the doorway, men with naked revolvers in their hands. The first, bow-legged, waddling of motion, carried a big blue-barrelled weapon in either hand.

"Here, you," he snapped. "Hoyt—and you, there, in the fancy rig—shove up your hands. Go through those boys, Lefty."

Lefty, gaunt of form, sidling of step, crossed the floor and removed from the clothes of Hoyt a huge Colt which had been stowed there quite unsuspected so far as Jack was concerned. Then he went to Jack Granville and patted his pockets.

"He's clean," he said, turning back to the short man who had given the orders.

"All right, folks," said the other, "you can put your hands down; but, mind you, no funny work with your hands. We're going to keep our eyes on your and keep our guns handy. We've stood by and watched a pile of queer things happen in these parts, and now it's about time that they stopped."

"I dunno what you mean—" began Hoyt with a frown.

"Shut up, Hoyt," said the short man sternly. "You know mighty well what I mean. Lying ain't going to do you no good. One of these days the only thing that'll do you any good will be that thick neck of yours when the rope is strangling around it."

Joe Hoyt attempted to answer. He merely scowled at the intruder, who now walked straight up to Jack Granville until only inches separated them. From this position he rocked back his head and stared up into the face of the latter.

"Big, ain't you?" he said.

"I suppose," said Jack, "that I'm large enough."

"You are, eh?" snapped the man of the bowed legs. "Well, son, I want you to know that a forty-five slug is a fine leveller and that you're in damn bad company here with that yegg Joe Hoyt and that safe-cracker Billy English."

There was a faint exclamation from the girl, but it was drowned in the angry response of Jack Granville.

"Look here, my friend," he said, "what right and business you have here I don't know, but the fact remains that you've come into this house without a warrant for an arrest or without a search warrant. You've shown weapons and you've given orders. Now, sir, let me see your legal authority for your actions."

This speech caused the other to step back a little with a smile. Now he nodded.

"Here's the judge that issued the order," he said.

He patted his revolver, which he had put back into his holster. The other two had done the same thing. Then blind fury swarmed into the brain of Jack Granville. He felt that he was being manhandled. He was being manhandled in the presence of the woman he loved.

Without a word, he jerked up his ponderous fist.

King Charlie

It cracked the bow-legged man just under the tip of his chin, which snapped his head far back and then sent his whole body lunging in the same direction, but before he had fallen a foot, the long left arm of Jack had darted out, piston like, at the next victim.

He was just a shade too late, however, for tall Lefty twisted out of the way, a gun flashing into his hand with the most uncanny speed. That weapon he now swung in the air, the long, heavy barrel cracked along the side of Jack's head—and a black curtain dropped over the latter's mind.

Chapter Five

He wakened with a feeling that he had been asleep for an hour. In reality hardly a second elapsed before he was sitting up, his head singing, and a lump rapidly rising on the side of his head, but otherwise none the worse off for his adventure. The bow-legged man was just in the act of scrambling to his feet. Joe Hoyt was halting where he had started to rush to the help of Granville and had been stopped by having a gun pointed in his direction. Jack came back to his feet.

In a corner of the room he saw Louise standing. She had not moved in the midst of the commotion. Neither did she move now. She remained perfectly cool, her colour neither white nor red. And, worst of all, her attention was not at all centred upon him, but impartially took in the entire situation.

Sam, the bow-legged man, was shaking his head to clear it, and grinning with surprising good nature at Jack.

"Never try that again, son," he said. "You got a kick

like a mule's hind leg in that fist, but no mule could ever kick me twice and keep a whole hide. I got a nervous gun that comes right out and begins asking questions. How come that you didn't get your fool hide punctured, anyway?"

"I seen he was a tenderfoot," said Lefty, who had dropped his gun back in its holster once more and was now rolling a cigarette. "I seen he was green, and besides, it sort of tickled me to think of one gent with his bare hands starting out to tackle the three of us— by surprise! I just slung my Colt and rapped him alongside the head and eased him into a short nap— that's all!"

"If he was Billy English himself," said the third man, who all this time had hung in the doorway as a sort of rear-guard and reserve force, "he couldn't have done that very well. But the point is, that he ain't Billy English."

Jack Granville crimsoned to his aching temple. It was the first time in his young life that he had been unfavourably compared with any other man so far as athletic feats were concerned. And it galled him to the soul to hear his prowess made light of in the presence of the girl. Had they been in the far East it would have been bad enough. But out here in the mountains, for some reason, it was incomparably worse. It was an abiding disgrace. He fixed a baleful eye upon Lefty.

To his surprise, the latter was looking upon him with undisguised favour.

"It sure tickles me to see a bulldog with the fighting grit like that," said Lefty. "Partner, the next time I come to windward of a shot of moonshine, I'll be drinking to you!"

He waved his new-lighted cigarette as though it had been a filled glass, and then blew a stream of smoke at the ceiling. Sam, also, showed not the slightest malice. They seemed to take this rather as a pleasant diversion than as a combat in which several men had come within an ace of death. For certainly if the diversion which Jack started had lasted long enough for giant Hoyt to come into action, there would have been breaking of bones.

"This will all be looked into," fumed Jack Granville. "I'll have this matter taken up, and it will not be allowed to rest until I've run you to the ground, all three! By the Lord, if there's a law in this land—"

He stopped. He was aware that all the three were smiling. .

He stepped back and saw that Lady also was smiling. It was bewildering! It was intolerable! Did they actually make open mock of the law of the United States?

"Sure," said Lefty soothingly, "most of 'em begin to act up like that when they feel the rope, but after they've got rope burned a couple of dozen times, they learn different. Don't you worry, son. If you stay around these parts long enough you'll get all the law that you want. Matter of fact, you'll get so much law that you'll be sick of the whole thing. Eh, Sam? Eh, Pete?"

Sam and Pete chuckled. Sam now crossed the room and accosted the girl by removing his hat in a great sweep towards the floor.

"Ma'am," he said, "I'm sure sorry that that tenderfoot had to start all that fuss. But there's some folks that never know when a fight ain't in order."

And to the unutterable astonishment of Jack Granville, Lady burst into a hearty peal of laughter.

He could not believe it. He turned bolt around and glared at her and made sure. Yes, she was indeed laughing at him. Or was she laughing simply out of the gaiety of her heart—a joyousness inspired by the arrival of an armed posse which was hunting for necks to stretch. Altogether it was a most amazing and bewildering proceeding.

Before he had a chance to think further upon the

matter, there was a returning roar of hoofs, though in a diminished volume, as they came back at a slower rate of speed. In another moment there was again the huge bass voice which they had heard roaring orders before.

"Stay out here, boys, unless you got some special errands inside. I'm going inside and find out what I can find out."

A tall and magnificently framed man stepped into the doorway. He boomed a vast greeting.

"Well, Joe Hoyt, the bird flew again, and this time just when I had my hand ready to scoop him up, damn the luck!"

"I dunno what you mean," said Joe.

"Why hell—," began the other.

"Cheese it, sheriff," cautioned Lefty in an agony of concern, and he pointed out Lady in the corner.

The sheriff started as though a knife had been slipped into the small of his back. His hat came off. His face mantled in crimson.

"It's Lady," he gasped. "It's Lady come back to us."

He crossed the room. He took her hand.

"Most likely you don't remember me?" he said. "Most likely you don't hitch me up with what I used to be when I knowed you before, Lady?"

"I remember you perfectly, sheriff. And I'm glad to see that they've elected such a good man for the office."

"I'm sorry to be here," he said slowly. "But it's duty that brings me."

"What duty?" she asked. "I've heard some strange talk here before you came."

"Was Billy English just here before I came by?"

"Who? Billy? I haven't seen him."

Jack Granville studied her face. She told the lie with the most perfect abandon. Granville admired her with all his heart. As for the sheriff, he drew back a little from her and bowed with an old-fashioned gallantry that it warmed the heart of Jack to see. He was beginning to feel that there were even points of manners which he could learn here in the wild West.

"I'm not trying to drag any information out of you," said the sheriff formally. "But I think that I may as well tell you as much as I know for the sake of sparing you embarrassment. We could not get in touch with the man who just started from the general direction of this house before we arrived. In fact, he left us behind so quickly that we formed the conclusion that it must be black Twister which was running away from us."

"H-m-m," said the girl thoughtfully. "Why couldn't it have been someone else on that horse?"

"Because there's only one Twister and, as everyone in the mountains knows, there's only one man who can ride the horse—and that man is Billy English. Twister killed two before Billy got him. But, of course, you know all that."

"I don't know it," said the girl, immensely troubled. "I've been gone five whole years, you know. And during that time, Billy has simply written kind, chatty letters, without giving me any real news. And now I come back and find that he runs away from the sheriff—why, that isn't like the Billy I used to know."

"You admit that he was here, then, and that he left when he was warned of my approach?"

She shook her head violently.

"I admit nothing. I deny everything," she said fiercely. "Good heavens, sheriff, you aren't asking me to talk against dear old Billy?"

The sheriff made a wry face.

"It's a bad business—the worst that I was ever mixed up in, I guess. I know, of course, everything that Billy English has done for you. But these boys that I've brought over here with me don't know a thing about you. Five years ago they'd never heard of him. It's since that time that Billy has become known. It's since that time that Billy began to ride over on the far side of the range and live a double

life. He was a cowpuncher on this side of the crest
and on the other side he was a—well, I won't say
what."

"But I want to know!" cried Lady. "There have
been all sorts of strange remarks made in here to-
night, and now I've got to learn the truth, and you're
the man to tell it to me. Oh, you won't shock me. You
need not fear that—for if you accuse him of anything
terrible, I'll know that Billy simply didn't do it."

The sheriff drew a great breath.

"All right, then," he said, "I'll do what I can to clear
it up; but it ain't a cheerful job, Lady. The point is
that Billy got tired of working the cows on his ranch.
He had to have more action than that, and he found
it by looking into the inside of the safes of other folks,
and that scoundrel, Joe Hoyt, yonder, showed him
the way."

Lady stepped back, looked from the sheriff to Joe,
and back again.

"Joe," she sobbed, "it isn't true?"

"True?" said Joe Hoyt. "Of course not. Of course
not."

But his voice was husky, and he kept his fascinated
eyes fixed upon the sheriff.

"Joe has a prison record that speaks for itself," said
the sheriff. "About Billy—well, facts are facts. He
hasn't been arrested yet, but that's partly because he
has friends like King Charlie and Joe Hoyt, who give
him word when the sheriff comes near, and partly
because Twister is a hoss that can outrun anything
in these parts. But that he's guilty—why, nobody in
the mountains can deny it, not even the best of his
friends.

"And he has friends, loads and loads of 'em that
would cut their throats if it would make Billy breathe
any easier. He's never done any dirty work. There are
no killings on his record. He's never picked out the
safes of some happy-go-lucky savings banks with the
nickels of widows and kids in 'em. He's gone after

the hard stuff, and he's got it. And that, Lady, is the long and short of it."

Lady had retreated until her shoulders and her head rested against the wall, and there she leaned with her face sickly white and her eyes closed. She seemed for an instant about to faint, and Jack Granville stepped a little closer to her. But then her eyes opened suddenly. She stared helplessly at the sheriff.

"Sheriff Watson," she said heavily, "it's true."

"Every word," he said. "I wish it weren't—partly for your sake and partly because Billy is the squarest man in the world in lots of ways. But now he travels with a price on his apprehension for the law."

"A price on his head!"

"He has. He's been as slippery as an eel in a coarse net, and now the Governor himself has got interested. The whole State is following the chase, and Billy has taken up the dare, you might say. He makes it a point of honour never to run into another State. He keeps inside our boundaries as though they were marked out with stone walls, and he's come back here time and again. That's the whole truth of the story, Lady, and the best thing that a friend of Billy's could do for him would be to tell him to go in and give himself up to the law."

He paused again, backed away, and faced Hoyt.

"Joe," he said, "we're watching you close. We have our suspicions about where you were on the night of the tenth of last month. Oh, you know what I mean. But—take care of yourself. Boys, come along with me."

Chapter Six

Jack Granville would never forget that scene, and that which followed the mounting of the wild riders as they mustered at the door of the shack for their return ride. The sheriff was the last to climb into his saddle. Seeing Jack step out of the house, the sheriff turned towards him.

"Young man," he said, "I don't know who you are, but while your record may be as clean as a whistle, I give you one word of good advice—if you want to keep it clean, get away from this house and those that live in it."

"Thanks," said Jack dryly, "and in return, sheriff, I wish you better luck on your next try."

"The next try is a matter of different colour altogether," said the sheriff simply, as though he had not detected the mockery in the voice of the other. "Miller and Warden are loose together; Miller and Warden and all that's left of the break."

"Miller and Warden?" echoed Jack.

The names started suddenly back upon his memory. It had not been six months before that the papers had been full of their daring escape from prison. Now, once more, they had not only escaped, but they had managed to escape together. It seemed impossible, and Jack said as much.

"It sounds queer," said the sheriff, "but what they've done since they got out is queerer still. They had eight men with them when they started. They've still got four, I think, and they've left a trail of murders behind 'em broad enough for a blind man to follow, you'd think, but still they can't be caught. They are spotted one place; they disappear the next. But, good-night, stranger. Good-night, Lady. So long, Hoyt."

With a cheerful wave of the arm, he threw himself into the saddle and rode off slowly up the hillside among his men. Perhaps they had ridden all of the day for the sake of making this blow at Billy English after dark; but now they rode back with their failure, uncomplaining.

Jack Granville went back into the house and found that Lady was pacing up and down the floor, while Joe Hoyt had retreated at once to a corner and sat there rolling a cigarette and frowning heavily.

Jack went to the girl.

"I'm mighty sorry," he said quietly.

She turned to him with despair in her eyes.

"Do you see what it means?"

"It means that poor Billy English is a goner sooner or later. I suppose it means that."

"It means that he's put his head into the noose for my sake."

"For you?"

"Oh, Jack, can't you see? He was perfectly happy here on the ranch until I went away to school. I remember writing back to him and telling him what some of the girls had—not in envy, but in wonder that there could be so much money in the whole world—and poor Billy must have thought that I could not be happy without the same things, and see what he did. He wrote back that he'd made some good deals; that business was beginning to boom; that he thought he could fix me up with plenty of fine clothes and most of the other things that I wanted.

"I replied that I didn't need anything like that at all; but he insisted. Money began to flood in, and presents. He made me buy this bracelet. He kept asking. I had to tell him that I had bought it, at last. No matter what I asked, he gave it to me. And how was he getting the money for those gifts? Oh, Jack, think of that!"

Jack Granville bowed his head.

"And that was the meaning," went on the girl, "of his refusal of permission for me to come West. That was why he insisted that I stay in the East. If I had vacations to spend, he wanted me to spend them abroad—he wanted me to coin all my opportunities into good times. Why? Because he knew that at any time—a bullet—might put an end to my source of income."

She buried her face in her hands and groaned. Joe Hoyt raised his lion's head and listened, vaguely troubled.

"Don't you go bothering Lady, stranger," he growled at Granville.

"How can he ever be paid for what he has done?" asked the girl bitterly.

"There's one way to begin," said Granville, "and that's for you to let me repay him for every cent that he's spent on you. I have money. You know that the family has so much money that it's of little consequence to us, really. Let me use enough of it not only to repay everyone who has lost a penny through Billy English, but to keep them from coming into courts to prosecute him."

She shook her head.

"Money can't repay him. Money can't hire the days

and the nights and the years of danger he has spent for my sake. Oh, think of what he has done! What a terrible, and a wild, and a noble thing to do. It was the sort of a thing that a child would do—a great, wonderful child. Wasn't it, Jack?"

He regarded her with a profound concern. Much as he admired certain of the qualities of Billy English, he felt that it was not at all to his interests to see the girl swept off her feet by such an emotion as that which had now seized her.

"It's easy to wave away that much money, Lady," he said, forcing a smile. "But even if you can't repay him spiritually, still it seems to me—"

"Besides, he's been outlawed because he refused to stand trial, don't you see? You can't buy him off. Don't you understand what outlawing means?"

She spoke almost savagely to him, as though he were an enemy for not understanding at once.

"It means," she continued rapidly, "that he has no recourse to anyone when he is pressed against the wall. It means that if anyone wants what Billy has, they can take it—at the point of a gun. He's only up for a reward payable for his apprehension. But if he's killed by treachery, can't the traitors simply say that they did it trying to arrest him in the name of the law? Oh, don't you see what it means, Jack?"

He did see, and what he saw sickened him. It was useless to speak of money where money could not help. So he stepped back to let the first torment of her grief and shame pass.

And up and down the floor stalked poor Lady, breathing quickly, desperate as she saw more and more clearly what had been done for her sake.

It was then that a great idea came to Jack. He stopped the girl in a corner.

"Lady," he said, "suppose that you and I were to go to the Governor, and suppose that we were to lay before him the full details of the motives on account of which Billy English committed some of the crimes

King Charlie

attributed to him—don't you think that he might be induced to grant a pardon if I guarantee to repay every cent that was lost from the safes which Billy blew up?"

He added, as she paused in her walking, considering the suggestion eagerly: "My money—and your smiles—I think we'd wear the Governor down, Lady."

Suddenly she threw her arms around his neck.

"Oh, Jack," she cried, "God bless you for that!"

And she kissed him fairly on the lips and was away dancing with joy.

"Was that partly for my sake," asked Jack Granville a little sadly, "or was it all for Billy English?"

"For both," she said. "And when can we start?"

She ran to Joe Hoyt and roused him with a shout and a stamp.

"Joe Hoyt!"

"Well, well," said Joe, "I ain't deaf, Lady. What d'you want out of old Joe Hoyt? He's getting so old and so slow that he ain't much account to nobody no more."

"Nonsense!" cried the girl.

She darted to the stove. She came back bringing a heavy rod of iron which was used as a poker.

"Once," she said, "you could bend this between your hands, Joe. I'll wager you still can!"

The dull eyes of Joe gleamed.

"I ain't tried that for years," he said. "I reckon I couldn't budge it."

So saying he took it. Under his ample grasp the massive bar shivered like a dry straw. He took it in both hands, his arms straightened, his wrists bent in, he sighed through his set teeth as his massive shoulders swayed forward, and then the iron trembled slowly into a curve. The pressure was suddenly relaxed and the iron was cast clanging upon the floor.

"Well," said Joe, "I ain't much good now, but I can still do a few tricks, maybe."

Sweat had stood out on his forehead with that great effort. Now he smiled sheepishly up to the girl. She was laughing with her pleasure.

"Suppose that were a man," she said. "He'd have gone in the same manner. And now tell us the shortest way to the railroad."

"And why that?"

"Don't ask why—it would take too long to tell. We have to start."

"Through the Jeremina Valley, I guess. And then down to Jerico."

"Can you guide us?"

"I ain't been over the trails that way lately. King Charlie could do it a pile better. Where is Charlie now?"

"Here," said a voice.

They found that the veteran had returned and sat now on the doorstep.

"I know the Jeremina Valley," he said. "I could go down them trails with my eyes closed pretty near."

"Then you can guide us by night. And Joe—you'll go along in case emergencies come up?"

Joe Hoyt stretched his long, thick arms.

"I reckon I got nothing else to do," he said.

Chapter Seven

Up through the hills they pressed, a hard-riding quartet. King Charlie, oppressed with the stiffness of age and with an exercise to which he had never become truly accustomed—namely, riding—nevertheless, clung in the lead, showing the way after they left the broad sweep of the valley and came to the intricate tangling of ravines which lay among the crests of the range.

It was a region of vast rocks, in sections where there was no soil for trees or even shrubs to take root-hold; and again there were stretches of dense forest; and everywhere a myriad little streams kept babbling, or chanting, or roaring down the ravines. There was never a time when they were out of hearing distance of the voices of waterfalls splashing here and there.

Through that region, of course, the trails were as broken and as uncertain as the country itself. No one riding them on horseback could have acquired a familiarity equal to that of King Charlie, however. The old tramp had gone over every inch of those mountains, following the wanderlust which had driven him here and there over most of the rest of the country during his youth. He had gone on foot, and, therefore, every bit of the trails was familiar to him.

He led them by the most gradual ascent up to the summit, but at that the work was bitter for the horses, sulking at the beginning of labour when the day was ended. When the summit was gained there was no gradual descent beginning at once, but for a time they took the course of the water-divide, holding straight down it towards the Jeremina Pass. The name had once been Jeremiah, but having been once corrupted it remained in the new and more easily remembered form.

It was a little valley with abrupt sides. It would have been the general thoroughfare from one side of the range to the other had it not been that, from the direction in which the party King Charlie conducted approached it, the way was a continual series of ups and downs through a myriad ravines. Therefore they came at it from the side, and presently they were dropping down a precipitous trail where King Charlie got off his horse and walked very slowly in the lead, calling out warnings to the others concerning the irregularities which he encountered.

In this fashion they came down to the floor of Jeremina Valley, with a fairly clear and smooth passage now levelled before them. No lofty mountains arose in their path. The peaks of the range now lay behind.

They went on in that thick darkness of the early morning. A thin sheeting of clouds covered the sky and shut away the usual clear starlight of the mountains. They went guided rather by the sound of water which continued steadily upon their left, the voice of the little Jeremina River shooting swiftly down towards the wide plains below.

There had been little talking during that night ride.

King Charlie

Joe Hoyt never spoke at all, King Charlie only to mention some difficulty in the trail, and only now and then Jack Granville murmured something to the girl. Those murmurs were bits of encouragement. As a matter of fact, the big man began to feel, as the journey progressed, that this trip to the Governor of the State in quest of a pardon for Billy English was the best undertaking in which he could have taken a hand. When they reached the capital of the State, it would be hard indeed if the Granville powers could not exert some pressure upon the Governor. He would be able to appear in the very best possible light; and the girl would be made to feel how long and how strong are the arms of wealth.

At the same time, through this effort she could not but feel that she was repaying some of her debt of gratitude to Billy English, and that would leave her free to spend some time in thinking of her own welfare. In that case, might it not well be that she would turn to him who had accompanied her on the quest of mercy?

It warmed the very heart of the big youth to think of these things. In the meantime, he would battle with all of his great strength to help Billy English.

As he reached this conclusion, there was a faint exclamation from King Charlie, who went in the lead. They were now winding through a dense and lofty growth of trees, and though Charlie was only a few yards in the lead, he had passed from view.

"What's up, Charlie?" asked Joe Hoyt suddenly, and pressed his horse on.

Suddenly Jack Granville saw a shadowy figure leap from among the trees and hurl itself directly at Joe. The impact rolled the latter from his horse, and while the girl screamed, Jack turned to defend himself from a second attack. It was delivered by two men, one in front and one to the rear.

There was no time for him to draw a gun. He struck down the man who leaped from the front, but

285

at the same instant an arm was whipped around his neck from the rear and he was jerked back in a strangle hold. He rolled heavily from his horse and struck the ground, by ill chance, beneath the other—an impact which knocked the wind out of his body.

Before he could recover, his paralyzed hands were tied behind him, and he sat up, helpless, while the two who had downed him leaped in to handle Joe Hoyt.

Jack Granville could see what the latter was doing only dimly, on account of the darkness, and yet by the strain of groaning breath he knew that a man was being killed. Then, as horror cleared his eyes, he made out that Hoyt was tangled with the body of another man, and that that man was bent back, far back, in a strange position.

Then there was a dull, snapping sound, a short shriek, and the body fell away from the arms of Joe Hoyt. There was no need of daylight to be sure that the victim would never rise again. At the same instant, however, Joe was himself jerked to the ground by invisible hands. There was a moment of brief rolling and twisting. Then a man stepped beside him.

"He's tied fast enough!" was the first word spoken in the entire affray.

Joe had been snared in a lariat.

"Munroe's down," said a louder and more authoritative voice, "and, by God, if they've hurt Munroe, I'll tear them all in bits. Light up a fire—start up a fire in some of these dry leaves. Damnation, do I have to stand here all night begging somebody to do what I tell 'em to do?"

His voice had risen to a terrible roar with the last words. Then another answered hurriedly:

"Don't be a damned fool, pal. What good'll a light do? It'll just show them who we are, and you can tell what's happened to Munroe by just leaning over him and feeling for his heart. I just done that."

"Don't tell me that's the end of him!" thundered the other.

"The last of Munroe—it sure is; and now we've got the horses, let's go on."

"I'll see you in hell first. I'm going to have a look at Joe Munroe's face. It was me that started him out on the job that landed him in the pen. It was me that started him out of the pen along with us. He didn't want to come. He wanted to wait till his term was up and then go straight, and now I'm going to have a light and a look at his face."

"Light a match, then. A fire might be seen."

"Who is there to see it? There's nobody in this neck of the woods, I guess."

"We've just met four."

"You talk like a quitter, Mugs."

"Don't say that to me, Miller!"

"Why not? Who are you, Warden?"

The terrible names brought a faint cry from the girl, and this cry, in turn, brought a fearful volley of oaths from all the gang.

"They've spotted us by our damned chatter, now," said Miller, "and they'll learn no more if we light a fire."

It was done at once. Someone kicked together a pile of the leaves and lighted a match. All that the flame of the match illumined was a pair of horny, grimy hands that held it. The next moment it was buried under the leaves. The fire shone milk-white through the ascending column of the smoke. Then a red edging of fire appeared and ran pyramiding to the top of the pile. In another instant the leaves were all alight and the whole scene started brightly into view.

Chapter Eight

What Jack Granville saw was King Charlie lying on his face just at a swerve of the trail among the trees, Joe Hoyt lying swathed in the ample length of a lariat, and another figure twisted oddly and prostrate near by, while a villainous faced fellow held the arms of Louise.

That was what he saw at the first glance. The second was for the captors who had thrown themselves upon the party. That glance showed him, beside the man with Louise, four of the hardest countenances he had ever seen. Their clothes were picked-up misfits. Their hats, limp and battered by many a rain and ill usage, slunk above their eyes. Their faces were covered with beards of several days' standing.

One glimpse of them was sufficient to announce them as outlaws. They had the manner of wild beasts. They had the same shifty eyes and the same stealthy manner, even towards one another. This, then, was the party of Miller and Warden, Mugs Warden and Jeff Miller.

There was only one mystery hanging upon the mind of Jack. Why had not these murderers attacked with guns? Why had they chosen to make the assault with their bare hands? This thought was almost instantly answered.

"This is what comes of your damned fool idea of tackling them without the guns. This is what comes of your saying that a trail of dead men is sure to be followed. And now look where we are. There's a dead man here, and it's Joe Munroe, Miller—your own pal, Munroe."

This was addressed to one who was by far the largest of the party. He paid no attention to the speaker, but crossing to the fallen body, he dropped upon his knees beside it and put his hand upon the breast, only a moment, and then he dragged off his hat, rose, and glared around at the others.

"That'll put me in hell," he said huskily. "It's worse 'n everything else that I've done. I started Joe out— and here's the finish of him."

He whirled and glowered down upon Joe Hoyt.

"You'll pay me for it," he said. "I'll have that out of you."

Joe Hoyt had struggled until he attained a sitting posture. Now he regarded Miller steadily, unabashed, unfrightened. With an oath, the outlaw leaned and struck his fist heavily into the face of the helpless man.

There was a shudder of Hoyt's big body, a creaking of the ropes that bound him, and then he sat quietly as before, looking steadily up into the face of Miller. A thin trickle of blood ran down from his mouth.

That silence on the part of Hoyt seemed to Jack Granville more impressive than a stream of terrible oaths and threats of vengeance. Even big Miller, red-handed from a dozen known murders, stepped back before the silence of Joe. The recovery of King Charlie from his swoon gave him a chance to turn his anger in another direction.

The old man came staggering to his feet, calling out: "Look out, Joe. Murder!"

He was shouting now the warning which had been in his mind, but which he had been struck down before he could utter.

"Shut up that old fool!" cried Miller.

One of his followers balled a huge fist and shook it in King Charlie's face. The latter at once recovered his scattered wits.

"Lady!" he cried in sudden agony. "Where's Lady? If she's been hurt—"

There was a sign from Miller. His man knocked Charlie flat with a blow of his fist. The old fellow struck a tree-trunk in his fall, spun upon his face, and then slowly, slowly dragged himself to his feet.

"That's right, Larsen," said Miller. "Give him the same thing again if he tries to yap. We got to have silence. We got to have a chance to think."

King Charlie, utterly dazed, came swaying to his feet, and Granville, with a shout of horror, saw that the brutal Larsen was prepared to knock the old man down again. But now Lady twisted suddenly free from her captor and ran in between. She faced Larsen with fury.

"If I had a quirt," she said, "I'd flog every inch of the skin off your body—you cowardly dog!"

Larsen retreated slowly before her rage.

"We got to take care," he said. "We can't have a lot of noise and such things around here. You ask Miller if we can. We may be followed close right now, for all that I know. That yell of the old one's might of told them where we are."

She answered with a shrug of scorn and disgust.

"Make up your minds, Miller," broke in Jack at this point. "Your man is right. You're losing time. You have the horses. The way is clear ahead of you. Staying here won't bring Munroe back to life. The best thing you can do is to start on. You can leave us here, tied, if you want."

This logical presentation of the difficulties in the position of Miller and his best way out of them only brought a snarl from the outlaw, as he turned towards the speaker. "Come over here, Warden," he said.

Warden obeyed. The two leaders drew a little apart, speaking earnestly together, and only half veiling their voices.

"The point is this," said Warden, "a man can't hang any more 'n once. Why should we leave all of these to take up the trail after us? That is, as soon as the posse catches up with 'em?"

"One of 'em has to die," said Miller calmly, "and that's him that finished Munroe."

Here he turned and looked full at Joe Hoyt, and Joe Hoyt looked silently back at the outlaw.

The wind blew on the fire and threw a high tongue of flame up, and by that light Jack Granville saw a dim form at a distance among the trees facing towards them. His heart leaped. The beat of it quickened so fast that he looked fixedly down at the earth, for fear that his expression might betray his joy.

"I only wish," said Miller, "that we could cage him with a wild cat. That'd be a fight. And I'd be half of a mind to bet on his big hands against the cat's claws and teeth. If he ever got his hold he'd wring the varmint's neck."

That pleasant suggestion brought a great grin from Warden and the rest of the gang.

"We could take the girl up the trail and across the hills with us," said Warden. "As for the rest of them— why, I've already said that every one of us is sure to hang if we're caught. And we can't be hung more 'n once. Ain't that reasonable? Let's march these birds off to the river and drop 'em in. Ain't that easy? I ask you, Miller, is there anything wrong with that plan?"

The other villain considered the horrible proposal

with his head bent seriously to one side. And when he finally raised it, there was assent in his glaring eyes. He turned upon the other three, who were standing about making no pretence of giving advice to their leaders.

"Boys," he said, "line up there—"

The rest of his speech was lost upon the ear of Jack Granville. He was far too interested in the appearance of the shadow which had been drifting steadily closer and closer through the trees until now it was close, and, staring fixedly, Granville saw the stranger drift silently and with uncanny speed to a tree comparatively close by.

He was roused from his happy dream by the toe of a heavy boot which landed in his ribs. He obeyed an order to rise.

"Now, boys," said Miller, "I hate to do what I've got to do. But a man has a right to live, I guess—yep, a man sure has a right to live. You fellows get together—you old one and you other two—and march ahead right towards the sound of that river until—"

A period was neatly supplied to his sentence by the explosion of a revolver on the far side of the clearing, and Warden leaped high in the air, like a wolf which deceives its death wound, and his yell ended before his body struck the ground with a heavy thump.

Jack Granville, at the same instant, flung himself back and rolled into the shadow of a tree. All of the others, with the exception of Joe Hoyt, who had not yet been liberated from his rope so that he could join in the march, had imitated Jack's example.

Instantly the little clearing in the centre of which the fire burned was emptied of men. Even Lady had managed to spring back into the shadow of a trunk.

Around that clearing there were four desperate criminals now furious for vengeance. And against them were opposed only a girl and an unknown man whose hands were free. The others were worse than helpless.

Jack, rising to his knees, saw big Miller, crouching low, work from one tree to another, and the face of the outlaw was contorted with a black passion. At sight of Jack he whipped up his revolver and fired. But the shaking and strange light from the fire was not conducive to good shooting. The bullet hummed wickedly in the ear of Jack as he hurled himself back into the shelter of a bigger trunk.

There was a stifled curse from Miller to attest his failure. Then a twig crackled. The big criminal was circling to get in another shot.

For the rest that forest was as silent as night. For everyone knew that the slightest sound might bring a bullet his way. Indeed, a mere whisper of a sound behind Jack Granville made him twist his head, feeling that all hope was gone, and as he did so he saw Billy English glide out of one shadow and into another and coming up beside him.

One slash of a knife freed Jack's hands. Then a revolver was pressed into his hand.

"God bless you!" whispered Jack.

But to his amazement, he saw that there was no serious and drawn expression of anxiety in the face of the other. Instead, there was a blazing riot of happiness. He responded to the blessing with a quick pressure of his hand, and as silently as he had come, he faded back among the trees.

Chapter Nine

A shout and a rapid explosion of revolvers a few yards ahead of Granville showed that Billy English must have been sighted working among the trees. But the shooting almost immediately died away.

The same terrible silence fell over the place. And the odds were still two to one in favour of Miller and his men. Indeed, the odds were greater than that, for in the list of Jack Granville's accomplishments, good marksmanship with a revolver was not included. He could shoot, but he needed a clear light and a large target before he began to strike home.

Now he edged around his tree, wondering when terrible Miller, a dead shot, as he was reputed, would come in view, and when he came in view, how long would be the lease of life of the heir to the Granville millions?

His own shoulder must have come in view. A gun exploded. A bullet sliced the bark off the tree and clipped the shoulder of his coat, just barely pricking his skin.

He winced back—then suddenly changed his mind. For that was exactly what Miller would expect—that the man he had just nipped with a shot would shrink back to the far side of the tree, and the outlaw would be working around to get in a finishing shot as Jack shrank back from the first wound. So Granville began to edge rapidly around in the original direction of his progress. So doing, he suddenly sighted half of the body of Miller lying prone behind a neighbouring tree and far closer than Jack had dreamed.

He pushed out his revolver, steadied it, and fired.

It brought a yell from Miller, who twitched out of view. But instead of groans came a series of wild curses, followed, at once, by silence.

But now a gun exploded from another direction, and another bullet cut past Granville. It could not be that Miller had multiplied himself and was in two places at once. Another of the gang had worked towards the sound of the firing and had finally reached a strategically important position.

But what could Jack do? To swing around to the farther side of the tree meant placing himself in point-blank view of Miller; to stay where he was meant to be killed by the newcomer; and if he bolted from his place he would fall under the fire of both men. Once they had a fair target they would not miss, he knew. They had both failed at a small target in the uncertain light, but given half a chance and they would show the same fatal skill which they had demonstrated more than once before during their retreat after the break from the prison. For every killing there had been a new headline in the papers. For every headline there had been a fresh accumulation of the rewards which were heaped upon the heads of the criminals. New posses had started out on to the trail.

Suddenly the mind of Jack flashed back to New York, where he had reposed at ease over his breakfast paper reading of the Western murderers and their exploits. It seemed unreal, dreamlike, this actual picture of himself in the wilderness with the Miller gang trying for his life.

He made out the second assailant. At the same time he saw a strange phenomenon. A shadow took shape, crawling up a long, slant, dead tree-trunk which had been blasted out of place by some mighty storm and had wedged in this place before it fell completely to the earth. It occurred to Jack at first that this must be his second enemy, but at that moment the shadow detached itself from the trunk and dropped catlike to the ground.

Where it dropped there was a shriek, a sudden stir of limbs, and then silence again, and by something in that swift and terrible attack Jack was forced back to the memory of the fiercely joyous face of Billy English a few moments before.

This was the explanation. Heart and soul the terrible fellow had thrown himself into the battle, and by this catlike stroke he had turned the odds from four to two to three to two. Quite another story. If he could only get to Joe Hoyt and liberate that giant, all would be well, or if old King Charlie could only lend a hand; but that, he knew, was impossible. King Charlie's tremulous hands could never support a revolver long enough to send a bullet true to the mark.

A heavy footfall beat just once beyond the tree. He started up just in time to see the height of Miller looming above him. Maddened by the prolonged suspense of that battle, the outlaw had closed. He had even dropped his revolver. He carried a surer weapon for hand-to-hand battle. His knife flashed as he jerked it up for the stroke.

As for Jack, sprawled out, with only half of his muscles collected, taken wholly by surprise, he could only act instinctively, and that instinct told him to drive at the legs of the other.

And that he did. After the manner of the warriors of the football field, taught to stand all manner of battering and gain their feet after no matter what falls, he lurched forward, and with his broad shoulder struck the legs of the other just below the knee.

Miller had been reaching for the stroke; but that impact toppled him completely off balance. In another instant he was tangled with Jack at close quarters.

And here it was another story. Unskilled with deadly weapons, when it came to battle with bared hands Jack was at home. All the strength of Miller, being unscientifically disposed, went for nothing. In ten seconds his face was buried in the forest mould and both his arms were twisted around behind his back. By a mere sharp pressure up Jack could break both of the arms of the criminal at the shoulders.

That he did not do it and, leaving a physical wreck behind him, rush on to find another victim was simply owing to his instinct for fair play. It was impossible for him to destroy a helpless opponent.

In the meantime, there was a sudden crashing among the trees, which began to grow fainter and fainter. A revolver barked twice. Then the voice of Billy English shouted cheerfully:

"They're done for. Two of 'em gone! Jack, how are things with you? Lady! Lady! Where are you?"

In two minutes they were assembled again, in the clearing, and a handful of leaves thrown upon the dying fire gave them light enough to compute their casualties.

King Charlie had a bruised head where he had been struck down, Joe Hoyt's mouth was split from the blow of Miller, and the ribs of Jack Granville were bruised.

But that was all. Lady was unhurt, and in addition they had recruited terrible Billy English to their party. His whistle brought in the black horse,

Twister, from among the more distant trees.

His story was quickly told. He had distanced the pursuit with the greatest ease, and he had then turned his course towards the upper mountains, following directly on the heels of the posse; because that, as he had learned before, was always the safest way to go.

Turning off at last, he had been giving Twister a long and needed rest when he made out a party of four horsemen passing through the night. He was consumed with curiosity, and slipping ahead down the probable trail which they would follow, he had left Twister at a distance, and coming close to the trail he had heard them talk as they passed him, and thereby recognized the party for his friends.

Why he did not announce himself to them at once he did not know. But a freak of fancy had kept him from doing this, and that freak of fancy, in turn, had enabled him to strike in from the outside and liberate them from Miller's gang.

In the meantime, they were ready to go on. They left behind them Munroe and Warden and Shrugue. They took with them Miller himself. As for the other two who had escaped, without the brains of Warden and Miller to direct them, they would doubtless be run to earth within the week.

They placed Miller between the horses of Hoyt and King Charlie, and with Billy English for a guide they went on again down the trail. Lady and Jack Granville naturally fell in behind. As for Billy, he simply announced that he would leave them at the next town. He had learned from Granville of the goal of their journey and, though he expressed doubt as to its feasibility, he did not attempt to dissuade them.

"The trouble is," he said, "that the sheriffs in these parts are mighty stubborn. They've been after me for quite a while, and, now they've formed the habit, I don't know how they're going to give it up, and they'll have something to say to the Governor if he wants to pardon me."

"But they've nothing against you, Billy," Lady had pleaded. "Tell me that they've nothing against you."

"I could tell you that," said Billy English soberly, "but I'd be telling you a lie. Lady, they've got plenty against me—plenty. I've busted enough safes to be run up for it a dozen times. I'm sorry, I know what you think—that you've been educated on stolen money—but I want you to look at it this way, Lady. You were such a plumb fine kid that you deserved the best the world could give you—the world owed you that—and all I did was to step in and act as a sort of purchasing agent, you see."

And as he said it he laughed gaily.

That laughter continued after they had stretched their party out along the trail once more.

"When we bring in big Miller," Jack Granville was assuring the girl, "we'll bring in the thing that will make the Governor pardon Billy."

She did not seem to hear him.

"Listen!" she said.

"Well?"

"Don't you hear?"

"I hear Billy singing down the trail there ahead of us. Is there anything else?"

"Isn't that enough? Don't you see what it means? It means that he doesn't care. It means that he's fallen so in love with his own wild way of living that he'll never be able to go straight again, and all because he wanted to give me—"

Her voice choked.

"Hush," said Jack. "If he hears you talk like that it will drive him mad. No matter what Billy English does, it'll be nothing that he really thinks is very bad. I've seen only a little of him, but I've seen enough to know that."

The girl waited a moment before she could speak again.

"I know all that," she said. "It's just beginning to dawn on me. Billy is only a child in one way; he really doesn't think that it's very wrong to steal. He doesn't take from the poor. He takes from the rich. And they guard their money with steel safes and armed men, and he matches his wits against them and beats them.

"So it looks to Billy like a legitimate game—particularly since all the profits have gone to support me in luxury. Of course, he knows that it's legally wrong and that the penitentiary is waiting for him if he's caught. But still it's more of a game with him than it is a crime. And some day—if he's cornered—suppose he should fight for his life to get away—he's such a terrible fighter—there would be a killing—and then—"

"You'll have yourself in hysteria in another moment," cautioned big Jack Granville. "Nothing like that is going to happen, you see. He's going to give up his wild ways and—"

"Jack, you don't know the West!"

"What has the West to do with it?"

"Simply that there are animals out here that nothing can tame—wolves, you know!"

And Jack Granville fell silent. Ahead of him the joyous voice of Billy English rose and floated back to them.

Chapter Ten

The Governor was a luckless man.

In the first place the powers of the great Granville family beset him. Not that he was cudgelled by fear of political results if he refused—politically he was a rarely fearless man. But every day or so another letter from another eminent man arrived for him, pressing upon his attention the fact that William English was really not guilty of any specially heinous crimes—that is, crimes which could not be overbalanced by his services in the matter of breaking up the Warden-Miller gang.

Of course the Governor shook his head and scowled at these letters, but he could not help being annoyed by them. They were all from men he hoped to know better when, if fortune so willed it, he went up to the United States Senate the next year. Washington was very near to New York and not so very far away from Boston.

In his own heart of hearts, however, he was con-

vinced that William English had far better spend the
rest of his life in prison. The criminal instinct, the
Governor held, was like the instinct for pretty clothes
in women—it was ineradicable.

But in the meantime, the pressure of not only famous men was brought to bear upon him, but also
he was subjected to a severe strain by the public
Press.

A clever reporter had attached to the name of William English the title "Knight Errant of the Mountain Desert." And that title stuck fast to him.
Henceforth he was referred to as the "Knight of the
Mountains." And long, long articles were written
about his exploits, his gallantry, his contempt for
danger. Much was made of a thousand little details
of his life; such, for instance, as the time he rode a
thousand miles and entered a town full of danger to
him in order to restore to a poor man money belonging to him which had been in a safe which English had looted.

That story thrilled the hearts of the readers. And
there were other stories to match—plenty of them.
When the reporters ran out of facts they blithely
leaned an ear to the thousand repeaters of hearsay
who spring up like mushrooms over night to whisper
tales about famous men. From these they learned
most wonderful things about William English.

In the meantime, while all of this was going on,
there was a third source of annoyance for the poor
Governor as he struggled on to do his bounden duty,
and that was the pressure exerted by lovely Louise
Alison Dora Young.

Of course she had no sooner appeared in the town
than she found friends who had known her in the
East. Through them she met the Governor's two
daughters. And the Governor's two daughters, being
hearty lasses more prone to swing golf clubs and
wield tennis rackets than to toss social chatter about
the circle at high tea, promptly decided that Lady

represented all that was charming and graceful and worthy of imitation in woman.

They placed her upon an altar and offered up incense which was constantly in the nostrils of the Governor when he entered his own home. This enraged him. And when the story of how English had taken the orphan and given up his life to raising her was told, the Governor so far forgot himself as to swear in the presence of the ladies.

The fact was that he was touched to the heart. It actually dimmed the gubernatorial eye to hear the tale. It haunted him during his office hours and set him smiling to himself during the lunch-time.

Indeed, had William English himself kept quiet, all would have been well, but that irrepressible rider insisted upon taking up his quarters near the State capital. Just where he was it was hard to tell. But it was known that he appeared here and there in the vicinity, and it was more than once rumoured that he was actually making his entry into the town itself whenever he pleased.

The sheriff nearly went mad with sorrow and rage. He himself would willingly have sat still and allowed the English case to be terminated in the mind of the Governor, one way or the other, before he took action. Besides, he was by no means inclined to go out and arrest a man whom the public was beginning to look upon as a hero.

If only Billy English would stay quiet!

But no. It actually seemed as though that strange fellow *feared* to be pardoned and wished to get in as much action as possible. He would not get away to the cover of the distant hills, and therefore the poor sheriff had to order out his reserves, so to speak. He wore himself ragged. He ruined the force immediately at his disposal. He had to conduct a man-hunt with posses full of men who wanted to shake hands with Billy, not shoot him!

But the climax of all of this was, one bright morning, that the Governor sat down to his desk and read through and through the record of terrible Jeff Miller.

It was a black, black tale. It began with petty thefts. It grew to burglary. It advanced swiftly to footpad work, and finally a butchered victim who attempted to fight for his wallet and its small store of money. It grew from this to gunwork at so much a head—in fact, as the story progressed the Governor began to feel small hearted to think that such a devil incarnate should be a member of the human race. And at length he threw the paper from him with an exclamation of disgust and rose and stood before his window with a broad shaft of the sunshine falling upon his face and upon his mind.

After all, was there not all the difference between Jeff Miller and William English that there was between noisome night and the good warm sunshine itself?

The Governor, at least, thought that there was. What had William English done that was really worthy of being called a crime when it was compared with the record of Miller?

And the Governor made up his mind.

Like Elizabeth of England, he knew how to make a concession in such a manner that he extracted from it the last possible ounce of credit.

First he pressed a button for his secretary.

"Jim," he said with a scowl, "please go for Miss Louise Young and bring her here in the car."

Jim, keen of eye at the thought of riding in the same seat with no less a person than Lady, disappeared at once. Then the Governor sent for the reporters.

He told them what he was going to do. He told them what he was going to say. And when Lady came, she marched to the tune of clicking cameras into his office and out again, and then they gave her a cheer as she departed, ere they rushed to their offices to write stories headed: "Justice *versus* Beauty!" or "Love or Gratitude!"

Any story was good enough for the front page as long as it gave an excuse to exhibit the picture of Lady with it.

As for Lady herself, she did not speak once to the secretary on the return trip. She could not. She was crying every bit of the way openly and unashamed, in the manner which is best for the heart.

Chapter Eleven

Profound silence reigned in the little cottage. It was a section of the town's best and largest hotel, arranged on the summer scheme of a number of cottages grouped around a central eating-house. Here Jack Granville and Lady and King Charlie himself and big Joe Hoyt were seated studying the floor.

Jack Granville had done his best to fill up the interval of waiting. Then King Charlie had come to the rescue with some thrilling narratives of his exploits on the road. But even the narrative vein of the old tramp gave way at last and silence covered the party once more.

For it was after ten and they had been waiting since noon to hear from Billy English. No sooner had Lady brought the pardon from the Governor than King Charlie was sent out to locate the lucky man of the hour. But King Charlie had returned having failed to locate English at their rendezvous.

And now they waited, gloomy, silent, wondering if

King Charlie

English would receive the message which Charlie had left for him, or if he were away that day, bent on some mischief which would need an entirely new pardon from the Governor—a second pardon which could never be gained.

The long, light chiming of the clock ended for eleven, and as the last murmur was still dying there was a light tap at the door, which was then opened, and Billy English himself entered.

He came like a breath of wind into a place filled with dead leaves. At once all was life, all was motion. They surrounded him in a chattering cluster. It had not died down when King Charlie spoke above the rest.

"Have you been gallivanting around the country today, Billy? Is that what you were doing when I didn't find you where you should have been?"

Billy threw back his head and laughed silently.

"The sheriff had two gents up from the south—two sure enough man-finders and man-killers from Arizona. They could of trailed a mountain lion on a dark night through a fog. That's how good they were. And they hooked on to my trail. I took 'em out for a spin today. That's why I was busy."

He laughed again, and then side-stepped into a corner.

"There's no way of looking in on me from a window or a door while I'm standing here," he said. "For all I know, they may come back here to headquarters—not trailing me, but trying to find sign again. And if they do, it might make sort of a fuss. They're the kind that go for their guns first and do their thinking afterwards, and a few slugs might smash a lot of furniture here."

King Charlie raised his hand.

He made a strange and scarecrow figure as he stood there. Good clothes had been procured for him by Jack Granville soon after the party arrived in the town. But the gaunt frame of the old tramp knocked the cloth out of shape at once. He had been the most gentlemanly of all tramps, and now he could not help but be the most vagabond of all gentlemen. Moreover, there were bulging places here and there about his clothes which, as the initiated knew, represented food supplies of various sorts. The habits of thrift which King Charlie had formed in days of penury and in days of frequent starvation now stayed with him even during what seemed a permanent period of prosperity. He could no more get rid of the habit than a camel can get rid of its hump. In times of easy feeding, it had been the custom of the King to provide for a lean day that might come tomorrow. He had learned to eat prodigiously until his stomach could hold no more. And when that happened, he knew how to purvey food into nooks and crannies of his costume. Many an apple and orange, therefore, went to the making of those lumps here and there about his person. And his coat was packed so tight at points that when he raised his arm his coat hitched up high with the gesture.

That signal brought silence upon the others. From Billy English it only brought a smile. He was more used to the dramatic attitudes of the old man.

"Billy," said King Charlie, "what sort of a life have you been leading the last few years, I'm asking you?"

"Tolerable bad," said Billy, grinning more broadly than ever. It was an exquisite pleasure to be lectured by this unprincipled old villain who had never lifted a hand in his life in honest labour.

"What d'you deserve from the world?" continued King Charlie.

"Bread and water and the shadows of the bars," said Billy English, now grinning more broadly than ever as he saw the King gather head.

"And what would you say," went on the King, "if the world was to offer you, instead of what's coming to you, velvet and wine, you might say?"

"D'you mean moonshine?" queried Billy.

King Charlie

The King snorted.

"Bad acts are one thing," he said, "but a bad heart is another. Pretty soon I'll be thinking that you get the badness deeper than your skin is thick, Billy. But to cut this short, I'm going to tell you the good news at once: Lady holds a pardon from the Governor for all that you've done."

The old man could contain himself no longer. He threw up both of his long, skinny arms and he uttered a shout of joy. At the same time he began a sort of war dance, heedless of an orange and two apples which were jounced from their hiding-places by this procedure and rolled upon the floor to the great amusement of the others. He clapped Billy about the shoulders. The others now pressed near. They wrung his hand. Tears were in the eyes of Joe Hoyt, and Lady was crying openly. Even big-hearted Jack Granville could not have spoken easily at that moment.

"And now," said Lady, "there's only one thing remaining. The Governor, when he gave me this, asked me to extract one promise from you, Billy, when I told you about it. Will you give it to me?"

"Of course!"

"Then give me your word that you'll never let temptation, or the needs of those you care for, bring you to break the law again. Will you promise me that, solemnly, Billy?"

To the amazement of the others Billy English stepped back a little, his head bowed in thought. Lady was too stunned to press her question home.

"I'm going to ask you other folks," said Billy, "to leave me alone with Lady for a couple of minutes. I got some things to tell her."

They nodded. Almost instantly the front door closed behind the last of them and the girl and Billy were alone.

"Lady," said he, "it's the worst thing that you could have done?"

"I'm not going to guess, Billy, but just tell me frankly why you're unhappy."

"Because what's best is for you and me to have a wall between us, so's I can't come near you."

"Billy!"

"I mean it."

"Then you're angry with me, and that distance and coldness I've felt in you ever since I came back—it means you no longer care for me, Billy!"

"It means I care for you more than ever; it means I've been fighting to keep from showing you how much I care for you."

She caught her breath and remained silent. Her whole attitude was that of one who hangs trembling upon the verge of a terrible discovery.

"Do you know, Lady, or shall I tell you word for word exactly what I mean?"

"Tell me—no—oh, Billy, what shall I do? And what do you mean?"

"Lady, I was pretty fond of you before, but when you came back I found you'd growed up. And all at once it hit me hard and straight—I loved you! And as a matter of fact, I'd always loved you. It was just the idea of you that stuck in my mind—the idea of what you were growing up towards—and that was why, all these years, women haven't bothered me much. It was because of you, Lady, though I never dreamed it. It was because, all the time, I was filling up my mind with the idea of what you'd be when you growed up. And then, when I saw you the other day, it wasn't like seeing a little girl grown up. Because I had a picture of you in my head, and you were as like it as one pea is like another. You see, Lady?"

He turned away from her and walked hastily back and forth across the room. She made a movement to follow him.

"But if it makes you unhappy . . . ," he said.

"Why, Billy, don't you suppose that I know I owe everything to you? And don't you suppose that if you want me, Billy, you can have me? Why, of course, you can!"

But Billy English turned sharply upon her, frowning.

"Never say that again," he said. "Never let the thought come into you head, Lady. When I say that I can't have anything to do with you, I mean it. And now I'll tell you why. . . ."

She started to speak. He hushed her with a raised hand.

"I know what you'd say," he said. "You can make yourself *think* that you like me pretty well. You're good enough to do that because you think that you ought to. But I'm going to tell you a thing now that'll make you root the idea out of your mind for good and all."

He walked to the front door and jerked it open. Outside, framed against the dark, crouched as he had been, to listen to the keyhole, was King Charlie.

The old tramp gave a half shrinking and half malignant glance up at the youth and then slunk away. Billy closed the door again and turned with a sick face to the girl.

"Why should he spy on us?" asked Lady indignantly. .

"Because he's a rat by nature," said Billy English. "Because he's got the soul of a thief and the heart of a sneak. That's why he had to listen. Because he has bad blood."

He spoke not in anger, but with a sort of dull despair.

The girl waited. She hardly dared to think. Too many new things were happening to her.

"And now," said Billy, "compare that old man with Jack Granville. He's the man for you!"

"But why should I compare them?"

"Because some day I'm going to be like King Charlie."

She cried out in faint protest.

"I tell you," said Billy English sadly, "that the best thing that was ever done to me was to get me that pardon. Because without that pardon the law would have kept a barrier between us and I'd never have had to tell you the truth about myself. But now you have to know and I've told you."

"Billy, my brain reels. I don't understand. What on earth do you mean by it?"

"I mean that King Carlie is a picture of what I'm going to be. Because blood is mighty thick. There's no escaping from blood, you know."

The girl gasped. She shrank away against the wall.

"Billy!" she breathed.

"I knew it would make you act that way," he said slowly. "I could see that sick look in your face, just the way it's come there. And I don't blame you none. Because King Charlie is my father! There's no chance of me ever getting better. There's no use in me giving you my promise that I'll stop breaking the law. I cannot ever stop. It's in my blood, Lady."

She threw her hands across her face and dropped into a chair heavily, sobbing.

Billy English stepped swiftly to her, leaned as though he would sweep her into his arms, and then turned and walked hastily away though the front door and into the garden beyond.

There in the dark he found big Jack Granville sitting with his head supported in his hands. He started up when Billy touched his shoulder.

"You better go inside to Lady," said Billy English. "She's been asking for you."